DON'T TRUST HER

CATHRYN GRANT

INKUBATOR
BOOKS

Published by Inkubator Books
www.inkubatorbooks.com

ISBN (eBook): 978-1-83756-200-8
ISBN (Paperback): 978-1-83756-201-5
ISBN (Hardback): 978-1-83756-202-2

PROLOGUE

2003

It proved her arrogance that she felt safe sitting beside a stream she couldn't hear, reading a novel. Earphones blocked every sound, including my footsteps, as the Walkman pumped music inside her skull. The words in her book filled the rest of her brain with an imagined world so that it might as well have been only her body sitting there alone, silencing all her instincts for self-protection.

I watched her for quite a long time, although maybe it only felt like a long time. Unlike her, I was hyperalert to every sound in the woods surrounding us. The trickle of water over rocks, the occasional rustle of undergrowth and dead leaves as squirrels raced for their last bit of food in the darkness that was falling fast.

Her head was bent forward. She hardly moved except her fingers flipping the pages. She was always reading thick books, maybe to prove to the rest of us how smart she was. Maybe only because we bored her.

Whenever it was hot, she came out to the wooded area behind our street, to the enormous flat rock beside the stream, and sat there with her backpack beside her, the headphones in place, and the book on her lap. She never swatted at gnats; she was so lost in the pages she didn't seem to notice them.

I moved closer. I stood beside a pine tree now, the sky impossible to see unless I tipped my head back until my neck ached. At the base of the tree was a rock the size of a woman's shoe. I picked it up and held it in my hand. The weight of it pulled at my shoulder. I wondered if it was too large. I let my arm go slightly limp, raising it up and down to see if I was able to control its movement.

Confident, I moved closer. I watched where I placed my feet, even though I knew she couldn't hear me. I wondered if a sixth sense might warn her that she wasn't alone, but I hadn't seen her look up for the entire time I'd been watching. Did that mean she might look up soon out of habit? Was the idea that someone could sense another's presence real, or just an idea that we believed after the fact?

I knew he was there all along. I felt her watching me.

We believe a lot of things after the fact.

I moved more quickly now, not wanting to risk that she might sense my presence.

A moment later, I was right behind her, and still her fingers touched the corner of the page, ready to turn to the next. I raised my arm. Without pausing to think or to plan how this might play out, I brought the rock down on the back of her head with every ounce of strength I possessed.

She didn't scream, as I'd thought she might. The damage was too great, even with a single blow. Instead, she grunted, and her upper body collapsed forward.

Without thinking, without hesitating, I raised my arm

again and brought the rock down as hard as I could. This time, I heard a crack. Or maybe I imagined it.

Then it felt as if I drifted out of my own body. I brought the rock down again and again until she was lying on her side. The huge, flat rock where she'd been sitting was covered with a thick pool of blood. Her headphones were dislodged from her head, but she still heard nothing. Her eyes stared blankly at the trees surrounding us.

1

NOW: EDEN

Celeste Campbell had been murdered when she was nineteen years old. Someone, a monster without a soul, crept up behind her and smashed the back of her head with a rock. Her murder changed all of us forever.

I was nervous about attending the memorial on the twentieth anniversary of her death. I hadn't seen my childhood friends, or anyone in our small town, since 2003, the year she died. How could two decades have passed so quickly? I didn't feel old enough to be counting my life in decades, but here I was.

From the day I met them at the age of seven, Parker and Dylan had been my best friends. During that first summer we began playing together, we vowed that nothing would ever tear us apart. Unlike a lot of childhood promises, ours stuck. All the way into high school. Celeste, Dylan's self-proclaimed wiser older sister, said a friendship like that wouldn't last. It couldn't last. None of us believed her. We thought she was jealous, cynical. Maybe a little bit mean.

But then it turned out she was right.

After she was murdered, we kind of forgot about her prediction. We were too numb. Nothing made sense. Our memories were distorted. We couldn't process the fact that someone we knew was dead. Teenagers don't know what to do with death. And murder? That's something else entirely.

Dylan never really got over it. But just a few weeks ago, he'd surprised everyone when he announced on social media that this would be the last memorial event. Did that mean he'd finally accepted his loss? I wasn't sure you ever got over the murder of your sister.

I walked from the rental car I'd left in the small public lot toward the park at the center of town. It felt as if I'd been walking along that street just yesterday, and at the same time, it felt so unfamiliar; maybe I'd never been there at all. The trees were huge now, as if they'd been there forever. The roses along the path to the plaza were lusher than I remembered. There wasn't an aphid in sight, and the lawn was beautifully manicured. The covered section of the plaza was filled with white chairs arranged in rows, more than one hundred of them. From what I'd seen in the pictures posted online, there was always a large turnout. In a small town, a town in which there'd only been a handful of violent crimes over its entire history, nearly everyone came to the memorial. It was held every five years and had become the social event of the summer each time, which was more than a little sickening, if you stopped to think about it.

The moment I drew closer, I saw Julian. I recognized him from his social media profile picture, but really, he hadn't changed at all. The same thin face and tall, thin body. His hair was still dark, almost black. He wore the same smug expression and had the same nervous gestures. The kid we'd all been slightly afraid of.

Maybe afraid is too strong a word. We had been creeped out by him, partially because he was different, but also because he was ... creepy. Julian's *hobby* had been sitting on the front porch of his parents' house, staring at the neighborhood through an expensive pair of binoculars. We never were sure what he was looking at. Was he watching birds when he angled them up, or aiming the lenses at Parker's bedroom window? Was he observing Tip's subtle moves as he slipped a small bag of weed to someone on the pathway leading to the woods, or studying something no one else had noticed?

We never knew. But no one liked him, and we rarely talked to him.

I wondered why he attended every single memorial because, in the photographs, he was always alone, as he had been all his life. He looked almost like a stalker, literally often standing in the shadows.

He'd never married, never found a life partner. He'd lived alone in his parents' house since their deaths.

As I watched, I saw him studying the others as they gathered, a superior smirk on his face. Did he enjoy being shunned because it increased his sense of superiority?

But no one enjoys that. As an adult, I'd wondered if he was terribly lonely, and if his arrogance and mocking laughter were simply a suit of armor to protect those painful feelings. I walked toward him without looking to see if Dylan or Parker had arrived yet.

"Hi, Julian. It's been forever." I smiled and held out my hand, feeling a little ridiculous, as if we were still kids, and shaking hands was pretend play. At the same time, I was conscious of myself as an adult woman who had been living in Milan for the past fifteen years, a woman who instinctively shook hands in social situations.

He surprised me by taking my hand, but I was not at all surprised when his expression turned to a gentle sneer. "Eden *Leone*. What made you decide to make an appearance after all this time?"

I shrugged. I wasn't about to tell him about my divorce, my life that was drifting without any direction right now as I tried to figure out where I would make my home when most of my friends and my career, for that matter, were tied to a country that didn't really feel like it belonged to me, or I to it, even after all these years.

"I guess the final memorial will bring all kinds of people crawling out of the woodwork." He laughed and let go of my hand.

"Even after talking to me on Facebook, you think I just crawled out of the woodwork?"

He laughed again.

Awkward laughter had always been his response to most questions, which was probably one reason why the police had questioned him so thoroughly after Celeste's murder. The repeated bursts of laughter in response to casual questions were unsettling, but I could see now how it might suggest social anxiety, or maybe a desire to speak, but a lack of certainty about what he should say.

In the end, they'd cleared him, but some people still wondered if he'd killed Celeste. A few probably had no doubt he'd done it. At the time, I'd assumed the police detective knew what he was doing. As a teenager, I never doubted whether law enforcement had a complete picture of the truth. But now I found myself wondering if Julian hadn't told them everything he knew. I wondered if other kids had done the same. We were teenagers, used to keeping secrets from adults. And what were cops if not stand-ins for parents and teachers? They were not to be trusted, and if you'd promised a friend you would keep a secret, that promise was more important than a question from a police officer. Especially a question that seemed as if it wouldn't elicit information that was guaranteed to help find her killer.

I asked him about his veterinary practice, and he started to warm up. We ended up talking for almost ten minutes. Then I saw Dylan.

He seemed taller than I remembered, but just as good looking and just as fit and slim as he'd been in high school. A tiny part of my heart melted, and for a moment, I was that thirteen-year-old girl with a mad crush on him. And fourteen and fifteen ... The feeling slipped away as he saw me looking at him. He brushed his curly brown hair off his face. His eyes were hidden behind dark glasses, and I felt as if I were looking at a stranger. So much had happened. Was he even the same person I'd been in love with through most of high school? I wasn't the same person. Not even close.

I walked toward him, and we gave each other a warm, comfortable hug. Again, I was fourteen, just for a moment. He stepped back. "You look exactly the same," he said, without even a whisper of amusement that would suggest he was being overly flattering and utterly ridiculous.

"So do you," I said, because there was no other easy response. It was mostly the truth.

I felt part of my mind detach, searching through the pieces of my memories to see how I felt toward him. He did seem like someone I hardly knew. Yet, within a few minutes, we were talking as if the twenty years had never unraveled into a chasm between us.

I didn't feel the overwhelming sensation of desire and need and whatever else I'd experienced as a teenager. I simply felt like I was talking to my best friend. And that was what the three of us had been until all those other feelings crept in and ate away at the roots. Three inseparable friends. Perfectly balanced. Three points on a triangle—the strongest shape—and yet ...

"How long are you here for?" Dylan asked.

I shrugged. "I haven't made definite plans yet."

"Where are you staying?"

"Laura Simon's B&B."

"Stay with us."

"I don't know ... I'm not sure how long—"

"You have to. You can't stay at a B&B. We can catch up. We have to catch up. After all this time? Don't argue with me. Okay?"

As he gave me another unanticipated hug, thanking me for coming to honor Celeste's memory, I pulled away to see Parker standing to my left.

Her blonde hair fell in long, loose waves. Her dark, dramatic eyebrows over her dark eyes were even more commanding than I remembered. She circled her arm around Dylan's and leaned into him. "This is a surprise. Where's your gorgeous Italian man?" She looked around expectantly, making a show of it.

"We split up."

"Oh," she said. "Sorry to hear that." She looked up at Dylan. "The guitarist is ready to start, if you think it's a good time." She rubbed his arm.

Dylan nodded.

"Nice seeing you, Eden." She turned and tugged Dylan away from me, moving toward the area at the front of the chairs where there was a small podium. A guitarist sat off to one side under a lattice arch woven with white, long-stemmed roses.

As they walked away, the warm June sun felt like it had been transformed to an icy globe in the still, cloudless sky. A sharp chill ran down my bare arms.

2

NOW: PARKER

I didn't want to pick a fight with Dylan on the day of Celeste's memorial. He was always fragile around the anniversary of her death. And I knew this year was more difficult than usual. I didn't ever want to *pick* a fight with him, and I didn't think that's what I was doing, but I only had about seven and a half minutes. That was the length of the drive from the park to our house.

In the rearview mirror, I could see Eden's silver rental car pull in behind us, ready to follow us home.

I also hated arguing, or discussing this at all, with Brianna and Maverick in the back seat, but I was hopeful they were involved in other things—Maverick with his game device, Brianna with the text-only phone we'd allowed her on her thirteenth birthday.

"Why did you do that?" I asked, trying to keep my voice calm to avoid piquing their interest, my question on a light note, to start. "Invite her to stay with us?"

"She's staying at a B&B. That's ridiculous. It'll be so good to catch up. Did you know she was coming? Why didn't you say anything? It's so great ... after all this time."

"I didn't know."

"I guess she wanted to surprise us." I could see his grin, even with his head facing forward as he waited for the traffic light to change to green.

"I'm not thrilled about having a houseguest for an indefinite amount of time."

"It's been twenty years. I thought you'd be ready to spread sleeping bags on the great room floor and make a bowl of popcorn."

I tried to force a laugh, but he was being absurd. "We're not fourteen."

"It will be so good having her around. I'm sure she won't stay that long."

"How do you know that? She's divorced. She doesn't have a home here. Her parents are on the East Coast now ..."

"Maybe she's planning to visit them after—"

"Is that what she said?"

"We didn't discuss it. What difference does it make?"

For several minutes we drove in silence. I wasn't sure how to get him to see what a bad idea this was. I didn't want her staying with us at all. And he was being so vague about what they'd discussed. It almost sounded as if she was moving in with us.

"Has she shipped her things back to the US?"

"We didn't get into that."

"So is this a vacation, or is she moving back?"

"I'm not sure if she's decided. We didn't talk about her plans."

"How can you invite her to stay if you don't know her plans?"

"Because it doesn't matter." He glanced at me, then back at the road as he started the wide left turn into our neighborhood. "You sound like you don't want her to stay with us at all."

"I don't. We don't even know her."

He laughed. "That's crazy. Of course we know her. We've been friends for over thirty years."

"No. We were friends for eleven years. When we were children. Then she moved across the country and became an Italian."

Dylan laughed. He laughed so hard, I thought he was going to have trouble focusing on the road. "She didn't *become* Italian. What are you talking about?"

"She's basically a stranger. We don't know her."

He glanced toward the back seat. I could tell by the way he moved his jaw slightly he wasn't going to say anything more. And he was probably right. Even when we thought the kids weren't listening, even when they weren't really listening, they had a way of absorbing things we were saying, as if they had antennae buried under their hair that were constantly scanning the air around us for unconscious sighs or comments, picking up on every sound we made and absorbing it into their psyches.

At home, I pulled Dylan into our bedroom while Eden was unpacking her suitcase, hanging clothes in the guest room closet, arranging cosmetics in the bathroom cabinet. Hanging her clothes! This wasn't a one-night visit. I felt ill, looking at how she appeared to be setting up a nest in our guest room, closer to our children's bedrooms than our own room was. "I don't like this, and I don't know why you did it without talking to me first."

"I didn't think I had to. She's our best friend."

"She *was* our best friend. Twenty-five years ago."

"Less than that. We vowed we'd be friends for life. Remember? I meant it, didn't you?"

"We were children."

"I still meant it."

"We don't know her. Look how much you and I have changed."

"Not at our core. We're the same people."

I shook my head. I folded my arms across my chest, my mind racing to think how we could be rid of her when she was already so entrenched. "How can you be so sure we ever knew her at all?"

"What's wrong with you? I don't understand where all this is coming from."

"I just feel invaded. You gave her an open-ended invitation, and I have no idea what she wants, why she's here, how long she'll be staying, what she'll be doing. She knows what's going on, but we're completely in the dark."

He stared at me as if I were a small dog barking at him, and he was trying to determine whether I wanted to go out for a walk or whether I wanted my dinner served. After a few minutes of staring at me, hardly blinking more than once or twice, as if he didn't really see me, wasn't even thinking about what I'd said, he shoved his hands into his pockets and took a step back. When he spoke, I knew he hadn't heard me, not really. "It's going to be so great to catch up. Having her here almost makes me feel like I'm fifteen again." He smiled, kissed my forehead, and walked out of the room.

Fifteen. He meant when Celeste was still alive.

A moment later, I heard him from the hallway outside the guest room, asking Eden what she'd thought, seeing everyone, and if they all looked the same or if everyone seemed to have aged. The sound of their voices continued, but their words became indistinct as I went into the bathroom, closed the door, and locked it. I sat on the small bench near the shower and opened the bathroom drawer. I stared at the contents, then closed it quickly. I pressed the back of my head against the wall and tried to think.

It wasn't any surprise to me that Dylan remembered the vow we'd made as kids. He always remembered the good parts of the past. I wasn't sure why I focused on the bad parts. Of course, I'd believed the vow when we made it. We were kids, and everything had seemed magical and special and real. But it hadn't worked out. Dylan didn't remember that part. Because he never knew.

He didn't know that Eden had tried to take him away from me. He didn't know that she'd been madly in love with him. He didn't know anything at all. Most of all, he didn't know why she'd come back. Neither did I.

3

NOW: DYLAN

We were sitting on the patio, almost finished with dinner. Bones from the chicken I'd barbecued and the remnants of Parker's outstanding potato salad were smeared across our plates. The conversation had flowed easily. It felt as if we'd been together just yesterday. It was a disconcerting feeling. Here we were adults fully into our careers, Parker and I with two kids, yet in some ways it felt as if we were still teenagers, still in junior high school, laughing and talking and giving each other a hard time.

Parker clearly wasn't thrilled that I'd invited Eden to stay, but it seemed like she might be slowly warming up to her. I hoped she would relax over the next few days and come to see that nothing had changed. We were the same people we'd always been. The same tight friends we'd been since we were seven years old. That wasn't something you tossed away easily, and it had nagged at me on and off over the years that we'd almost completely lost touch.

Sure, it's hard to keep things the same when your lives

take such different routes, especially when one person is living halfway around the world, but sometimes I was aware that we hadn't put much effort into it. Now, it felt easy, knowing we really didn't have to try very hard at all.

Brianna and Maverick had gone into the house to watch TV, and we were drinking wine, watching the darkness settle over the backyard and the woods that lay just beyond the fence. The woods that were so quiet and beautiful, yet held such dark memories, knowing that my sister had taken her last breath among those trees, that her heart had beat for the final time beside the creek that ran through the forest.

I took a sip of wine, turned my face up to the sky to look at the emerging stars and the thin slice of moon.

"I talked to Julian this afternoon," Eden said.

"Why would you do that?" Parker's voice was snappish and cold.

I took another sip of wine. Just when I thought she was easing into a more accepting attitude, she changed. Why did she have to be like that? I didn't get it. I wanted us to recapture what we'd lost. It was a simple statement, and she didn't need to be so edgy, no matter what she thought of Julian. She wanted me to let the past go; maybe she needed to take some of her own advice.

"I thought he looked lonely."

Parker snorted.

"I wonder about him," Eden said. "He never had a good relationship with the police."

"That's his own fault," Parker said.

"I just wondered if he didn't tell them everything."

"What does that mean?"

"Not just him. I'm wondering that about a lot of people. Think about it. Teenagers. It's not like we told our secrets to our parents or teachers. Why would we tell the cops? They asked so many questions. And a lot of them seemed pointless. Don't you remember?"

"Not really." Parker stood and began stacking the plates on top of each other, scraping bones onto one plate for easier stacking, moving the utensils into a pile.

"It would have been so easy for people to not tell them everything. Not lying, exactly, but to leave things out. To not mention something they saw because it didn't seem important."

"What are you talking about?" Parker asked.

"I was just thinking, because I remembered how Julian always laughed when you asked him a question. He still does. He didn't always answer. And I remember how many questions were a little open-ended. Questions like, did you see anything unusual? What does that even mean?"

Parker picked up the stack of plates. "Do you have a point?"

I stood and moved around the table toward her. "Let me help with that."

She took a step back. "I have it."

"Yes," Eden said. "My point is, if five or six or ten teenagers didn't mention some small detail. What if several people knew small pieces of information that seemed unimportant, but they said nothing, and all of those missing details added up to something that would have helped the police investigation."

"No one knew anything. It's wishful thinking. Like I've been telling Dylan for years, it's way past time to let it go." Parker smiled at Eden, but she looked angry. She walked toward the back door. I took a few steps, moving ahead of her, and I opened the door to the kitchen.

I returned to the table to see that Eden had refilled all our wineglasses. I turned my chair to face the woods and picked up my glass.

"Don't you see how that could have happened?" she asked.

"Yes." I took a sip of wine. Julian had always been a strange kid, and he was an equally strange adult. Reclusive was the best way to describe him. Sometimes I wondered why he'd stayed in the neighborhood. He never socialized with the rest of us. He had a thriving veterinary practice, but we didn't have a pet, so even though we lived across the street, we rarely spoke. I knew he went for long walks in the woods in the early morning because I often saw him emerging on the path that went between our house and the neighbor's when I was leaving for work.

"It just makes you wonder."

Parker returned carrying a plate of chocolate chip cookies she'd made the day before. I grabbed one before she'd placed it on the table. Her cookies were the best. I touched her hand, hoping she'd lean down so I could give her a kiss. She seemed upset, and I wanted to enjoy the evening. Three friends, finally together again.

She moved away from my touch.

"What are your plans, Eden?" Parker asked.

Eden took a cookie and placed it on her paper napkin. "I'm not sure yet. One day at a time."

Parker gave her a grim smile.

"It's fascinating to me that the police are so dependent on witnesses and the general population to solve crimes," Eden said. "Sure, there's forensics and all that, but it seems like half the time when you hear about a crime getting solved, it's because a normal person reported something."

"Do you follow true crime, then?" Parker asked.

"Doesn't everyone?"

"No. It's morbid." Parker took a sip of wine. "Let's talk about something else."

"Eden has a point," I said. "I wonder what it would take to get them to reopen the case."

Parker looked like she might cry. "Oh, Dylan. Come on. The whole point of today was our final goodbye. Your final goodbye. That's what your talk was about."

"I know." I thought about my sister. Sometimes, it seemed as if she'd never even existed. I couldn't even remember what her voice sounded like. If someone died now, you had megabytes, gigabytes of recordings of their voice, their laughter, their movements. Back then, we had only a few videotapes, if we were lucky, and my parents hadn't owned a video camera. Celeste and I had tape recorders, but we'd used them to record songs off the radio. I didn't have a recording of her voice, and the sound of it had faded from my head. I had photographs, but most of those were in albums or on CDs from my old digital camera.

There was a frame in the hallway that had snapshots of my family, my dead family, all collected in a single frame. But as Brianna and Maverick got older, the frame seemed to grow smaller and less significant, surrounded by a growing collection of our family photographs. Maybe that was a good thing. Any therapist or self-help guru would tell me it was. Parker had certainly told me that repeatedly. Not about the photographs themselves, but about the importance of moving on. The necessity of moving on.

But the murder of my sister ate at me, year after year. She had been a brilliant, happy, funny teenager, just finished with her first year of college. What if she hadn't come home for the summer? What if she hadn't gone out to read by the creek that evening after dinner? What if she hadn't been listening to music with her headphones on, unaware of the sounds around her? *What if, what if, what if* ...

And then the police had eventually decided it was one of the twenty or thirty faceless kids and young adults who hung out in those woods sometimes, smoking crack, buying crack, at the height of the crack cocaine epidemic that touched even our small town.

They saw her upscale watch and her Walkman and her oblivious absorption in her book—all of which represented a chance to get stuff that would provide them with cash for drugs. It was senseless. It destroyed my parents. Both of them gave up living before I'd graduated from college myself.

"Dylan." Parker's voice was sharp. I knew from her tone what she would say next. She wasn't nagging me. And I knew she was right.

I looked at her. In the spreading darkness, I couldn't see her eyes, but the tight set of her lips was clear because the skin around them was white and bloodless. And of course that thought made me think of the blood that had poured out of my sister's beautiful head and soaked through her hair. I took a sip of wine.

"Please don't," Parker said.

I couldn't see the tears filling my wife's eyes, but I heard them in her voice. She hated it when I sank back into the past, grieving for what I'd lost, twisting my brain into knots as I asked the same unanswerable questions over and over. After twenty years, I should have given up. Some questions can't be answered, but when there isn't an answer, it's that very lack of an answer that keeps the mind circling around asking. Why? *Why? Why?*

And ... *Who?*

"You promised," Parker said.

"What did he promise?" Eden asked.

Parker ignored her.

The silence gathered around us. I tried to shake off the feeling that I could never let go of, wanting to know who had killed her. It wasn't a drug-hungry teenager or dropout. It wasn't a dealer. It wasn't a random crime. I couldn't accept that. It wasn't as if the woods were crawling with addicts. Sure, we saw them out there sometimes. But it was still a beautiful area with the peacefully moving creek and trees that had been there longer than the town itself.

If all they'd wanted were her possessions, they could have taken them and beat her up, hurt her badly. But I never thought they would have killed her. It wasn't necessary.

I finished my glass of wine.

"Are you looking for a job around here?" Parker asked. "Or are you still doing the fashion design thing? What's going on with you?" She laughed. "We haven't heard from you in two decades except a few Facebook thumbs-ups. It's such a surprise to have you suddenly show up like this."

"A nice surprise, I hope," Eden said.

"Absolutely." I leaned across the table and tapped my glass against hers. "Cheers. Adults drinking wine on the patio. We never imagined this, did we?"

Neither of them said anything. The chill from Parker was palpable.

4

1997: EDEN

Parker was lying on my bedroom floor with her blonde hair spread across the pale pink rug like the fur of our golden retriever. Her lower legs were on my bed, and she was staring at the ceiling. "It's so hot in here. I hate it that he chased us into the house. We should just sit out there and give him the bird so he knows he can't intimidate us."

"I guess."

"Don't be so wishy-washy. He's a creep, and someone should do something," she said.

"Like what?"

"Call the cops."

"He's not breaking any laws."

"Peeping Tom. Ever heard of that?"

"But he's not looking in our houses."

"How do you know?"

"I'm pretty sure he can't see in the window."

"Those are expensive binoculars. That's what Dylan said."

"They still can't see around corners or up and through glass."

She flexed her feet, making her tendons stand out, which always made them look like an old person's feet. I hated it when she did that. It was so gross, and I wondered if she knew it made them look old. She relaxed them again. "Want to paint my toenails?"

"Sure. What color?"

"Red, of course." She got up, and we went into the bathroom.

She sat on the toilet, and I knelt on the bathmat in front of her. I put down toilet paper on the floor in case I dripped polish. I pulled out the brush and spread a thin coat on her big toenail.

"Don't get it on my skin."

"I won't."

"Hey." Her foot jerked.

"Be careful," I said.

"I forgot to tell you what the queen said."

When she talked like that, it was hard to know whom she meant.

"Celeste."

"Oh." Dylan's sister. I liked her better than Parker did, but not a lot more, if I was honest. She acted like she didn't want us to be friends with Dylan, and I could never figure out why. We'd been best friends since we moved onto their street when we were seven, and from the very first day, Celeste acted like Dylan belonged to her and he shouldn't be playing with us.

"She said we should start getting used to the idea that in high school we won't be friends anymore."

"Why not?" I dipped the brush into the polish and wiped the extra on the edge of the bottle.

"Everything changes."

"Like what?"

"You know Celeste. She likes to be all mysterious. She just said everything changes, and being friends with a boy won't last."

"Okay. Whatever."

"That's what I said."

"What did she say?" I painted the baby toenail, which was so tiny it was hard not to get polish on her skin.

"Careful." Parker reached down and wiped a smudge of polish off the tip of her toe. "She laughed. She said we'll find out soon enough. It changes, and it won't last. Just wait. She made it sound like a warning."

"You know what she means," I said.

"Of course I do. I'm not a moron. She thinks one of us will fall in love with Dylan. Or he'll get the hots for us."

"Yeah." I felt hot. Hotter than I had all day, and it was the middle of summer, and I was hot most of the time. I wondered if my face was red. I bent my head forward, letting my hair fall over the sides of my face.

"Hey! Be careful your hair doesn't get in the polish," Parker said.

I moved back.

She complained about Celeste while I painted the toes on her other foot. Then we went back to talking about Julian and his binoculars while she painted my toenails purple.

After we got a bowl of potato chips and two cans of soda, we went back upstairs to my room. We sat with our backs against my bed and our legs out straight so our toenails would finish drying.

"We should make a vow," Parker said.

"A vow for what?"

"That we won't fall in love with Dylan."

I felt the heat rush up through my body again. I liked Dylan a lot. I'd always liked him. He was one of my two best friends. But the past few months, I was having strange feelings about him. When he looked at me, I thought about how my hair looked, and I wondered if he noticed I was wearing a bra now. Every time he touched me when we were playing board games or messing around in the backyard, I felt that heat rush through me. I tried not to think about him like a crush because it wasn't like that. He and Parker were both my best friends, even though everyone said you couldn't have two best friends. Best meant one person. But all three of us agreed—we were different. We were equal best friends.

"Don't you think that's a good idea?" Parker asked.

"Probably."

"You don't sound very sure."

"No, I'm sure."

"Love wrecks everything," she said. "We need to vow we won't do that. So that we all stay friends for the rest of our lives."

"Okay."

"Don't you want that?"

I did want that. I couldn't imagine my life without both of them. She was right. We did need to make a vow. It would help me not think about how I felt. And I wouldn't be tempted to start writing stories in my diary that imagined different things happening with Dylan and me, as if Parker weren't there. It was disloyal. "I do. That's a good idea. We should do something to seal the vow. So we don't forget."

"Like blood sisters?"

"Maybe not that. But something."

"I don't know what it would be."

"It doesn't have to be a big thing."

"I know." She wove her fingers into her hair. "I'll pull out three hairs, and you do the same, and we'll give them to each other. Then we'll promise, and we'll keep each other's hairs."

It sounded silly. Dylan would probably even laugh at it, but it also sounded like a really good idea. "Okay."

After deciding how we would do it, we moved the bowl of chips to the side. We touched our toenails to make sure they were dry, then sat facing each other with our legs crossed.

I pulled three hairs out of my head at the root, and Parker did the same. I handed mine to her, and she placed hers onto my open palm. Looking at each other, we promised we would stay friends with each other and with Dylan. When we went to high school, we would fall in love with other boys. We would never kiss Dylan or even hold his hand. We would never think of him *that way*.

When the words of our vow were spoken, we went downstairs and got two plastic sandwich bags out of the drawer to hold the hairs.

"It's too hot in here," Parker said. "I'm sick of Julian making us prisoners in our own houses. Let's go sit on the porch."

We went out to the front porch and sat on the double swing, moving it back and forth, talking about how we would always remember this day because of our vow. We talked about how lucky we were to be friends and how we were the best girls in the school and how Dylan was amazing and he'd been so much fun to play with since we were little kids. We imagined how it would be in high school and how maybe we could all be roommates in college.

"There he is," Parker said.

She was staring at Julian's white house with the dark green trim. He was sitting on the front porch in a lawn chair. It was the only chair on the porch because his parents never sat out there, and he was an only child. The porch was empty. There weren't any potted plants or anything to make it look welcoming like the other houses on the street. He was leaning so the back of the chair rested against the wall of the house. The binoculars were pressed against his face and pointed straight at our porch.

"He gives me the creeps. I feel like I have worms crawling all over me." Parker wriggled around, shaking her arms as if she were trying to shake earthworms off her bare skin, making faces like she was going to be sick to her stomach. "I want him to stop. Why isn't it against the law? You can't just sit there and watch people. Especially with binoculars. Who knows what he can see?"

"It's not like they're X-ray and he can see through our clothes."

"I know that," she said. "But it's creepy. Why can't you say how creepy it is?"

"It's creepy. But I don't see how we can make him stop."

"I should tell my dad," she said.

"Will that make him stop? Julian's dad will get pissed off, and then we'll have a whole neighborhood war over it."

"We're just supposed to sit here and let him stare at us? No," she declared as she got off the swing. She moved so fast, the swing lurched back, and I almost fell off myself.

"I'm going over there," she said.

"What are you going to say?"

"I don't know. I'll follow my instinct. Are you coming?"

"Okay."

We slid our feet into our flip-flops. Parker walked down the steps, and I followed. I didn't have a good feeling. Julian was just going to laugh at us. That was what he always did when you talked to him about anything. I didn't believe he was going to stop just because we asked him to.

"Julian!" Parker sounded almost like a teacher when she shouted his name from where we were standing at the bottom of his porch steps.

He didn't move the binoculars. He laughed. "Yeah. That's me."

Before we left my house, I'd thought he was looking at us close up on the swing, but the binoculars were still pointed in the same direction, and now we were standing below him. It didn't make sense that he would be looking at the empty wooden swing, but it was hard to say. He was strange. Maybe the direction we thought they were pointed in wasn't really the spot he was looking at.

"Stop staring at us," Parker said.

He laughed.

"Put the binoculars down and look at me," she said.

He laughed. "I thought you wanted me to stop staring at you."

"You know what I mean. It's creepy to be staring at people all the time. You're going to end up in a lot of trouble if you keep doing that."

He lowered the binoculars to his lap. "Why would I be in trouble?"

"Because it's an invasion of privacy to look at people's houses with binoculars."

"What makes you think I'm looking at people's houses?"

"It's obvious."

"Is it? How is it obvious?"

"Because I can see."

"You can't see anything. Maybe I'm watching for drug dealers. I thought people liked having a neighborhood watch. That's supposed to be a good, community-minded thing."

"This isn't a community watch."

"It's not?"

"No." Parker's voice was shrill, and I could tell she knew she was losing the fight. She thought she would scare him or make him feel bad or embarrassed, but he was never embarrassed. She should have known that.

"Well, it's a free country. I could be looking at birds and other wildlife. I could be watching aircraft flying over. I could be keeping an eye out for illegal drug use, which is an increasing problem. Everyone knows that. So, is there anything else you want?"

"I want you to stop staring at our houses. I want you to stop looking in my bedroom window."

He laughed. "I have zero interest in looking in your bedroom. Thanks for stopping by." He raised the binoculars and pointed them right at us. I imagined our faces looked large and swollen at such a close distance. I turned away and started walking.

After standing there for a few more minutes, Parker followed. When we were back on my porch, sitting on the swing, with Parker making it move so hard the stand came partway off the floor, she said, "He isn't going to get away with this."

I had no idea what she thought she could do about it.

Ignoring him was better. He would probably grow out of it. That was what my mom said.

I planned to do the same thing with Dylan—ignore how I felt. I would grow out of that, too.

5

NOW: PARKER

It was coming back to me how stubborn Eden was. Passive-aggressive-class stubborn. She'd decided she wanted to come stay with us, for a reason that was still a mystery to me, and she had no intention of leaving. All her comments about what she planned for her life after her divorce and her move back to the US were vague. More than vague. Sometimes, she simply answered with questions. She wanted to start over, maybe? She was thinking she *might* want to reconnect with her past and see old friends. She wondered if this was a good place to *figure things out*.

Mostly, she wanted to plant herself in my house and drag my husband down the rabbit hole, into the past. I didn't like it. I was worried about him. But I couldn't say that because he didn't like it when I worried about him. Most men don't, I suppose.

She was at our dinner table, talking to our children, every single night. I couldn't complain that she was creating extra work for me. She cleaned up the kitchen every evening and helped with the kids' breakfast, cleaning the kitchen then, too. She'd even done a load of laundry and weeded the vegetable garden at the side of the house.

She'd cooked two Italian dinners, but that ended up being a bit of a stab in the back. Dylan and Brianna went on and on about the food, as if I'd never made a nice meal in my life. I didn't say anything to Dylan because I knew I'd sound petty and insecure, but it hurt. A lot.

Now, she'd been with us for three days, and there was no sign of her leaving. She'd bought a bag of her preferred blend of coffee so she could make her own after we finished with our pot every morning. The fridge was stocked with greens for the enormous salads she made for lunch and the tofu and mushrooms she liked to eat for breakfast. Stir-fried. It was weird. She said there was nothing Italian about it, she just liked it.

I worked in our home office except when I was meeting with my clients, so I didn't see her all day. Most days I had lunch meetings, so I only knew about the oversized salads because she told me about them to explain all the space she was taking up in one of the crisper drawers.

When I opened my office door at the end of the day on the fourth or fifth day she'd been with us, I heard voices coming from Brianna's room upstairs. It wasn't a friend of hers, two girls chattering and laughing like I was used to. It was Eden's voice. They were talking at an excited pitch, Brianna doing most of the talking, asking questions in a long, flowing stream.

I walked up the stairs and across the landing to her bedroom. Brianna and Eden were sitting on the bed, their heads bent over Eden's phone. Eden was scrolling through something.

"Hi," I said.

"How was work?" Eden asked without looking up. Her waist-long, tangled dark hair fell over her shoulders and almost hid her small face with its delicate features. When she did raise her face, my first thought was that she almost looked Italian, even though she didn't have a single drop of Italian blood.

"Good. What are you doing?"

"I hope we didn't disturb you," Eden said.

"Not at all." I stepped into the room, moving closer so I could see the phone screen. Photos from an Instagram account.

"What are you looking at?"

"Eden's Instagram."

"Let me see." I took a few steps closer. Was it my imagination that Eden moved closer to my daughter until their hips were touching, that she pulled the phone in so I couldn't see it quite so easily?

"Maybe I could give you some tips if you're trying to promote your business on social media." I laughed, hating how my laughter sounded nervous, almost insecure. I took a deep breath to steady my voice. "I'm pretty good at helping my clients grow their influence and engagement."

Brianna laughed. Not just a little chuckle, but a full, gut-bursting laugh that went on for several seconds. "I don't think Eden needs your *help*, Mom. She has thirty-nine thousand followers."

I felt a gasp in my throat. I hoped they didn't hear it, but I felt Brianna's eyes on me, so she must have sensed my reaction, even if she didn't hear me. "That's impressive," I said.

"Yeah. What do you have? Like fifteen thou?"

"My job isn't to promote my own account, it's to help my clients." The defensiveness was so loud in my voice you could feel it like a thick blanket had fallen over my head and I was speaking from beneath it, my voice and all my self-confidence muffled by cotton.

"It's just for fun," Eden said. "I post food, so of course I get lots of followers. Everyone loves food, right? You can't go wrong."

"Food is popular," I said.

"I wish I could have an account," Brianna said.

"Let's find something else to do. I don't want her focusing on this right now. Even if food is fun and harmless."

"Don't talk about me like I'm not here," Brianna said.

"I'm sorry. I didn't mean to ... Let's go start getting our own dinner ready. It's a lot more fun than looking at pictures of food someone else ate months ago, right?"

"These are scrumptious," Brianna said. "You should see them. It looks like you could stick your fork right into the screen and take a bite. It's making me hungry." She laughed and touched Eden's phone, moving her finger up the screen, scrolling past more images. "You have so many comments. People love, love, love you."

"Eden." My voice was like a blade, slicing through my daughter's gushing adoration.

Eden looked at me, finally.

"That's enough social media. It's not allowed yet. Let's go, Brianna. You can slice onions. You always love doing that."

"Since when?"

"You used to love doing it."

"Yeah, when I was ten."

"Strangers clicking a heart does not mean love, we've told you that. And thinking it does proves you're not anywhere near ready for social media."

"Don't treat me like a little kid."

"I'm not. I'm trying to help you understand."

Eden put her phone on the nightstand. "I'd love to help with dinner. I can show you a way to slice onions really thin that's a little easier than how most people do it. Do you want to learn?"

"Sure. I'm all about easy," Brianna said.

I felt the muscles in my jaw and neck tighten. I didn't like the way Brianna was talking, I didn't like hearing her treat Eden like some sort of quasi-peer, and I didn't like that she seemed to be more interested in anything Eden had to say than what I was telling her. I was being childish and petty, but it hurt. Of course Eden had the glamor of someone new, someone Brianna had hardly known existed. Eden had the cachet of having lived in Italy and probably, for all I knew, of being divorced and childless. Everything about her was different from what Brianna was used to.

It was natural she would be awed by her, but Eden didn't have to feed it like she was. And there was absolutely no doubt she was feeding it. She might think she was being subtle about it, that she wanted to look like she was on my side. But that was not what this was. She wanted my daughter to think she was cool. She wanted my daughter fawning over her and thinking she was more successful than I was at my own career because she'd oh-so-casually picked up thirty-nine thousand Instagram followers. How on earth had she done that? Posting food pictures? Sure, food was popular. But millions of people posted pictures and videos of their food. Their accounts didn't grow like that.

I turned and walked out of the room, seething all the way down the stairs.

My sour mood deepened and spread while we prepared dinner. Eden and Brianna chattered away like the best of friends. Everything Eden did was fabulous and amazing. Everything I said or did earned me an eye roll or a put-down.

By the time Dylan was home and my family was seated at the table, with Eden enthroned as the queen bee at the center, both my children across from her with adoring looks in their eyes, I was exhausted. I poured a bit too much wine into my own glass and took a long, calming swallow. The problem was it didn't calm me at all. Why was she here? What did she *want*? Besides my family.

6

NOW: PARKER

I t felt like my kitchen, which had always been a creative space for me, had become a battleground. In less than a week, thanks to Eden Leone, it was no longer a place where I felt fully at home, where I spent my time preparing meals to nurture my family. Where I put together delicious combinations that would create memories and a welcoming place for our children to feel safe and loved and accepted around our dinner table.

Today, I'd stopped work early and gone to the gym for a workout because Dylan said he would take care of dinner. I should have figured that Eden would be involved, because her whole game plan was to be oh-so-helpful in every way. Maybe she thought we'd invite her to live with us indefinitely if we found her indispensable.

She and Dylan were making dinner.

At first glance, they looked like a couple themselves.

As I stood in the doorway, they didn't even notice I was there.

Dylan was at the center island, mixing something in a bowl with a wire whisk.

Eden was next to him, giggling softly and holding her hands in a fan shape over the bowl. "You can't be so wild. It's splashing out." She giggled again. "It's tickling my hands."

Dylan laughed and beat the whisk more furiously. She shrieked with laughter.

"Are you making dinner or a mess?" I asked, walking into the room and dropping my purse onto the chair at the head of the dining table.

Eden laughed. "A little of both." She poked Dylan in the ribs with the handle of the spatula she was holding. Then she raised it to her mouth, stuck out her tongue, and ran it up the length of the spatula. "Yum. It's so good."

"I'm so glad you approve." Dylan gave a dramatic sigh, which elicited another childish giggle from Eden. He turned and dropped the whisk into the sink.

"What are you making?" I asked.

"It's a surprise," Eden said. "It was Dylan's idea."

"Why is it a surprise?"

"Because surprises are fun. Don't you know that?" She laughed and glanced at Dylan. He grinned at her. For half a second, I thought he might give her a peck on the lips. I wasn't sure if that thought came from the self-doubt simmering inside my chest or if it was something between them that my instinct was picking up on.

"Why don't you go take a nice hot shower, and dinner will be ready by the time you're cleaned up," Eden said.

Of course I planned to shower. Who didn't shower after the gym? Her tone was so condescending, as if she needed to tell me to wash my sweaty body before I was allowed at the dinner table. Or that she had to give me permission to use the bathroom inside my own home. The more likely intent was that she wanted me out of the kitchen so she could continue flirting with my husband. Had it been like this when we were teenagers? Dylan and I got together when we were sixteen. I didn't remember her flirting with him, at least not right in front of me.

She was acting like the ugly stereotype of a divorced woman, coming on to every man she was near. Needing the attention and sexual electricity of someone else's man because she didn't have one in her life right now.

I pulled off my tank top and tucked it into the waistband of my workout pants. I really didn't want to leave the kitchen. I wanted Dylan to say something, to do something to make me believe I'd misinterpreted his behavior. But he was ignoring me. I might as well already be in the shower. What had gone on before I came home?

"Where are Brianna and Maverick? Usually they like to be involved helping with dinner."

"It's a surprise for everyone." She sounded like a songbird; her voice was so high-pitched and full of sweetness. "Get going with that shower, or you'll miss dinner."

I picked up my bag and trudged out of the room. I felt like I was dragging lead weights up the stairs and into the master bathroom.

The grand surprise of dinner was nothing surprising. They'd made chicken Kiev. The sauce she was so delighted with was a rather ho-hum cream sauce. Maverick picked at it with a wrinkled nose since he didn't like ham. Dylan should have remembered that.

In our room, after we'd had a long, somewhat tedious lecture from Eden about life in Italy, I tried to think about how I was going to bring up the flirting with Dylan. It had nagged at me all through Eden's lecture. I knew she didn't see it as a lecture. Dylan had hung on every word as if he'd waited all his life to hear a Wikipedia overview of the history of Milan and the modern-day culture and attractions of the city. If I said he'd been flirting with her, he would deny it. If I put it on her, he would consider it an attack, which was how he viewed even the slightest criticism of her behavior. Then he would shut down. I decided I was going to have to go with self-pity and insecurity, even though I hated making myself into that kind of pathetic figure.

I arranged the pillows on my side of the bed and climbed in beside him. His eyes were already half-closed.

I leaned my head on his shoulder and wrapped my arm around his waist. "You know, I felt left out when I came home and you and Eden were having so much fun making dinner."

"Why?"

"You were ... it seemed like you were flirting with each other."

He laughed. "That's crazy. I thought you were thrilled to have a chance to go to the gym instead of cooking."

Normally, I would have been thrilled. But normally, there wouldn't be a woman who used to be ... or still was ... in love with my husband dancing around my kitchen, giggling and playing with food. Making a meal she would later post on social media so my daughter could see how absolutely amazing she was.

"Yes. But why were you ..." There was no way to explain this in a casual way. I abandoned my meek attitude. "She was flirting with you. Wasn't that obvious?"

He sat up suddenly. "What are you talking about? We

were making dinner. We haven't seen her for twenty years. Why are you being like this?"

"Because you were flirting with her!"

"I wasn't flirting. I'm glad she's here. Aren't you glad to have her back in our lives?"

"Honestly, I'm not sure. I really don't know who she is anymore."

"You're not trying very hard to find out."

"Why didn't you stop it?"

"Stop what?"

"The flirting."

"We weren't flirting!"

"Shh. She'll hear you."

"Then stop saying ridiculous things like that. We were having fun."

"Giggling and teasing each other with food and standing so close like that is not harmless fun."

"Oh my God. I don't get where this is coming from." He punched his pillow, leaned to the side, and turned off the light. He lowered himself onto his side, his back toward me as if he was the one to decide the conversation was over.

"Can you at least promise you won't do that anymore?"

"I don't even know what I did. I miss our friend, okay? *Our* friend. I don't even know what happened. How did twenty years go by with nothing more than a few messages on social media at Christmas and birthdays? Not even that every year?"

I was tempted to turn on my bedside light. I wanted to see his face, but that might irritate him even more. "She moved away. She took off to New York for school, got involved with Marco, and the next thing we knew, she was moving to Italy."

"It wasn't that fast."

I didn't say anything.

"Everything is so blurry from that time. I was in a fog because of Celeste. Sometimes I can't even remember college. And then my mom's cancer. My dad's heart attack ..." With each word, his voice grew softer.

It was hard sometimes for me to understand why he was still so emotional about the loss of his family. Maybe because it all started with the murder of his sister. Maybe because he'd been so young, and they'd all died within a few years of each other. Still, it had been twenty years. My parents were also gone. It had been over ten years, and I missed them terribly, but I didn't feel the deep ache that Dylan seemed to experience.

I knew it was his sister. His age. Losing his parents and that connection to his sister. His family, especially Celeste, hung like a cloud over our lives sometimes. I wanted to be supportive, but I also wanted it to fade. Why couldn't he let go? After all these years? We'd completely remodeled his parents' home when we moved in after they died and we were married. That had been my condition.

Dylan had a condition as well. Celeste's bedroom would remain as it had been. I hated it. And I didn't think that made me a bad person. The addition we'd put on the house had been done so her room was tucked behind the stairs. Our bedroom, our children's, and the guest room opened onto the second-floor landing. Celeste's bedroom door was hardly even visible unless you deliberately looked in that direction. There was no reason to, but I still felt it there, more often than I liked.

"I just don't remember how it all happened," he said. "How we lost touch with her."

"It doesn't matter now. It happened."

"We should have visited her in Italy. I wonder why we never did."

"Friendship is a two-way street. She and Marco never visited us either."

"But now she's here. And we should be welcoming her with open arms."

Should we?

He leaned, turned over and kissed me, his lips half-missing mine. It meant the conversation was over.

7

2000: EDEN

Usually, Parker and I walked home from school with Dylan, but he had a group project due in history, so he'd stayed at school to meet with the other kids on his team. When we didn't walk home with Dylan, Karin Shapiro liked to tag along with us. Parker didn't seem to mind, but I didn't like it. Karin was okay, but sometimes I felt like Parker might like her more than me.

We'd promised a long time ago that Dylan, Parker and I would be friends for life. I didn't want someone to come along and mess that up. Another person would change everything around. Karin was more like Parker, a little wilder and crazier and always wanting to do things that I was more careful about. I felt like I was a good influence on Parker. Karin was a bad influence. It wasn't as if she got in trouble, she was just ... unpredictable.

We turned onto our street, and like always, Julian was already home. He must have left school early, or maybe his mom picked him up, but every single day he was already on the porch, waiting for us to walk by. His binoculars were pressed against his face, and he was watching us, moving them slowly to follow us every step of the way.

My parents told me to ignore him. He was lonely, they said. He wasn't hurting anyone. So I ignored him. After that one day when Parker had told him to stop, she tried to ignore him too. Most of the time.

But, like I said, Karin was a bad influence.

"I can't believe you've let him watch you for all these years," Karin said.

I moved away from Parker a bit, taking up more space on the sidewalk, forcing Karin to walk on the lawn of the house we were passing. That didn't stop her from talking. From stirring up Parker.

"I can't either," Parker said. "I told him to stop a few years ago. My dad even talked to his dad, but that guy is a total asshole. That's what my dad said. He just said *mind your own business. He's on our property, and he can look at whatever he wants. He likes birdwatching.* My dad said, 'Birdwatching, my ass. I know what kind of birds he's looking at.'"

Karin laughed.

We kept walking until we were almost up to Parker's house, right across the street from Julian's. I still hadn't looked, but Parker and Karin were staring straight at him.

"Tip said he's stepping over a line," Karin said.

"Why is Tip the expert?" I asked.

"I didn't say he was an *expert*. But guys know what other guys are up to, ya know?" Karin moved off the lawn and bumped her shoulder against mine, pushing me toward Parker. "He said what Julian is doing is predatory."

"How is it predatory?"

"Don't you know what a predator is?" Parker asked.

"Of course I do. So why is looking through binoculars predatory? Tip's exaggerating."

"Guys know how other guys think," Karin said.

"It's not like Tip can read his mind," I said.

"It's predatory. Trust me. You just know he's looking in windows."

"Yeah," Parker said. "I have to keep my drapes closed all the time. It's not fair. I shouldn't have to be worried in my own house about someone looking into my room."

"It's really sick," Karin said.

When we reached Parker's front path, Karin turned with us, talking about how weird Julian was. She kept talking, following us to the front porch. "You shouldn't just let him get away with it. Someone should do something." At the door, Parker invited her inside, and I knew she would be spending the rest of the afternoon with us.

Luckily for me, after Karin finally went home, Parker's mom invited me to stay for dinner. While Parker and I were doing our homework, but mostly talking, then taking a break for a math problem, then talking some more, she went back to the topic of Julian.

"I think Karin's right. We can't let Julian get away with this. He's a pervert. It's not like he's a junior high kid doing this anymore. It should be considered more serious at our age. I'm going to tell my mom she should call the police. She talked to my dad about it once, but they never did it. I think they—"

"Are you sure that's a good idea?"

"Yes. It's the only way to get him to stop."

"What are the cops going to do?"

"They should arrest him."

"I don't think they will. Is it really illegal? You can't prove he's looking in your window. We can't even prove he's looking at us. He can just say he's birdwatching or doing the neighborhood watch like he told you that time."

"But the cops will scare him."

"They might not. And even if they do, after they leave, he might get worse."

"No. That's not how this works. You don't let the bad guys do whatever they want because you're too afraid they'll do something worse. Then all the bullies and creeps and criminals will take over the world."

I erased the answer to my algebra problem and wrote it more neatly. "I just don't think it will work. He'll be mad, and he might find another way to bother you."

"Are you going to spend your whole life letting people do whatever they want to you because if you stand up for yourself they might do something worse? People respect it when you push back."

So she did it. And her mom called the cops. We didn't want to be too obvious, so we watched from Parker's bedroom window when they came.

We saw the cop car pull up to the curb in front of Julian's house. Only one officer, an older guy, got out of the car. Julian made it easy because he was sitting on the porch with his binoculars. I wondered if he'd watched the cop car turn the corner and drive up to his house.

The cop stood there talking to him for less than five minutes. When he was finished, he walked across the street to Parker's house.

"That's not good," I said.

"What?"

"He shouldn't have walked right over here. He should

have called your mom or something. Now Julian will know who reported him."

"He probably knows anyway, if the cop said don't look in bedroom windows. Which is what my mom complained about specifically."

We slid off her bed and hurried down the stairs to hear what the cop said to her mom. They were standing in the front hall. He didn't even come into the house, so Julian was probably watching through his binoculars, staring at the cop standing just inside Parker's front door. Maybe he could even see us. I took a step back.

"Did you issue a citation?" Parker's mom asked.

"I already told you he's not doing anything illegal," the cop said. "I told him your daughter felt uncomfortable with him appearing to stare at her bedroom and watching her whenever she's outdoors."

"Appearing?" Parker said. "He doesn't *appear* to watch me, he does!"

"Let's not make unfounded accusations," the cop said.

"He's been doing this for years. Tell him, Mom."

"My daughter feels harassed. She has a right to feel safe in her own home."

"Has he done something to make you feel unsafe?" the cop asked.

"Yes. He stares at me."

"Well, he can't see through draperies or blinds. And he's probably harmless," the cop said. "Unless he's said something threatening to you or approached you ... has he?"

"Not yet," Parker's mom said. "I can't believe there's nothing you can do to make this stop."

"As I said, he's probably harmless. And since his behavior hasn't changed over the years, I think we can assume that. He says he likes to watch birds and planes and keep an eye out for people dealing drugs. That's a good thing."

"That's not what he's doing," Parker said.

The cop looked at Parker's mom. "If you have any trouble, please don't hesitate to call us." He handed her a business card. "Have a good day, girls." He gave us a fake smile and left.

"Well," Parker's mom said, "we tried. You'll just have to ignore him as best you can. Eventually he'll get bored and grow out of it."

"Yeah, right. He hasn't gotten bored for, like, five years." Parker stomped up the stairs.

I followed.

In her room, she flopped on her bed.

I went to the window and looked out.

"What's he doing?" she asked.

"Are you sure you want to know?"

"Of course I want to know."

"He's standing at the porch railing. He has the binoculars pointed right at your window."

"This is so unacceptable." She punched her pillow. "I hate this."

"I told you we shouldn't call the cops."

"It's not fair that I have to just sit around and let someone wreck my life," Parker said.

I didn't think he was wrecking her life. And I thought my mom was right, ignoring him would have been better.

8

NOW: PARKER

On Wednesday mornings I took a yoga class at Karin's studio. After I was blissfully stretched and relaxed, my thoughts calm and centered, Karin and I went into her adjoining health food shop and café, where we drank tea and snacked on nuts, trying to focus on the health benefits and not the calorie content of cashews, walnuts, and pecans.

Karin looked like she was still in her late twenties, with her long, straight brown hair and cosmetics-free skin, which literally glowed with health. Her eyes were light hazel, clear and alert. Her body was slim, and she had so much energy. I wondered how she managed her multifaceted business, cared for her son, Cole, ran a half marathon every three months, and taught ten or twelve rigorous yoga classes a week. She was a walking advertisement for her yoga classes and health food offerings, and her business was thriving in our small community. Her evening and weekend classes had waiting lists.

I sometimes wondered if she even needed me to manage

her social media accounts, because most of her social media activity was driven organically by enthusiastic students and customers.

The vast majority of people would never in a hundred years guess that her partner and the love of her life since junior high school, Tip Darby, still had a steady business selling weed, along with a few other controlled substances. He never got into meth or fentanyl or any of that really dangerous stuff, so I think that helped Karin justify it to herself. Once weed became legal, he could have gone that route, but he still liked doing it on the down-low because he didn't want to be handing over taxes to government entities, which he believed misused eighty percent of every tax dollar they collected.

He was basically a good guy, but a lot of people probably wouldn't see it that way if they knew what he did. Karin adored him, and he was devoted to her. He was a great dad, although I could see a day of reckoning coming once Cole was old enough to start asking hard questions.

Karin placed two mugs of green tea on the small table in front of us, along with a tiny hand-thrown pottery bowl filled with nuts.

"Let's get right to the most interesting thing that's happened in a while. Maybe years." She popped a cashew into her mouth and chewed it slowly. "How is it having Eden back? The fearsome threesome." She laughed.

Her laugh was pleasant. The hurt feelings of being excluded from our group that had plagued her in elementary school and high school had dissolved. Yoga and her associated pursuit of spiritual thinking had emptied her mind *of all that gunk*, as she put it. When I listened to the lightness of her tone, I was jealous. She truly sounded detached from all those teenage feelings that, for the rest of us, seemed to grip like leeches at times, still clinging to the dark places in our minds.

"I want her out of my house," I said.

"I thought you were the three musketeers. Best friends for life."

"Please don't. You know that all ended a long time ago."

"Actually, I don't really. You never really said what ..." She popped several nuts into her mouth and picked up her mug of tea, holding it with both hands in front of her face, letting the steam drift across her skin. She closed her eyes for a moment as if she were taking a steam bath in green tea.

"Dylan is so excited. He loves having her here, but I feel like I don't even know her. We've all changed a lot. It's been such a long time. It honestly feels like having a complete stranger living in my house."

She took a sip of tea.

"I don't know anything about her except what I've seen on social media, and we all know what a lie that can be."

She laughed.

"I have absolutely no idea how long she's planning to stay."

"Why don't you ask her?"

"Dylan thinks it's rude to ask. Besides, he doesn't really care."

"It's a natural question."

The bells hanging on the door chimed as someone entered the shop. Karin glanced toward the door, but the woman who managed things while she was teaching had already eased her way out from behind the counter and was offering a low-key greeting and asking if any help was needed. Karin returned her attention to me.

"I don't even really know why she came. I guess because she heard it was the last memorial, but why? And because she's divorced, so she had nothing else to do. It sounds like she's done with Italy. So ..." I shrugged. "That's all I know."

"That sounds undefined."

"It does, doesn't it. But not to Dylan. He's too busy pretending we're fifteen years old."

"That would feel comforting. Forgetting Celeste is gone, maybe."

I sighed. I took a few nuts. I stared at them in the palm of my hand. I was suddenly ravenously hungry, and nuts were not going to satisfy me at all. I popped all of them into my mouth at once and chewed them furiously, washing them down with tea that was still too hot.

"You look upset," Karin said.

I put down my mug and nudged it to the side. I leaned forward and lowered my voice. "She keeps flirting with Dylan. And she's all over my kids, especially Brianna, trying to prove how cool she is, and better than me, somehow."

"Really?"

"You can say I'm paranoid or insecure or whatever, but it feels like she's trying to take my family away from me, or something." Saying it out loud made me sound like I was definitely paranoid. And insecure. But saying it out loud didn't change my mind even a little bit.

Karin laughed. "She can't take your family away. They adore you."

"I know. It sounds crazy. But she's trying to be Dylan's go-to girl for brooding about the past again. She's dragging him right back down. After all the work he's done to let go, finally. I'm hearing Celeste's name every single day."

"I guess that would be natural, since you haven't seen

Eden for years. When you connect with an old friend, you're going to talk about the past."

"Maybe. But the flirting. It's so blatant. And he doesn't see it. He gets irritated when I point it out. So I'm stuck. But I know what I feel, and I trust my gut. She's planted herself in our house, and she doesn't seem to have any plans for looking for a place to live. Supposedly she was designing all these clothes and selling her designs in Italy, but I haven't seen her doing anything like that. She's not working. She does Instagram, but it's just food pictures that she brags about to Brianna. I mean, there's design stuff too, obviously. It's a little pathetic, actually. Trying to impress a preteen with how great you are for having thirty thousand followers or some bullshit because they all like your food porn."

Karin laughed. "Are you jealous?"

"No. To be honest, I'm scared. I'm worried. She's here for a reason. And she's not leaving for a reason. I don't know what it is, and it's driving me insane. I think it's about my family."

"Have you tried talking to her?"

"Yes. I just get nonanswers."

"What's the story with her ex? Is she moving back here permanently?"

"I don't know."

"You just need to put a deadline on her visit. Instead of trying to get information out of her, just tell her it's been nice, but time to go."

"Dylan won't have it. And she's getting him wound up about feeling like the cops did a bad job investigating Celeste's murder. She was even talking to Julian about it at the memorial. She's got this idea that people didn't tell the detective everything. She thinks that if enough people kept little pieces of information to themselves, then it might have impacted the investigation."

Karin put down her mug. It thumped the table. She stared at me. After a long minute, she blinked slowly. "What does that mean?"

"Just what it sounds like. If two or three or more people kept little details to themselves, maybe all those details put together would have helped them find the real killer."

Karin took a deep breath and let it out slowly. "Wow. That's ... that's something. After twenty years. Why didn't she say that at the time? Or ten years ago? Or whenever?"

"I have no idea."

"Maybe she's worried."

"Worried?"

She spoke so softly, it sounded like a whisper. "You know what they say. The killer always returns to the scene of the crime."

I gasped. I didn't mean to, but it just happened. "Is that what you *think*?"

She shrugged. "It was so obvious she had a crush on him in junior high. Maybe she never got over him, and it festered all the way through high school." Her eyes widened, and she leaned over the table, getting caught up in her story. "Maybe when you and Dylan broke up for those few days, she thought if Celeste was dead, he would fall into her arms, looking for comfort since he didn't have you."

"Maybe she never got over her crush on my husband. Maybe she never even *married* Marco," I said. "None of us ever met him. It feels like she's still in love with Dylan."

"It's possible." Karin pushed the bowl of nuts toward me.

I took a cashew.

"If she's talking to Julian," Karin said, "it sounds like she's a little worried about whether there's something he knows that he didn't tell the police. Maybe that's why she came back. It is a little strange how she suddenly started connecting with him on social media a few years ago. She reached out to me once or twice."

"I don't know why she's talking to him. But I know for sure she's flirting with Dylan." My throat felt tight when I said the words. I remembered how angry Eden had been when Dylan and I got together. "I think she came back to get him. And she wants me out of the picture."

Karin took a sip of tea.

"It would make me feel better, if you see her around, if you could just let me know what she's up to."

"Absolutely." She smiled. She placed her hand over mine. It was warm against my cool skin.

I wondered if Karin had been thinking this way for a while, or if the idea had come to her just now. But what consumed my thoughts more than anything she'd said was my increasing certainty that Eden was here for Dylan, and that I was in her way.

9

NOW: EDEN

When I came back from a run just before lunch, I saw Julian sitting on his front porch. That glimpse of him was like a smack across the side of my face, sending me reeling back to the age of fifteen, remembering how he was always there, balancing his lawn chair so the back rested against the side of the house. We rarely saw his face because it was covered by those enormous binoculars permanently pressed against his orbital bones.

Now, the binoculars were nowhere to be seen, the aluminum lawn chair had been replaced by a beautiful redwood chair, and he was holding a coffee mug. Although he wasn't using binoculars, he was staring directly at me. I didn't feel the trickle of self-consciousness, the discomfort bordering on fear that had run down my spine when I was a teenage girl. This time, I felt a surge of curiosity and an urgent need to get inside his head and find out what he'd seen and what he'd been thinking all those years.

I jogged across the street and up the front steps to his porch.

I leaned against the railing. "Hi, Julian. What a gorgeous day, isn't it?"

"It usually is in the summer. They're all the same."

I smiled. "Enjoying your late morning coffee?"

"Maybe it's Irish coffee."

I laughed. "Mind if I sit for a minute? I'm a little tired."

"Then why did you run so far?"

"Is that a yes?"

"Help yourself."

I pulled the other chair around so it faced him. "We got interrupted the other day, and I just wanted to finish catching up."

He smirked.

"You don't have to be at work?"

"There are three vets in my practice. I was there late last night with an emergency."

"It must be hard caring for animals in pain. I admire you for being able to do that."

He shrugged and took a sip of whatever was in his mug.

"I've always wondered ... why did you watch everyone through binoculars for all those years? Didn't it bother you that you made people uncomfortable?"

He laughed. "I like knowing things other people don't know."

I could see how that would be something. It probably made him feel powerful, especially since he was such an outsider. "Like what?"

He gave me a slow, lazy smile, as if he really did know things, maybe even things about me. "I liked that people were afraid of me. And I liked knowing there wasn't a damn thing they could do to stop me." He laughed. "They tried. But no one could stop me from doing what I wanted on my own front porch."

He was right about that. I wondered what his parents had thought about it, if they resented the police being called, if they worried about their son. But he'd become a veterinarian; they must have been proud of him, must have been relieved, thinking he'd turned out to be a good person.

"What do you know that other people don't?" I asked.

He smiled.

"Are you going to tell me?"

He laughed, going on for longer than was natural.

"Why is it funny?" He was making me uncomfortable, which was probably exactly what he wanted.

"You're so curious. Are you worried?"

"No."

"Then why are you here?"

"It seems as if you're implying you might know something about Celeste's murder. Something you never told the cops?"

"I know it wasn't me, like some people still seem to want to believe, even after I was cleared, even after all this time."

"Oh. That must be—"

"Yeah. Whatever."

He stared at me, jutting his head forward. He laughed again, then took a sip of his drink.

I waited. The silence became uncomfortable, and still I waited. He didn't look at all uncomfortable. I wondered how long I would have to wait until he spoke. Would he just sit there until I repeated the question, and then he would do nothing but laugh? Would he wait until I left? "Do you?"

He laughed.

"I saw a picture on Facebook of you and Karin. It was taken at the fifteen-year memorial for Celeste."

"So?"

"You were having a really intense conversation."

He stared at me, shaking his head slightly as if he expected me to explain what this meant.

"You both looked upset. What were you talking about?"

"Are you serious?" He laughed. "How am I supposed to remember a conversation from five years ago? I probably didn't remember it five minutes after it happened. Normal bullshit small talk."

"That's not what it looked like."

He chuckled. "How can a conversation *look* like anything?"

He was lying. He had to be. He and Karin had never been friendly. They never spoke to each other. They hadn't gone near each other at the memorial a week ago. From the emotion they both showed in that photograph posted on social media, they'd looked like they wanted to kill each other. I was certain he remembered.

"You're sure you don't remember?"

"I'm sure."

"Why didn't you ever move away from here?" I asked.

He gave me a scornful look. "My mom had Parkinson's. I took care of her. When she died, my dad was ... anyway, I took care of him until he passed last year."

His voice wobbled slightly on the last few words. I wanted to touch his arm, but I knew he wouldn't respond well to that. "I'm really sorry to hear that. Marco's mother has Parkinson's. So I know it's ..." I wasn't sure what else to say. I didn't need to spell it out for him. "It's really hard."

"Yup."

"It must be awful if some people still think you killed Celeste."

"Only at the memorials. Two pieces of hate mail every five years. Predictable." He slurped his drink, then put his mug on the table beside him. "I need to get to work."

I stood. "See you around." I walked down the steps, feeling his eyes on my back, and all the discomfort of my fifteen-year-old self washed over me, growing more intense with each step. I didn't relax until I was safely inside Dylan and Parker's house with the door closed.

A long hot shower settled my nervous energy, but the conversation wouldn't stop replaying in my mind. That and the fact that I still didn't know what he knew, if anything.

JUST BEFORE DINNER, I was sitting at the desk in the guest room, responding to email on my laptop. The door was partially open, and from the corner of my eye, I saw it move slightly. I looked up. Parker was standing there. She stepped into the room and closed the door. "I saw you talking to Julian this morning. From my office window."

I nodded.

"What were you talking about?"

"Why did you close the door?"

"Because I want to know if you were asking Julian about this idea of yours—that there are some so-called missing pieces around the question of Celeste's murder. I don't like it. Dylan has finally put all of that behind him, and now you're stirring things up again."

"If you want to hear what Julian said, Dylan should hear it too. There's no need to close the door; it's not a secret."

"Please don't."

"You can't force him to let go; he has to come to that himself."

"I don't want—"

I got up and stepped around her, opening the door. I called for Dylan to come upstairs.

A moment later he was standing in the doorway. "What's going on?"

"I had an interesting chat with Julian this morning, and Parker was curious to hear what he had to say."

Parker glared at me. She moved to the doorway and slipped her arm around Dylan's waist.

"This'd better be good," she said.

I repeated the conversation, almost word for word. I remembered it clearly because I'd been repeating it in my mind all afternoon, trying to make sense of what Julian might be trying to say. It felt as if he wanted me to ask, almost to beg him to tell me his secret, yet he refused to answer a direct question or tell me anything meaningful. I couldn't figure out if he'd actually seen something the night Celeste had been murdered, or he just wanted everyone to think he had.

I'd barely finished when Parker started talking over me. "He just wants attention. You need to ignore him."

"That's not it," I said. "He knows something."

"Is that what he said?"

"Yes." He hadn't said that, but I knew in my gut it was the truth, and if I told her that it was simply my instinct, she wouldn't believe me.

"He doesn't know anything. Can't you see how he's winding you up? It's almost funny how naïve you are."

"I'm not sure about that," Dylan said.

She leaned into him hard, pushing him against the door-frame. "Eden was always gullible, and Julian can see that. He loves playing games with people's heads. I wish I'd known that when I was a teenager."

"Why would he bring it up now?" Dylan asked. "After all this time?"

"Exactly," Parker said. "Eden is back, and he knows he can manipulate her. Please stop giving him airtime." She moved away from Dylan. "I'm starving. I'm going to get dinner started. Come open a bottle of wine, Dylan. It would be nice to have a midweek celebration."

"Of what?" he asked.

"I don't know. Does it have to be something specific?"

"Maybe we should celebrate that Julian is going to speak up," he said.

"Don't do this." Parker's voice rose. "Sorry. I didn't mean to ... he's playing games. Can't you see that? It's what he's done his entire life. Trying to mess with people's heads, trying to make everyone think he's someone when he's not. He can't get along with human beings, so he spends all his time with animals."

"People who care for animals are usually kind-hearted," I said.

"Yes. Sure. But we've already spent too much time talking about nothing."

"If he saw someone, or there's something he didn't tell the police, that's really ... I don't even know what to think," Dylan said.

"Dylan, *please* don't do this. If he knew anything, the police would have gotten it out of him twenty years ago. They questioned him several times. They even took him to the police station. They aren't idiots. They know how to get

people to talk. It's their job. You want there to be something
because you don't like it that her murder was random. But
we've worked through this. Dr. Bilan said ..."

"I know what Dr. Bilan said."

"We agreed it's time to let go. Please."

She turned and looked at me. The coldness in her eyes
was so fierce I felt a chill run through my body.

"Don't encourage Julian anymore," she said. "It's time for
dinner." She took Dylan's arm and tugged on it, pulling until
he was forced to stumble out the door after her.

He looked troubled. I wondered how long he'd been in
therapy, and I wondered if he was finished with it. Celeste's
murder had haunted all of us, but I felt almost guilty for
thinking that what I'd experienced in the wake of her death
was even in the same universe compared to what he'd lived
through.

10

NOW: DYLAN

I t was clear to me what Parker was doing, but I let her do it because part of me was glad. For the first time since Eden had arrived, she was acting as if she wanted to rebuild our friendship. After biting my head off because I was interested in what Julian Taggart might be hinting at, her mood appeared to do a complete about-face.

Urging me to open a bottle of wine, she abandoned her plans to reheat a noodle and sausage casserole for dinner. Instead, she called a Spanish bistro and ordered takeout delivered. After a leisurely meal during which she was overanimated, engaging Brianna and Maverick in nonstop conversation so that neither Eden nor I could say anything beyond *wow* or *that's awesome*, she settled the kids on her office sofa. She turned her large desktop screen to face them and put on a movie.

We sat in the great room, the candles Parker had lit for dinner still glowing on the dining table across from where we were seated. She started up another conversation that felt mildly contrived—sharing memories of college, urging Eden to tell us all about what it was like studying fashion design and how she'd met and fallen in love with Marco. Eden didn't look thrilled to be talking about the man she'd recently divorced after sixteen years of marriage. She kept changing the subject back to school and her other friends.

When the movie was over, Parker hurried the kids to bed and came back downstairs. She opened a second bottle of wine and began yet another conversation that she'd outlined and was directing according to a plan that was almost visibly unfolding behind her eyes. She began telling stories from when the three of us first met as second graders.

My family already lived on the street. It was the only house Celeste and I had ever known. Parker and her two older brothers moved in next door when she was seven. Eden and her younger brother moved into the house on the opposite side of Parker's just a month after that.

We did everything together, and now, Parker was determined to recall, seemingly month by month, the smallest details of the games we'd played and the things we'd talked about. I'd loved playing with the two girls because I reveled in their wild imaginations. Knowing I wanted to be a video game developer because I already loved the rudimentary offerings that were on the market when I was little, I too loved make-believe play. Most boys I knew preferred riding their bikes and running around in the woods, trying to break the largest possible tree branches they could or setting fire to pine needles on the sidewalk.

Now, Parker was going to recount all the games, try to resurrect the stories we'd told. She was going to get us reminiscing about the backyard campouts and our attempts to catch tiny fish in the creek.

After a while, Eden got caught up in her memories. I did

too, because I did like thinking about those years. I liked living in the world of childhood freedom and our utter lack of awareness that the monsters in our games truly existed.

Still, as we talked, part of my brain whirred in the background, wondering if Julian really did know something about Celeste's murder that had never been investigated by the police. Parker hated it when I wondered about it, hated it that I wouldn't fully accept the outcome. When the police decided that one of the kids who sometimes went into the woods to smoke meth had seen the Walkman and the expensive watch Celeste had been given for high school graduation and had decided to repeatedly bash her head until her life was gone, we told them they were wrong. That couldn't be the answer. It couldn't be *someone* but *no one*. It was an ugly, horrific, but opportunistic crime, they'd said. That was all.

I couldn't accept that. My parents couldn't accept that. We refused to accept that!

Sometimes, I wondered if that lack of resolution ate away at my mother and transformed itself into physical cancer cells, devouring the healthy cells in her body. If that rage stopped my father's heart from beating. It's fantastical thinking, but I know the toll it's taken on my sleep and the headaches I've endured, and I know there is something physical to it all.

Parker yawned. "I guess we've had a little too much wine."

Eden laughed softly. "Probably."

"I'm going to bed." Parker stood and grabbed the neck of the wine bottle.

"I'll wash the glasses," Eden said.

"You can leave 'em." Parker put the wine bottle back on

the coffee table as if she didn't even realize she'd been holding it. She waved her hand limply, turned and headed toward the stairs.

As she disappeared from view, Eden picked up the bottle and one of the glasses. I picked up the other two and followed her to the kitchen. After she dropped the bottle into the recycling bin, she turned on the water and squirted a bit of soap into each of the glasses.

It was soothing watching her soap the glasses. There were no rings on her fingers, and she maneuvered the glasses with perfect care despite the slippery surface. The silence was calming after Parker's frantic conversation. I'd liked bringing back all the good memories, but at the same time I was angry that Parker was so determined to make sure I didn't have a chance to speculate any further about what Julian had said.

Of course, she was probably right. He did like to play games. There was no reason for him to hold onto a crucial piece of information for twenty years and suddenly start taunting one of us with it now. He liked being important, and he had a new audience with Eden coming back home. That was all it was.

But I was still angry. If she'd let me talk it through, I'd have seen that hours ago instead of a vague feeling of hope and dissatisfaction gnawing at me all evening. She acted as if simply mentioning Celeste's death was wallowing in trauma and living in the past. She thought I was filled with despair. It wasn't like that at all. I'd accepted my sister's death a long time ago. I'd even, finally, accepted the lack of closure and, worst of all, the senseless brutality and utterly unjust nature of it. You have to accept things like that, or your own life is over. But in Parker's mind, any mention of it was proof that I was living in the past instead of focused on our lives now and on our future. It exhausted me how she stood guard over every word I said about Celeste.

She hated that I'd insisted we leave Celeste's bedroom undisturbed when we remodeled the house. Her only comfort was that the bedroom door was tucked out of sight from the second-floor landing.

I knew she thought she was looking out for me, that she wanted me to be happy, and she worried I never would be as long as I entertained any thoughts about the tragedy, but she had it wrong. I could be happy and think about all the facets of my life. I didn't have to pretend perfection every moment of every day to be happy.

Eden rinsed the first glass and handed it to me to dry. She still hadn't said anything, and I felt another wave of gratitude for her easy silence. Nothing felt awkward. I felt no pressure to fill the space with small talk, letting the effects of the wine carry me along in a slightly numb, dreamy state, mesmerized by the sparkling glasses.

When the glasses were dried, we walked out of the great room toward the stairs. We both paused to turn out the lights; both of our hands reached for the switch, hers brushing the back of mine. As the lights went out, she left her hand on mine. Her fingers were warm from the hot water, and I felt the blood pulse in my hands and wrists. She took her hand away, then turned and placed it on the side of my shoulder. I felt my body relax as my brain whispered I should move away from her, I should start climbing the stairs.

Her hand moved up to my neck, and she pulled my head down gently. Lifting her face toward mine, she began kissing me. The warmth of her lips and tongue did something to me beyond just what I was feeling from the blood pumping hard against my skin. Somehow, I felt as if she knew what I'd been thinking, or at least understood what I felt when Julian pretended to know something that might identify my sister's killer. For a moment, I let my mind go quiet.

I pulled away slowly. Not wanting to stop but overcome with guilt. Parker would be so hurt. What was I doing?

Eden let me go.

"This was a mistake," I said.

"But it was nice." She took her hand away from my neck.

"Yes. I guess ... I really missed our friendship—the three of us. I don't know what happened. And I'm sorry for my part, for our part, in not making an effort to stay connected. The three of us together again has made me too sentimental. And the wine." I laughed softly. Was it the wine? Maybe, partially. "It won't happen again."

"No."

We started up the stairs, parting at the top without speaking.

Lying in bed with Parker breathing deeply beside me, I relived the brief kiss. It had been kind of incredible. I shoved that thought away. It was situational. I had been caught in a weak moment because of a slightly unstable guy who liked watching people squirm. That, and all those stories of the past. And the wine. It would never happen again.

11

2001: EDEN

Surrounded by ancient pine trees, Parker and I were standing in the creek where it ran through the clearing in a secluded part of the woods. It was the place where we'd played our make-believe games with Dylan once we were old enough that our parents allowed us to go into the wooded area alone, and the place where we'd sprawled on our backs, looking at the sky, and where we'd talked about our dreams.

It was a hot summer afternoon, and we liked going out there to stand in the icy water. Just having our feet and ankles in the clear cold water was enough to cool our entire bodies. We no longer walked over the pebbles looking for fish, or pretended we were fairies hunting for magic stones. We stood there talking, sometimes sharing a beer if one of us was able to sneak a bottle out of the fridge. Usually, Parker had more luck than I did because my dad tended to count the beer bottles.

Today, we were drinking soda because we'd both failed in our quest. Dylan wasn't with us. He'd gone with his sister and parents for a premature look at colleges that Celeste was considering.

Parker gulped the soda.

"Hey, leave some for me."

She took another swallow and handed over the can. I took a sip. It was still nice and cold because we'd put it in the creek when we first got there. I took another swallow and handed it back to her.

"I have something to tell you," Parker said.

I laughed. "Why don't you just tell me instead of announcing it like you're giving a speech."

"You might get annoyed with me."

"I never get annoyed with you."

"You might." She took a sip from the can, then held it against her cheek. "Ooh, that feels nice."

"Don't. You'll make it warm."

Parker handed it back to me. "Sorr-ee."

"So, what's the big announcement?" I insisted.

She looked at me, and something in her eyes almost took my breath away. "Dylan and I made out last night."

The can slipped out of my hand and splashed into the creek. Soda bubbled out into the water.

"Pick it up," Parker said. "You're polluting the water."

I couldn't pick it up. I could hardly think. I suddenly wanted a drink of soda so badly I thought my throat would shrivel up, but it was too late now.

Parker bent over and grabbed the can. "What a waste."

"How did that happen?"

"I've had a thing for him for a while. For ages, actually." She gave me a gooey smile.

I turned away from her. I couldn't look at that smile. I started walking carefully toward the edge of the creek, taking extra care to watch where I was placing my feet so I didn't slip.

"Where are you going?"

"I need to sit down. Or go home."

"Don't be like that."

She splashed through the water and grabbed at my arm. I wrenched away from her before she could touch me. My feet slid across the rocks, and I fell, landing in the water, smacking my tailbone into a rock, sending pain shooting up my back. I started crying from the pain and from the freezing water soaking my shorts and legs. I tried to get up, but everything felt slippery now, and I couldn't see because I was crying.

"Let me help you."

She grabbed both my arms and tried to pull me up.

"Let go of me."

"God, Eden. Calm down. I like him. A lot. And he feels the same about me."

I shoved myself to my feet and made my way to the side of the creek. I walked to the fallen tree where we'd left our sandals.

"Where are you going?" Parker stepped out of the water and came over to where I was sitting, buckling my sandals onto my wet feet. "Don't be so upset," she said.

"What about our vow? We promised. We pulled our hair out and said we would never let a crush break apart our group."

"It doesn't have to break apart our group."

"It was a vow!"

"Love takes precedence."

"*Love?!*"

"Yes. Love is more important than some silly childhood promise. It's not like we're nuns or something."

I hadn't thought it was silly. I took it seriously, and I thought Parker had too. I stood and started walking, my wet feet sliding around in my sandals.

"Come back here." She pranced across the dirt and pine needles in her bare feet, holding the soda can in one hand and the straps of her sandals in the other. "We're sixteen. It's time to grow up."

"Whatever." I continued walking. She hurried after me, arguing all the way about how I wasn't being fair, and I didn't understand, and when I fell in love, I would realize how it was. That it was too powerful to fight, *impossible* to fight. She insisted we'd been children and we didn't know what we were doing. We didn't know anything about love when we were twelve. It's not an unbreakable vow if you don't know what you're talking about. We were clueless; we were kids. On and on she went. I wanted to smack her face to get her to shut up. Maybe I should have.

I NEVER SAID a word about it to Dylan, and he never said anything about it to me, although he looked a little embarrassed the first few times they held hands in front of me. And, of course, just like Celeste had predicted, everything changed. The three of us still hung out together. Parker and I still hung out together. Sometimes, Dylan and I hung out together alone. We still talked about school and gossiped and complained about Julian and the druggies and homework.

But it was never the same. I felt like I didn't quite belong when the three of us were together. I was in the way. It was a little embarrassing when she sat on his lap or did other stuff and I had to look away. And we didn't see each other as much. They wanted to be alone, so they didn't always invite me. They didn't deliberately make me feel left out, they just didn't always tell me what they were doing, and I would find out later. Besides, before that, we saw each other every single day. Now, we didn't.

I don't know which part was worse. That I realized Parker didn't care about me and our friendship at all, that she would throw it away like that. She broke her promise like it meant nothing.

Or that I hadn't told Dylan I had a crush on him. That I would never have a chance with him. She got him because she didn't care about our promise, and I gave up the one guy at our school whom I really cared about because I was loyal to my best friend. But that loyalty and our promises, they were all for nothing.

12

NOW: PARKER

He thought I was asleep. But it didn't take that long to wash three wineglasses, and I didn't understand why he wasn't coming up to bed. So I went to the doorway of our bedroom. I stepped out onto the landing and saw them. Right at the bottom of the stairs. Making out like teenagers. I doubled over as if someone had stabbed a knife right into the center of my stomach, the blade penetrating all the way to my spine. The pain was that sharp and quick and deep.

I wanted to scream, but I have a lot of pride. Maybe too much. I was not going to let her have the satisfaction of seeing me cry, of seeing that she hurt me. That my husband was so easily lured away from me; all it took was a few glasses of wine, some mild flirting, and she had him. I bit my lip so hard I tasted blood in my mouth. I wanted to spit that blood in her face. When they finally managed to let go of each other, I slipped back into our bedroom. I wanted to hear what they said, but I couldn't let her see me.

I got back into bed and turned on my side. I bit my lip

again and squeezed my eyes shut. I tried to take long, slow breaths, tried to make myself feel like I was falling asleep. I had to think. I had to decide what I should do, how I would tell him I knew.

She was absolutely not staying in our house. If he didn't see that now, there might not be any hope for us. That thought made a sob rise from my belly, but I forced it back down. By the time he came crawling into the room like a teenager past his curfew, I sounded like I was asleep and dreaming.

In the morning, I woke early and made a pot of coffee and toast. I brought it up to our room on a tray and closed and locked the door.

He'd only had two sips of coffee when I put my mug on the nightstand and folded my arms across my chest.

"I saw you."

At least he didn't try to play dumb. He didn't lie to me. The guilt was all over his face, in his eyes, twisting his lips, making his nostrils twitch slightly.

"It was an accident."

I laughed. "An accident is when you trip and fall down the stairs."

"We'd had so much wine. I'm sorry. I'm so sorry." He put down his mug and moved toward me awkwardly, trying to put his arms around me.

I scooted away from him. "Why? Why would you do that? Aren't you happy with me? Don't I satisfy you? What's wrong? Are you—"

"No! No, no, no, not at all. I mean yes. Of course you satisfy me. I adore you."

He moved toward me again, but I pushed him back.

"I'm so sorry. I ... I don't know what happened. Too much

wine. Way too much wine. And the things Julian said, I was feeling ... I don't know. And I've been missing what the three of us used to have. I'm really, really sorry, Parker. It didn't mean anything, and it will never happen again. I promise. I adore you. You're the only woman I've ever loved. You know that. I hope you know that."

I appreciated his gushing. It did make me feel better, but it was also just words. "You're right, it won't happen again. She needs to leave. Today."

He closed his eyes. I waited for him to nod his head, to tell me I was right. I waited for him to tell me he didn't really want to be around her after that. I'd seen the whole thing. She'd come onto him. At least I had that to comfort me. He'd done nothing, at first, to push her away from him. But it had been all her, and most men might have done the same. After a surprisingly decent night's sleep, I could see that, even though the pain was still there, wrapped tightly around my heart and filling my chest and belly with a heavy feeling.

He still wasn't talking. He should be rushing to agree with me, telling me he didn't want her around, that she'd done something awful, and he couldn't bear the thought of looking at her.

"Today." My voice was louder, raw and so ugly, on the verge of tears again. "You need to tell her."

"It was a terrible mistake. But it didn't mean anything. It really didn't. She's our oldest friend. Doesn't that matter?"

"No."

"Why?"

"Because she betrayed me."

"Please. I don't ... I love you, Parker. And she ..."

I got out of bed and walked to the bathroom. I closed the door and turned on the shower. Obviously, I would have to tell her myself. I got it that he thought it meant nothing. And for the most part, I believed him. For him, it was probably, hopefully true. But that didn't mean she should stay in our house! Because, for her, it was a crack in the door. I could almost feel her lying in her bed right that minute, gloating, planning her next move.

When I faced her in the kitchen, while Dylan was mowing the lawn and the kids were doing their Saturday chores, I felt calm. "I saw what happened last night."

She looked at me without a trace of guilt on her face. She pushed her tangled dark hair off her face, slowly, gracefully, as if she were getting ready to pose for a photograph.

I wanted to smack her. "Don't pretend. I saw you kissing Dylan."

Her eyes widened, but she still said nothing.

"You need to leave."

She nodded and turned away. She poured the remains of her coffee down the drain, rinsed her mug, and placed it on the counter. "I understand."

I didn't know what to say. It wasn't the answer I'd expected. "Thank you." I regretted the words the moment they formed on my tongue, speaking them as if by rote. Why was I *thanking* her?

She turned to face me, smiling, with a look so smug, so superior, my fingers flexed of their own accord. I felt my arms wanting to move. I wanted to wrap my hands around her neck and choke her until that smile turned into a grimace and her eyes bulged out of her head.

"I can see why you're upset."

"Can you?"

Her smile lingered. For half a second, I thought she might try to give me a comforting hug. What was she up to?

She certainly didn't appear to feel guilty at being caught, or for kissing my husband in the first place. She wasn't at all regretful, and she hadn't apologized. What was she thinking? What had they been talking about while they spent upwards of fifteen minutes washing three wineglasses? Were they making plans? Did she ... what if she left but didn't really leave? She would return to the B&B. She would be less than two miles away.

Was it possible she was thinking it would be easier this way? She'd already plotted devious ways to meet up with Dylan. She was smiling because she had pictures in her mind. When he left for work, she would be waiting around the corner to meet him for coffee. She would drive to his office at noon so they could go running together, and those runs would turn into hookups in her room? I might be making a terrible mistake.

"Thank you for letting me stay as long as you have," she said. "It's been so good to reconnect with Dylan after all these years ... and you. Of course." She gave me a smile that could only be described as wicked. "It's been absolutely lovely getting to know your children, although only slightly, obviously. You can't know people in such a short time. But they're incredible human beings. You're doing an amazing job raising them."

I felt crushed under the weight of her flattery. I was making a mistake. She wasn't apologetic. Telling her to leave my house was not going to keep her from going after Dylan. Now she was hinting that she adored my children! She'd already won Brianna's admiration. What next?

"Why did you kiss him?"

"You know. Nostalgia. Too much wine." She laughed.

"Maybe I overreacted." I hadn't, but I couldn't let her

leave and slowly take Dylan with her outside the scope of my ability to keep an eye on what she was up to.

"Did you?" Her eyebrows lifted gracefully.

"I ..." Letting her do as she pleased, without any clue as to what that might be, was far worse.

She put her hand on my arm.

It took everything I had not to recoil. "Imagine how it feels to see your husband kissing another woman," I said.

"It's—"

"I know how that feels, actually." She looked sad, but I wasn't sure it was genuine. "Hopefully you had a good heart-to-heart with him. If this damages your marriage ... I would hate to see—"

"Our marriage is rock solid. You're right. We all drank too much." I laughed sharply. "It's silly to tell you to leave when we're just getting reacquainted after all these years. Dylan said it meant absolutely nothing, and of course it will never happen again." I smiled, feeling my lips pulling taut, as if the skin were about to crack.

"So which is it?" Eden asked.

"Forget what I said," I told her. "Let's forget it happened."

"If that's what you want."

"Absolutely," I said.

If either of us were telling the truth, we would have hugged each other. Instead, we both let our fake smiles linger for another few seconds, and then she left the room.

13

NOW: EDEN

Kissing Dylan had been an experiment of sorts. When I'd first seen him, I felt a faint thrill through my body, and I hadn't been sure if it was an echo from the past or a feeling that was still there. How could it be, after twenty years? In the days following the memorial, it had been difficult to sort out whether I was feeling nostalgia, a loneliness brought on by my divorce and the loss of most of my friends in Italy who were shared by Marco and me, or something else entirely.

At the same time, I felt his confusion and unfulfilled desire—the wanting to know something he hadn't been able to know for decades—emanating from him like heat from the embers of a fire that refused to die.

So I kissed him. It hadn't answered all my questions. The kiss was nice; it felt good. I wasn't sure if that meant anything. I wasn't trying to steal Parker's husband from her, although I'd known she would think that.

When she demanded I leave their house, I was a little shocked. I hadn't realized she'd seen us. She was awfully quiet. I didn't know if I would have the wherewithal to watch my husband kiss another woman so deeply for such a long time and remain silent. But she had.

I would have given anything to know what was going through her mind as she stood in the kitchen, staring at me, her eyes bulging with rage, telling me I had to leave. Then, without a change in expression, she suddenly decided Dylan and I were both telling the truth. Our kiss would be forgotten, and I was welcome to stay. I was glad to stay, but the experience left me a little off balance. It made me recall how I'd spent a lot of time as a teenager wondering what was in that girl's mind.

We retreated to sort things out—me to the guest room, Parker, I assume to her bedroom or her office. I wasn't sure, because I didn't see her again until much later that day.

When Brianna and Maverick were finished with their chores, I found them in the backyard. Brianna was sitting on the lounge chair, trying to figure out a knitting project for a summer school class she was taking, and Maverick was reading a book about dinosaurs. I settled in one of the patio chairs with a glass of water beside me and watched them. They didn't speak to me, which was fine, because I liked watching them. I hadn't spent much time around kids their ages. Most of our friends in Italy had younger children.

It was an eerie feeling watching Brianna, especially. She looked so much like Parker; sometimes when I glanced up suddenly, I felt like I was twelve and Parker was standing in the doorway to my bedroom with that mischievous smile on her face. It shook me. It threw me into the past, like shoved me hard, and it took a moment to catch my breath.

She had the same thick blonde hair with its gentle waves, the same large dark eyes, the same elegant nose and finely shaped lips, the same slender fingers that I saw manipulating the knitting needles now.

It was haunting, and it brought back memories of Celeste as well. The girl who had barely become a woman before she vanished. Celeste haunted all of us in different ways, and despite our reminiscing the night before, we'd hardly talked about her. We hadn't spent a lot of time with her when we were kids. It was always the three of us. But she was there, a backdrop to our lives, and a pillar in Dylan's life. A force that he wasn't even aware of until she was ripped out of the world.

After a while, Brianna dropped her knitting to her lap. When a crow screeched, she turned her face toward the wooded area behind the house.

I wondered if she ever looked at the trees and thought about her aunt's murder. Probably not. I wasn't even sure how much either of them knew about the details.

"It's so peaceful, looking at the trees. You're lucky to live here," I said.

Brianna nodded, mostly disinterested in my romanticized view.

"I like to remember that when your aunt Celeste was killed, the one thing that comforted us was we all knew she was happy in the minutes before she died. She loved going into the woods and sitting by the creek, reading her big fat novels. They were so heavy everyone teased her that she was going to break her back carrying them. Hardback books that were five or six hundred pages long."

"Yeah," Brianna said. "Dad told me she liked to read."

Maverick looked up from his book. "Like me."

I took a sip of water.

"But how do you know she was happy? I wouldn't be very happy getting murdered."

"She didn't know. It happened so fast, the police said she probably didn't know."

"Really?" Brianna said.

"Maybe not, but I suppose it made us all feel better to imagine it that way."

Brianna shoved her yarn and needles into the canvas bag.

"It makes me feel like she's there when I go to that spot," I said.

"Well, she's not," Maverick said. "There's no such thing as ghosts."

"That's not what I mean. It just feels peaceful. As if ... it's hard to explain."

"You know the exact place?" Brianna asked.

"You've never seen it?"

"No."

I took a sip of water.

"So do you? Know the exact place?" Maverick placed his book on the patio and leaned forward.

"Yes."

"Can you show us?" Brianna asked.

I glanced at the back doors, open to let the warm summer air inside. The house was silent. I was sure Parker was still hiding out, conflicted about whether she'd made a mistake in allowing me to stay. Or maybe she was interrogating Dylan about his feelings for me or giving him rules for his behavior going forward. Maybe they were in their bedroom, having whispered afternoon sex.

"Sure. If you think—"

"I want to see it," Brianna said. "Maybe we'll feel her presence too."

"It's just a feeling I have. I don't think you can expect something like that. It's probably just my memories because we always played there as kids and hung out there when we were teenagers."

"We'll see," Brianna said. "We never even got to meet her. We never met our grandparents either. It's totally not fair."

"You're right, it's not," I said.

Without saying we would go, we all stood at once. We crossed the backyard and turned toward the path that cut between Dylan and Parker's house and the one next door, leading into the woods. Brianna and Maverick walked in front of me as if they knew exactly where they were headed, but once we were among the trees, they slowed and let me lead the way.

We walked along the dirt path that had been worn smooth for nearly forty years now, since the homes in the neighborhood had been built. When we reached the clearing where Parker and Dylan and I used to hang out, I felt my heart pounding. It beat so hard, I felt as if I'd been walking up a steep incline. I put my hand to my chest, trying to slow it, trying to catch my breath.

As we neared the bend in the creek and the flat rock where Celeste always sat, where Parker sometimes accused her of hiding behind a larger boulder so she could spy on us while we played our games, I paused.

"Is this it?" Brianna asked.

"Yes."

"Where?" Maverick asked.

"That flat rock. Your aunt Celeste would sit there and

read. When it was really hot, she'd sit near the edge and put her feet in the water."

"How do you know?" Brianna asked.

"We played here a lot. Sometimes she came out here when we were playing. She didn't start coming out in the early evenings until she was in college."

Brianna walked away from me. She stepped onto the rock and moved closer to the water. She stood there, staring at the creek. After a moment or two, she turned to face me. "I don't feel anything." She walked back, jumping off the rock. "But it's okay. She doesn't feel like a real person to me."

"Yeah," Maverick said. "She's like a picture on the wall. And she makes Dad feel sad."

"Not even any good pictures, really," Brianna said. "Just a bunch of snapshots in a collage, and her high school graduation. And graduation pictures always look fake."

I put my arms loosely around both their shoulders. To my surprise, they didn't pull away. "I have some photos of her. Maybe I could get a few of them framed."

I felt Brianna's head nod against my arm.

"Anyway, thanks for showing us," she said. "I never saw where someone died. It's kind of creepy, but also interesting. I wonder what the last thing was that she thought. And I wonder if it hurt, or if she screamed and she was crying."

"There are a lot of questions," I said. "But I like to think about how she loved it here."

They pulled away from me then, and we walked back to the house without saying anything more.

Parker was standing on the patio. One hand was on her hip and the other was against her brow, shading the sun from her eyes. She was shouting the moment she saw us.

"Where were you?" she yelled as she began walking across the lawn.

When she reached us, she grabbed Maverick's wrist and pulled him toward her.

"We saw where Aunt Celeste was killed," Brianna said.

"What?!" She glared at me. "Maverick, Brianna, please go inside."

"Why?"

"I need to talk to Eden."

"It wasn't a big deal," Brianna said. "I was curious."

"Go inside like I asked."

They trudged across the yard. Parker followed. I remained where I was. Without turning, Parker yelled, "Come inside, Eden. We need to talk."

Inside, she nearly shoved me into her office before going into the garage to get Dylan. When they returned, he looked upset, although he didn't have the rage flaming in his cheeks like she did.

"What the hell were you thinking?" Parker asked.

"They were curious, like Brianna said."

"I seriously doubt that," she said. "They have never been curious before."

"Have you ever asked them?"

"Of course not," Dylan said. "It's not healthy."

"It's morbid," Parker said. "Inappropriate."

"You shouldn't have done that, Eden," Dylan said. "Not without asking us. It's not good for them to—"

"You need some serious boundaries if you're going to stay here. Got it?" Parker asked.

"Absolutely." I thought they were both overreacting. Kids are curious. If you make a big deal out of something, tell them it's forbidden, it's like an engraved invitation to stir up their interest. Not that I knew anything about how to be a parent, but I had been a kid, and you don't forget that part of it. In fact, that's part of human nature. In some ways, we never outgrow it. Someone tells you no, and you want to do it more.

When they were finished telling me how out of line I was, I went upstairs to the guest room. I closed the door and thought about what I'd done. I didn't regret it. Their kids would be fine. Parker and Dylan would calm down and realize they'd overreacted. Meanwhile, maybe the kids wouldn't feel so disconnected from Celeste if there were a few more photographs of her about the place. I opened my laptop, launched the photo app, and began scrolling back through the years.

14

2003: EDEN

Parker had something on her mind, but she was taking forever to tell me. She kept opening her mouth like one of my brother's guppies, then closing it again. I thought she might start hiccupping because she was swallowing so much air. I could see her eyeballs rolling to the side, looking across my bedroom like they did when she was trying to remember the answer to a question when we quizzed each other before tests.

I sort of wanted to ask her what she was thinking about, but I also wanted to see what she would do. It must be something big if she was taking so long. It had been like this for over half an hour. School was over. We were all graduated. Done with prom, done with high school, supposedly ready to become adults. It felt weird, like it wasn't real. It always seemed so far away, and now, here it was.

We'd eaten our way through a bag of cheesy tortilla chips, a box of red vines, and slurped two sodas. We were listening to Pink. Usually, we would be talking while we listened, but not today. Now we kind of moved with it, wiggling our feet and shoulders, but that was it.

Maybe she was pregnant. Maybe she and Dylan were planning to elope instead of him going away to college. Maybe they would elope, and she would go to his college with him and be a housewife in an apartment while he went to school instead of the current plan where she would go to a two-year college to be a secretary, and he would go away to study computer programming so he could be a game developer, which he'd wanted to be since he was a little kid and first discovered video games.

"I guess Dylan and I are taking a break for college," she said.

My heart started thumping so hard it hurt a little bit. I wondered if she meant what I thought she did. "What kind of break?"

"Like it's okay to see other people." She laughed. "Just go on dates and stuff. So we're more experienced."

"He broke up with you?"

"Just that we should see other people. Since we've always been together. But then we'll know it's real. Because we'll see that we still love each other and that there's no one else."

"Is that what you think?"

"That's what Dylan thinks."

"He said that?" I asked.

"Why are you being so mean?"

So he hadn't said it. "I'm not being mean. I'm just confused. Are you broken up?"

She glared at me, then looked away. "I love this song."

"Me too."

"Anyway, it's so romantic that he knows we'll prove it's real."

"It's probably good to go out with other people."

"Yeah, I think it probably is. I should have thought about that."

I felt my heart still beating so hard I couldn't stand it. This was my chance to tell Dylan I loved him. It was only the beginning of summer. None of us were leaving for college until the middle of August. I couldn't believe this was happening. I wasn't going to tell Parker. She would get pissed. I didn't have to tell her anything. She didn't care about me when she broke our vow, so I didn't have to tell her. The vow was dead. I'd flushed her three strands of hair down the toilet. She didn't own him. She wasn't the one who got to decide whom he would go out with.

And I didn't believe for one minute that he wanted a break to prove their love. No one does that. She was telling herself that because she didn't want to believe he didn't love her anymore.

TWO DAYS LATER, after writing in my journal to build my courage, just when the sun was starting to go down, I went over to Dylan's. I figured that by then Parker would either be at someone's house or watching TV, so she would be less likely to see me walk past her house.

Dylan's mom answered when I rang the bell. Dylan came outside, and we sat on the porch. We talked about a lot of stuff, because it was taking me forever to get my nerve up. I really wanted to tell him. I loved him so much; it didn't seem real that I was sitting there next to him. It didn't seem like I finally got the chance to be with him myself. I'd given up after all the time he and Parker had been together. And now, here we were.

But what if he said he didn't like me that way? What if he only wanted to be friends? What if he just wanted to go away to college and meet girls there? In two months, he was leaving for Chicago, and I was going to New York. Maybe this was a bad idea. But I had to do it. After all these years, I had to. This was my one chance.

I was hardly paying attention to what he was saying, my brain was spinning and asking itself so many questions.

The front door opened, and his mom stepped out onto the porch. "Dylan, I'm really worried."

"What's wrong?" He stopped the swing from moving back and forth and looked at his mom.

"Celeste. I don't know where she is. Her car's here. She said she'd be back by seven, and it's almost eight. I was busy, and I'm not sure she said where she was going, but I know she said seven. I've called Kim and Daniella and Kirby. None of them have heard from her."

Dylan got off the double swing. "I know where she is."

"You do?"

"Probably reading by the creek. She always goes there."

"It's dark."

"More like dusk. There's still enough light, and she never notices when she's reading until she can't see the words. Sometimes she brings a flashlight. I'll go get her." He glanced at me. "Want to come?"

This wasn't how I planned it. I didn't want this to happen. I almost had my courage up, and now he was leaving. When he came back, Celeste would be with him. I'd have to start all over again tomorrow or the day after or ...

"No. I'll ... I'll see you later."

"Okay. Sure." He hopped down the porch steps and onto the pathway. "See ya."

I walked slowly down the steps. He had disappeared from view by the time I reached the end of the front path.

15

NOW: DYLAN

After dinner, Eden told us she had a surprise. When Brianna shoved her chair away from the table with an excited smile on her face, it was obvious my children were in on it. I glanced at Parker. She looked upset, which seemed to be her permanent expression lately. She'd told me repeatedly that she didn't like Eden fawning over Brianna, whatever that meant, so I expected whatever the surprise was, and whatever Brianna's involvement had been, I was going to have to soothe Parker's feelings again. Was this all my fault because of one drunken kiss, or was something else going on with her?

Eden led us up the stairs. When she turned sharply to the left and walked past the guest room toward Celeste's old bedroom, my dinner turned to a doughy lump in my gut. This wasn't going to be good.

I realized that it had probably been years since Parker had been in Celeste's bedroom. The door was usually closed, and because it was tucked out of the way after the remodel, it was easy to ignore it. The door had taken on the appearance of an extra closet, even though the room was spacious and its large window looked out onto the backyard. Because she didn't like leaving it entirely undisturbed, I was the one who went in there from time to time with a dust cloth and to run the vacuum across the carpet.

I'm not sure why I'd wanted it left untouched. Or maybe I was absolutely sure. I couldn't bear the thought of carrying her furniture out of the house and carting it off to a thrift store. I couldn't begin to imagine what we would use the room for. I certainly didn't want to use it as a guest room or even a spare room for games or craft projects that Parker was involved with. I didn't want my children sleeping there. Not because I thought it was jinxed. I'm not a superstitious guy, although my insistence on keeping it untouched might suggest that I was lying to myself.

The room comforted me. That was what I'd told myself over the years, and I was fairly certain it was the simple truth.

Leaving it alone didn't bother anyone, and it didn't interfere with our lives.

Eden opened the door and stepped inside.

"What are you doing?" Parker asked, as if it wasn't obvious.

"I have something to show you."

"Whatever surprise this is, we don't use this room, so your effort will be wasted."

"You should open it up more," Eden said. "There's so much light in here. Maybe you could get a daybed or something and use it as a sitting room."

"We don't need your advice on how to decorate our home," Parker said. "Are you finished?"

"You haven't seen the surprise yet," Brianna said.

"It's cool." Maverick pushed ahead of everyone into the room. He went to Celeste's bed and sat down. I was a little surprised he felt so comfortable, but also glad to see he wasn't intimidated or spooked.

Eden followed him, with Brianna on her heels.

I stepped inside while Parker remained in the doorway, her arms folded across her ribs, her shoulders tight.

Eden swept her arm toward the wall in a grand gesture.

Across from the bed to the right of my sister's dresser were three sixteen-by-twenty-inch black-and-white photographs of Celeste. They had simple black frames, drawing the eye to the images themselves.

The first showed Celeste sitting on the back patio. She was about fifteen. She was holding an ice-cream cone. It must have been a hot day, because the ice cream looked slick and ready to start dripping. Her hair was swept up on the top of her head in a tight bun. She was smiling, her head tipped back slightly so the sun, which was low in the sky, was splashed across her neck and shoulders and the side of her face. In the second photograph, she was seven or eight. She was standing in the street, straddling her brand-new bicycle. I remembered that bike—turquoise with turquoise and white streamers coming from the handles. She looked confident and ready to race anyone who showed up on a bike of their own. In the third photograph, she was standing on the stairs the night of her junior prom. Or maybe it was senior. I couldn't recall. She wore a long dress with thin straps and a corsage on her wrist. Her hair was a waterfall of curls around her face and shoulders.

"Those are incredible. They ..." My voice caught in my throat, so I stopped speaking.

"It was my idea!" Brianna said. "Because her senior

portrait is so fake. With that black thing across her shoulders that no one ever wears their whole life."

"I love them," I said.

"Thank you for showing us," Parker said. "Brianna, will you and Maverick please go start loading the dishwasher."

"But we—"

"You know we do the dishes after dinner."

"Do you like the pictures?"

"They're very nice." She smiled and moved a lock of Brianna's hair off her shoulder. "Now ... dishes are waiting. Let's go." She nudged Bri and Mav toward the doorway without looking back at me.

I knew she expected me to follow, but I wanted a few more minutes to drink in the pictures of my sister. It seemed as if she came to life again, just for a moment, on the walls of her bedroom. It was partially the size of the images, partially the moment-in-time sensation that black-and-white photography always evoked in me. Maybe it did in everyone. It made me feel as if time had stopped.

As Brianna and Maverick descended the stairs, Parker pulled back, almost shoving me into the alcove in front of Celeste's room, where Eden still stood in front of the open door. Parker reached around Eden and pulled the door closed. "What is that about? It's not your call to start decorating our home."

"Brianna said—"

"I don't care what Brianna said."

"But she—"

"You have no right to be in that room, much less to decide what should be hung on the walls."

"I'm sorry. I thought you'd enjoy them."

"No you didn't."

"I think they're great," I said.

Parker glared at me. "I want them taken down."

"No," I said. "I love them. And that's beside the point now. It was Brianna's idea, and the kids feel part of it. They'll be crushed and confused if we take them down."

"They never go in there. They won't even know."

"They might now," I said.

I watched as Parker's shoulders rose and fell as she took deep breaths, trying to control her frustration, or whatever it was she was feeling. "I need to speak to you, Dylan." She walked away, into our bedroom.

"I love them. Thank you." I wanted to kiss Eden's forehead or give her a hug, something to show my appreciation, but I wasn't stepping into that again. Instead, I smiled, hoping all the things I'd felt looking at those photographs were still exposed on my face.

"I'm glad." She went into the guest room and closed the door.

Parker was sitting on the chair near the doors that led to a small balcony off our bedroom. "Sit down."

I sat cross-legged on the floor.

"Not there."

"Just tell me why you're upset so we can get back downstairs with the kids."

"Isn't it obvious? She's acting like this is her house! She's acting like Celeste died a month ago. She's stirring up all these feelings, and it's not healthy."

"It was Brianna's idea."

"You actually believe that?"

"Yes."

"You're not seeing things clearly. She's taking over my

role. Spending time with Brianna and Maverick like they're the best of friends, like she's their aunt, like—"

"What's wrong with that? She's not taking your role. That's not even possible. You're their mom!"

"It's not her job to hang pictures in our house. That's my job."

I got to my feet. "That's a little unfair, babe. You've had fifteen years to hang photographs of Celeste. So ..."

She stared at me.

"Can we just let it go?" I asked. "Can we just not make an issue out of every single thing she does?"

"You mean me. Can I not make an issue out of everything."

I shrugged.

"I don't want to fight," she said.

"Then let's not." I walked over and kissed her forehead, remembering my impulse to kiss Eden's and feeling suddenly strange that I was doing the same to my wife. I pulled her to her feet and kissed her gently. She relaxed into me for a moment, then pulled away.

It was all too much. No one would ever really look at the photographs, because we never spent any time in that room. But from here on out, maybe I would, once in a while.

16

NOW: PARKER

As I heard sounds coming from behind the door, the poster of dolphins on Brianna's bedroom door seemed for a moment as if it had come to life. I stared at the perennially smiling creatures and for the hundredth time wondered why my daughter wanted it on the outside of her door rather than inside where she would see it. I suppose she wanted us to consider the dolphins before knocking, but I was never sure what message I was supposed to take from that. The poster did nothing to enhance the decorating style in our spacious landing, but I knew it was important to let our children feel like they had some say in all the parts of our home, not just their bedrooms, so I'd allowed it. Which made me think of those photographs of Celeste.

I shoved the thought out of my mind and knocked on the door just as I finally made sense of what I was hearing from inside her room. She was practicing her French lessons from the summer enrichment class she was taking. But there were two voices. I had no doubt whom the second voice belonged to. Eden had made no secret of the fact that she was not only fluent in Italian after living in Italy for over fifteen years, but she'd also learned to speak some French and a bit of Spanish.

Brianna's voice sang out, "*Entrez.*"

I opened the door.

Eden said something that sounded lovely, but it made me want to scream at her to shut up. Brianna responded, much more slowly, stopping abruptly. Eden gave her a prompt, and Brianna continued.

Eden laughed. She spoke again in that beautiful language, her words flowing like a stream of clear, fresh water.

How could I feel so awful hearing such gorgeous words? I'd been thrilled that Brianna wanted to take French, and now I hated every sound that came out of her mouth as she responded. Why was my own daughter speaking in a language I couldn't understand right in front of me? I knew why Eden was doing it. She was going out of her way to get under my skin, for some reason I couldn't fully pin down. I knew it was payback but wasn't entirely sure for what.

For breaking our silly vow? For loving Dylan? For my mere existence because I was the one he'd chosen to love? Or because I'd cut her out of our lives after she zipped off to New York City? I never knew, and I wasn't about to ask her. Just like I wasn't about to ask what they were talking about.

"I'm glad to hear you practicing," I said.

Brianna looked me in the eye and spoke in French. It was really irritating, but I smiled and gave her a nod as if I appreciated the effort.

Eden let out a flood of words. She'd told me she knew a little French. This was a lot more than a little. She sounded like she'd lived in the country half her life. I couldn't believe Brianna would be able to pick up on all of that. She spoke too fast and said too much. I was right, because Brianna responded with a few words that sounded like a question, so I assumed she'd asked for an explanation, a simplification.

Eden spoke more slowly, a single sentence this time. Brianna responded.

My irritation was growing to the point I didn't think I could control it much longer. I'd forgotten why I'd even come looking for Brianna. I backed toward the doorway, ready to leave, trying to remind myself it was good that my daughter was improving her skills.

I was almost out the door, my hand on the knob, when Eden spoke again, just a few sentences, but among the flow of musical sounds was the name Julian. Not once, twice. Brianna responded. Eden spoke again, and then Brianna said a few words and spoke his name.

"What are you talking about?" My tone was so sharp and bitter they both looked as if I'd slapped them.

The French evaporated instantly.

"Nothing," Brianna said.

"You mentioned Julian."

Brianna shrugged. "Just practicing."

"How is Julian part of your homework?"

"I'm supposed to talk about everyday topics."

"So what were you saying about him?" I was asking Brianna, but my gaze was fixed on Eden, who was looking directly at me, but giving no indication that she planned to answer my question.

"Just talking about the neighborhood."

"What about it?"

"Chill, Mom. It's not important. What are you freaking out about?"

"I'm not freaking out."

"You actually are."

"I'm not. I asked a simple question. What does Julian have to do with your French homework?"

"And I told you, I'm supposed to talk about everyday things, and we were talking about our street and the houses and people who live here."

"I didn't hear any other names."

She rolled her eyes.

"Don't roll your eyes at me. I've told you—"

"O-kay. Do you want me to do my homework or not?"

"I want to know what you said about Julian, Eden."

"Brianna told you."

"She didn't tell me a damn thing. She said you were talking about the neighborhood. That doesn't tell me what you said about him."

"Please don't make a big deal out of nothing." Eden got up.

"Don't patronize me."

"I'm not. I apologize if you—"

"Brianna, I asked you a question. I expect an answer. What were you saying about Julian?"

"Oh, my God. I can't believe this." Brianna slammed her textbook closed and shoved it to the floor.

"Brianna!" I stepped to the side. "You need to leave, Eden."

Eden walked out of the room.

"What's going on with you?" I walked to the bed and sat beside my daughter.

She moved away from me. "What's going on with *you*?"

Her voice trembled with tears. "I was practicing French, and Eden was helping me, and you came in here and flipped out for no reason at all."

"Because I asked a question, and you refused to answer me."

"It wasn't anything, and you sounded so threatening. Like you're worried I was saying something bad about you or whatever."

"But you weren't talking about me, so how could I—"

"I don't know. You just sounded crazy."

"I'm sorry. Okay." I put my hand on her leg. I felt her stiffen, but she didn't push me away. "I'm really sorry. It's unsettling to hear people speaking in a language you don't understand and ..."

"You wanted me to learn another language." She laughed tearfully. "What did you expect?"

"I'm really sorry." I moved closer and put my arms around her, pulling her head onto my shoulder. She allowed me to cradle her head for a few seconds before I felt her try to straighten.

I apologized again before retreating to my bedroom. Closing the door, I fell on my bed and let the tears pour out of me. Eden was tearing my family apart, and so far, it seemed as if there was nothing I could do about it. No matter what happened, I always came out looking like the bad guy. She'd caused a fight with my precious daughter, and even though I thought everything was now okay with Brianna and me, she would remember. She would remember how I over-reacted, and she would wonder what was wrong with me. She would see Eden as the calm, easygoing one, and me as the hysterical, insecure, unstable one. It was so unfair. I wanted Eden to leave, but Dylan had this ridiculous fantasy we could all be friends like we were children again. And if I shoved her out, I might shove him right into her arms.

There was no way I could tell him what had happened with Brianna because he would think I was the one with a problem, just like Eden did, just like Brianna did. He would be utterly confused about why I didn't want her speaking French. He would think it was fabulous she had this chance to practice with someone who really knew the language, instead of with classmates who knew only the rudimentary phrases she did and had no sense of the proper accent.

He would say I was out of my mind.

And buried under all of that, the question remained— what had they been saying about Julian? Had Eden spoken to him again? Maybe she hadn't told us everything he'd said, despite her dramatic throwing open of the door to make absolutely sure Dylan heard every word. Had he spoken to Brianna about it? I had no way of knowing, and now, I couldn't ask without further alienating my daughter.

17

2003: DYLAN

Leaving Eden sitting on my front porch was a relief. She seemed so awkward. One minute she would be talking ninety miles an hour, jumping from one subject to the next, hardly seeming like she was breathing. Then the next minute she would be really quiet, and if I asked her a question, she wouldn't answer; then she would seem like she sort of woke up and would ask me what I'd just said. It was tiring. I wondered if she wanted to talk about me and Parker breaking up. Or maybe there was something else on her mind; maybe she was just having feelings about the three of us going our separate ways in a few months, spreading out all across the country.

I wasn't sure if she'd changed or what. While I was walking along the path into the woods to find Celeste and tell her mom was worried about her, I realized I hadn't been alone with Eden in a long time. Probably a year—ever since Parker and I got more serious.

It was dark once I left the paved path and was walking on the dirt trail. It wound through trees that towered into the inky blue sky, where quite a few stars were showing themselves. After a few minutes, I heard the sound of the creek, and then the trail veered in that direction, headed toward the large flat rock where Celeste liked to sit.

In the darkness, I couldn't see her, but maybe she was leaning against the boulder. She had to be there, although I had no idea how she could be reading now that it was this dark. Maybe she'd closed her book and was just listening to music on her Walkman. She was always wearing her headphones, half-dancing instead of walking like a normal person. Or maybe she'd taken a flashlight with her, like when we were younger and snuck flashlights under the blankets to read after we were supposed to be asleep, just like a million other kids did.

I was almost at the rock, and I still didn't see her. I wished I'd brought my own flashlight. Still, there was enough moonlight that I could make out the tree branches and see the edge of the creek. Now I saw her. She was lying on her side. That was weird. It looked super uncomfortable. Had she fallen asleep? It made sense to lie on her back to look at the stars and listen to music, but why would she be on her side?

I stepped up onto the rock, and my foot slid on something thick and wet. I lost my balance and fell back. What the hell? I wiped my foot on the ground, but mostly the dirt and pine needles stuck to whatever was on my shoe. I moved to the side and stepped up again.

"Hey! Celeste, what are you doing?" Even though I raised my voice, I realized she still might not hear me with her headphones. I went to her side and reached down to pull them off, but I realized they weren't there.

I touched her shoulder, and she kind of rolled toward me. Her eyes were open and so ...

A howl came out of me. It sounded like a coyote or something else. Some kind of supernatural monster or prehistoric beast. Something from a nightmare.

Her eyes were so ... dead. Celeste was dead.

LATER, when I was sitting on the couch in the great room at home, I could hear my mom wailing from my parents' bedroom. She hadn't stopped except maybe to breathe. In the entryway, my dad was standing guard by the front door, as if he could protect our family or some stupid pointless bullshit like that. There was a knock on the door that was loud enough for me to hear in the great room.

Parker was beside me on the couch. She'd come over the minute she found out, even though we were broken up. Eden was there too, sitting on the floor facing us. There were other people in the house, but I felt like I couldn't be sure who they were. The cops were outside, and maybe one cop was in with my mom or somewhere in the house.

The knocking shocked me because everyone else rang the bell when they came over to tell us how awful and horrible it was and to ask us how this could happen.

I heard my dad open the door. I heard talking. A minute later, my dad and this guy in a suit came into the great room.

"I'm Detective Franz."

No one said anything.

"I'd like to speak to you for a few minutes, Dylan. As I told your father, he's welcome to join us."

"Why?"

"Because you're a minor," the detective said.

"No, why do you want to talk to me?"

"I'd like to ask you a few questions about your sister."

"I told the cop everything."

"I have some additional questions. Your father said we can go into the den."

"I don't feel like it."

"I don't think you have a choice, Dylan," my dad said.

"Why not?"

"It's just a few questions." My dad's voice sounded a little whiny, like he didn't want to deal with this.

I groaned and got up off the couch. I followed the detective, who led us into the den, which seemed a little messed up, having a cop telling us where to go and showing us the way in our own house.

My dad sat on the old couch where we watched TV. I sat next to him, and the detective stood in front of the TV. Then he started asking me questions about where I was all evening, about how I knew to go into the woods to look for Celeste, and a bunch of other stuff. I was numb. I was using all my energy not to cry in front of people. It took about five questions before I realized what was up. He thought I'd killed my sister.

This asshole was asking me all this stuff to find out if I'd bashed a rock into my sister's head; my sister, who was pretty much my favorite person on the planet.

I shot off the couch. I felt like my head might explode, so I clenched my teeth, which made me sound like a robot. "I would *never* hurt my sister. I love her. This is bullshit!"

"Hey," my dad said. "Just answer the questions."

"Sit down, son," the cop said.

"No."

"I only have a few more—"

"Then just ask the one you really want to know. Ask me straight out if I picked up a rock and walked up behind my sister and pounded it into her head until it turned into a bloody pulp. Ask me that."

He stared at me.

I glared at him, knowing I'd won, but not really feeling like I had.

"It would be helpful if I can have your permission to search his room, sir. We can get a warrant and come back, but it would be simpler ..."

"Yes," my dad said. "That's fine."

I stood there as they walked out of the room, the detective leading the way again, my dad following.

I was never sure if they were shocked they didn't find anything in my room or in the laundry room or anywhere in the house. He never came back to talk to me. When that guy came back to update my parents on *the case*, I stayed in my room, and later, when they came back again, I was away at college. It didn't matter because he never had anything useful to say. Just lazy answers from a lazy detective.

18

NOW: PARKER

After brooding about it to the point of near insanity, the very thing I usually accused my husband of doing, I realized that even though I couldn't ask Brianna what Eden had said to her about Julian, I could ask Julian. It was such an obvious solution. I had no idea why I hadn't thought of it immediately.

He was right there, across the street, still spending far too much time on the front porch. He no longer rotted away his time as he had in his teens, peering out at the neighborhood through binoculars, trying to see into windows, keeping secret the things he saw, or making up stories about the things he hadn't seen at all, but there he sat, still watching.

I went over there as soon as I saw his car in the driveway. Luckily for me, Dylan was still at work, and both the kids were at their friends' homes. I had no idea where Eden was, but she wasn't in my house, for once. With my family gone for the day, she had no reason to hang around.

I changed out of the work clothes that I wore even when I was spending the day in my home office. I never knew

when I would have a video call, so I liked to dress profession-
ally and walk into my office every morning with a mental
attitude that said I was presenting my best self to the world.
Sitting around in pajama pants and my husband's T-shirt
with my hair in a messy bun wasn't my style.

To help put Julian at ease, I wore jeans and a summery
top and flip-flops. I put my hair in a ponytail. Nonthreat-
ening was the image I wanted to project. I hoped he didn't
still hold it against me that I'd called the police on him when
we were kids. He probably did. Why was I fooling myself? Of
course he did. But I wasn't going to let that stop me. I had to
know what Eden and Brianna were talking about. It sickened me that I couldn't find out from my own daughter, but
here I was. Desperate.

I crossed the street, carrying a container of brownies to
help pave the way.

The expression on his face changed with each step I took
toward his front path. I could see it even from the street, he
was so dramatic about it. I paused at the bottom step. "Hey,
Julian. Do you have a few minutes for a quick chat?" I raised
the container. "I brought brownies."

"How about that?! Brownies. Are they laced with weed?"
He chortled at whatever joke he thought he'd made.

"Of course not. Can I come up?"

"It's a free country."

His favorite phrase. He hadn't outgrown it. I climbed the
steps and settled in the chair beside him without asking
permission. I'd been subservient enough. I took the lid off
the container and held it out to him. He took a brownie and
one of the cocktail napkins I offered. No one can turn down
brownies. I smiled to myself and took half a brownie to
nibble on, just to be sociable.

He took a large bite. His lips turned dark as he chewed. Two more bites and the brownie was gone. He licked his lips, his tongue equally stained. "That makes me thirsty. You should have brought a beverage."

"I didn't think about that."

"I need something to wash that down." He stood and went inside, leaving the door standing open.

I called after him, "Can I come inside? I'm a little thirsty too." I gobbled the rest of the brownie.

He called back out the door—"Free country, as I said."

Stepping inside sent a slight chill down my arms. I'd never been inside his house. The floor plan was similar to ours, without the extension from our remodel, so it felt somewhat familiar. I waited in the entryway, listening to him opening and closing drawers in the other room. I moved slowly to the center of the entryway, then stopped, unsure how far the welcome of a free country extended.

"Iced tea or water?" he called.

"Water's fine."

I heard the clink of glasses and the sound of water running.

A moment later, he was back with two glasses. I took the glass. It felt almost warm. My stomach wavered slightly as I took a sip, but I gave him an appreciative smile.

He gestured toward the couch, and I took a seat. The room was open and light but still felt claustrophobic because there was far too much furniture. They'd broken up the open flow of the great room by adding a three-quarter wall between the dining and living areas. In addition to the couch, there were two recliners, two armchairs—both with footstools in front of them—an enormous coffee table in front of the couch, oversized occasional tables between the sets of chairs, another long table filled with empty, slightly dusty glass vases behind the couch, and an eight-foot entertainment center behind that.

"So, what did you want to chat about?" He gulped his water. "After how you've treated me all these years, I have to say, it's shocking to see you sitting there. Am I supposed to feel honored by your presence? Grateful that you made brownies for me? Oh!" He smacked his forehead with his free hand. "You didn't make them for me. You made them for your international guest. What a moron." He laughed.

"I didn't make them for anyone in particular." I tried to give him a friendly smile, but he gave me the same creepy feeling he always had. "I just like to bake."

"Uh-huh. So, the chat."

"I'll get right to the point."

"Of course you will."

"Eden mentioned that you said there's something you know about Celeste's murder that you never told the cops."

"Did she?"

"Is that what you told her?"

He laughed.

Why was he so strange? I never understood it when we were kids, and I didn't understand why he'd never grown out of it. "Do you know something?"

"Maybe."

"Did you tell her what it is? Or did you talk to my daughter?"

He laughed.

I did not want him talking to Brianna. I was deeply sorry I'd mentioned her, but I wanted to know if he'd approached my daughter as much as I wanted to know what he'd said to Eden. If he hadn't spoken to her, had I just planted a horrible idea in his creepy brain? I felt queasy again.

"I don't think your daughter would give me the time of day. Like mother, like daughter."

Relief washed over me. I hoped it didn't show, but he smirked, so I wondered if he sensed it anyway. "Do you know something you never told the police or not?"

"Demanding as always, aren't you, Parker. So entitled."

"I'm not entitled."

He laughed. He laughed so hard, I knew it was genuine. Even though I had no respect for him, hearing him laugh like that hurt a little bit. I never thought of myself as entitled, and it upset me that he thought I was. Did other people think of me that way? Probably not. I needed to stay centered. Of course they didn't. Julian's brain was stuck in high school, and that was what he'd thought then. That was all it was.

He sipped his water, peering at me over the rim of the glass.

"I'm just asking a simple question," I said.

"Are you hoping they'll reopen the investigation?"

"There's not really anything to investigate. They knew it was drug related. I just wondered if—"

"Then why are you here?"

"Obviously, they never figured out the person who did it. Are you saying you saw a drug deal or something else? It's not as if you could see into the woods from your front porch, so I was mostly curious, I guess." Mostly, I wanted him to stop saying things that were probably nothing. It had taken Dylan so long to accept the uncertain closure. No one was ever punished, and that ate at him for years. He'd finally put it to rest. Now, I felt like we'd been suddenly flung back in time.

"You don't know the things I saw," Julian said.

"You're right. I don't. But I'm asking a simple question. And it's a little tiring going in circles."

"Oh dear. Is it *tiring* for you? Then maybe you should leave."

I wasn't going to get a straight answer out of him. I wondered if Eden truly had. Was he playing these games because he hated me more, or had he done the same with her? I picked up my glass and took a few sips of water. Maybe if I said nothing, he would start talking. I looked around the room.

It was so cluttered. How did he live like this? Every surface had things on it. The three-quarter wall that was built between the dining and living areas was topped with open shelves that extended from the solid wall all the way to the ceiling. Every single one was filled with stuff. Not decorative objects, but stuff.

My eyes were drawn to the third shelf up near the corner where it joined the side wall. On top of a stack of paperback books was a Walkman from the nineties. I felt the air stop moving in my lungs. The cord hung down over the side of the shelf, the headphones placed haphazardly on top of the Walkman itself.

"That's almost a collector's item," I said as I pointed at the Walkman.

Without turning, he tilted his head and grinned.

"What is?"

"That Walkman."

"Not that rare, really. All of us had them."

"I suppose." I took another sip of water. Everything in me

was screaming that I should ask him about it, that I should ask to see it up close. But I said nothing. What was I even doing here? Celeste had been gone for twenty years. Dylan had said there would be no more memorials. He'd finished therapy. We'd decided we no longer needed couple's therapy. We were in a good place. Our family was thriving.

Eden had swooped in and stirred up everything. Just because she was speaking French to Brianna, I'd let self-doubt and some long-forgotten petty jealousy take over. I was being ridiculous. I had an amazing family, and I was not going to let her take over my life. I was not going to let her turn my husband into a grieving recluse, or whatever it was she had in mind.

I stood. "Thanks for the water."

"I thought you wanted to chat."

"We did. And I appreciate it. If you have a plate, I'll put these brownies on it, and you can enjoy the rest of them."

"No, thanks." He remained seated. "You can find your own way out, right?"

"Absolutely." I picked up the container and walked to the front door.

19

NOW: DYLAN

Parker came crashing through the front door as if she were running for her life. I walked into the entryway to see her leaning against it, holding a plastic container with both hands. It was easy to guess why she was upset. I'd been standing in her office because I'd come home after picking Brianna and Maverick up from their friends' houses, and then gone looking for Parker.

She wasn't in her office, but while I was in there, I happened to glance through the front window to see her walking down Julian's front steps. I stared in fascination as she took each step primly, staring straight ahead, hardly watching where she was placing her feet. She walked along the path slowly, then crossed the street without looking.

Before I could ask her why she was over there, and why she looked so upset, I saw Eden at the top of the stairs. I knew I should probably wait, but I was curious. My desire to know got the upper hand over my weak impulse toward discretion.

"What were you doing at Julian's? Did you go inside?" I

couldn't hide the shock in my voice. I was sure she hadn't set foot inside his house at any point in her entire life.

"I needed to talk to him."

"Why?"

I heard Eden coming down the stairs.

"Because I don't think we heard the full story."

"About what?" I asked.

"All of those exaggerated head games Eden fed us. I think she was lying to us."

"I'm not a liar." Eden had stopped halfway down the stairs.

I looked up at her, long dark curls of hair spilling over her shoulders and covering half her face as she bent her head down slightly to look at Parker.

"Did he tell you anything?" I asked Parker.

Parker turned away from me. "I need to start dinner."

"What did he say?"

"We can discuss it later," Parker said.

"Why not now?" Eden said. "If you're so sure I was lying to you. What did he say?"

Parker placed the container she was holding on the kitchen counter, yanked open the fridge door, and began pulling out veggies. Her entire body was hidden behind the open door.

"Why won't you talk to us?" I asked.

"Us?" She closed the door.

"What's going on? You can't make an accusation like that and then just shut down the conversation."

Right on my heels, Eden stepped around me now. She put her fingertips on the counter, breathing deeply. "I don't appreciate being called a liar without being told why. I told you every word he said."

"You didn't tell me what you were saying about him when you were speaking French."

Eden smacked her palm lightly on the counter. "Grow up. I'm not a liar. Brianna told you; we were practicing conversation about the neighborhood. You're imagining things. Did Julian tell you if he saw anything or not?"

"I already told you. I don't want to discuss it right now."

"So you'll call me a liar and I'm supposed to stand here and take it?"

"You can do whatever you want."

Eden crossed the room. She opened the back door and stepped out onto the patio. I watched as she stood there for a moment, staring at the trees beyond the property line. She stepped off the patio and began walking slowly across the lawn toward the woods.

"Why are you doing this?" I asked. "Did Julian tell you anything or not?"

"Not really."

"Why couldn't you just say that?"

"Because she was speaking French right in front of me and ..."

Two bright red spots emerged on Parker's cheeks. She must have realized how childish she sounded. She turned away from me and opened the fridge again, pulling out a bottle of white wine. She plucked three wineglasses from the cabinet over the center island. That was a good sign; at least she wasn't planning to exclude Eden from the dinner table. She opened the bottle, still refusing to make eye contact.

Before she could pour wine into a glass and hand it to me, I went to the back door and out onto the patio.

Eden stood near the edge of the lawn, hands in her pockets, gazing at the trees. Her head was tilted back slightly so that her hair hung to her waist. I walked across the lawn until I was standing next to her.

"I want to know what Julian is playing at just as much as Parker does," she said.

"What was that about the French?"

Her laugh had a bitter edge to it. "I was helping Brianna practice French conversation. Parker freaked out. I think she assumed I was telling Brianna something about Julian that I hadn't told the two of you." She laughed. "It was so ridiculous it was funny. It still is. Instead of recognizing how insecure she is, she calls me a liar. Unbelievable."

"I don't think she means it."

"Ha."

"I certainly don't believe that."

"Thank you."

We still hadn't looked at each other. I wondered if Parker was watching us. I wanted to turn to check, but she might take that as a guilty move, so it was best to continue as we were. "She's overprotective of me. She knows how I can go to some dark places when I start brooding too much about the past."

"I get that. It's just so ... she's so hostile."

"Julian has stirred things up. If he wasn't trying to hint that he knows some secret, things would be different. It's so great that you're here. We've lost all those years, and I really want to recapture what we had. Some of my best memories are the times the three of us spent together."

"I've realized that's not realistic."

"It is. People don't have the kind of friendship the three of us had and lose it entirely. That connection is still there."

"It's not like this is a new thing. It's not like Julian is the entire cause of the problem. Parker didn't even want Marco and me at your wedding."

"That's not true. I addressed the invitation myself."

"She told me not to come."

Now I turned to face her. From the corner of my eye, I saw Parker standing in the open doorway. She was holding a glass of wine. I nodded at her, hoping it would serve as an invitation for her to join us. She didn't move or acknowledge me. "She told you not to come?"

"Yes."

"I don't ... but you were on the guest list. She never mentioned ..." I was confused. As far as I could remember, Parker had compiled the guest list, then shown it to me for approval and additions. Why would she turn around and tell Eden not to attend? "I'm not sure what to say. But I do know this, I'm not going to stop believing that childhood bond is still there. It hasn't broken. We just need a little time."

"You were always the optimist." She smiled.

"I still am."

We returned to the house, where Parker poured wine for us. We drank, then ate the delicious salmon dinner with salad and pasta that she'd made.

In our bedroom later that night, I asked her why she'd told Eden and Marco not to attend our wedding.

"I never said that."

"Eden told me you—"

"She's misremembering."

"She was very definite about it. And please don't call her a liar again."

"She's not remembering it right, or she overreacted at the time. Maybe she took it the wrong way when I was trying to be nice. What I told her was that she shouldn't feel obligated to come. I told her I knew how expensive international flights are, not to mention the expense of staying somewhere for at least a week, since we couldn't offer them a place to stay in the house."

"Why not?"

"All my aunts were staying here, remember? Anyway, I was trying to be sensitive. I knew she had a lot of loans to go to that expensive design school, and I was trying to be nice. If she's choosing to remember it as I told her not to come, that's her decision. But that's not what happened."

She kissed me gently, then more deeply. All her animosity from earlier seemed to have dissolved. In fact, it had dissolved by the time we sat down for dinner. She'd been a completely changed person from the woman I'd seen leaning against the front door after she'd walked home from Julian's.

Maybe this was all about hurt feelings and misunderstandings and miscommunication between the two of them, a female thing that I didn't understand, which had been allowed to fester for two decades. Nothing else really made any sense.

I took her into my arms, and everything about the way her body relaxed into mine felt normal and pleasant, as if none of the sharp words had been said.

20

NOW: EDEN

Because I'd obsessed for years over that photograph of Karin and Julian having what looked like an intense conversation, I wasn't sure if I'd made it into something more than it was. I still thought Julian was lying when he'd said he couldn't possibly remember what they'd talked about, but maybe he didn't. Maybe he'd simply been taunting her the way he had me.

Still, it was likely that Karin remembered, and I wasn't sure why I'd waited so long to meet up with her. Probably because I knew she was now close friends with Parker. There was a good chance she would run to Parker and tell her the minute I even suggested getting together, and she definitely would after I asked her about the photograph. But why did I care? I was curious, and it had nagged at me for five years. Not constantly. But enough that I still had the photo sitting in a separate folder in my photo app.

I sent Karin a message and asked if she wanted to catch up over a glass of wine. She said yes. Simple as that.

We sat across the table from each other and talked about

some of the highlights of what had passed through our lives over the course of twenty years. She'd stayed with her high school boyfriend, Tip. They had a son, who was nine. Tip still sold weed and, reading between the lines of her vague phrasing, a few things that weren't legal. He wasn't even selling the weed in a way that complied with state laws, collecting *outrageous* taxes and all that. His legit job was working as a security guard, which seemed mildly ironic.

Karin's health food store and yoga studio were doing well, and she felt incredibly lucky to have work that *satisfied her soul*. I wondered how many people knew that the seed money for her soulful business came from the sale of drugs. Because of his security job, not many people realized Tip was still in that business.

It seemed like a strange mashup of health enhancement with health-destroying substances, but as far as I could tell, that contradiction didn't bother Karin at all. It also didn't seem to bother her that her son was growing up in a family that was poised to be blown apart at any moment. I suppose we all tell ourselves stories that justify our choices, and she was happy with how their lives were going.

She asked me about Italy and was extremely sympathetic about the end of my marriage. She recognized how untethered I must feel now that I had no country and no mate and a dissolving social structure, because those pieces of my life had been tied to Marco. When he and I were happy together, it never seemed as if it all belonged to him. But once the split was final, it felt as if I didn't really belong in Milan, that none of the people I'd thought were my closest friends truly belonged to me either.

My phone had been lying on the table while we talked and sipped our wine and ate lentil chips that were so light, we'd already gone through two baskets without even thinking about it.

"They buy these chips wholesale from me," Karin said. "Aren't they amazing?"

"They are, but I can't stop eating them!"

"I know. Dangerous." She laughed and took another chip out of the bowl.

I picked up my phone and opened it to the photograph. "I have a picture from Celeste's memorial—the fifteenth anniversary. I don't know if you remember it, but it's nagged at me on and off for a few years." I turned the phone toward her.

She moved her glass to the side and took the phone. She spread her fingers across the screen to make the image larger.

"Do you remember talking to Julian that day?"

"Yes." She handed the phone back to me.

"I didn't know you were friends with him, so it caught my attention. And you both look so intense. I couldn't get it out of my mind."

She looked down at her wineglass but said nothing.

"Do you remember what you were talking about? I know it might sound like a ridiculous question after all this time, but it looks ... I don't know ... serious."

She took a sip of wine and glanced at the table beside us. She turned her attention to the intricate silver ring on her index finger, twisting it around several times. "I'm not ..." She sighed. "It's probably fine. Maybe it would be good to say something and get it out of my head. He already knows anyway, so it's not like I'm risking something telling you." She twisted her ring some more. "But ... well, actually, yes. I do remember. Celeste's memorials are the only time I talk to him. And it's the same conversation every time."

I ate a lentil chip and waited.

"He's always taunting me. Like he's threatening me, but not really. It's hard to explain." She took a deep breath and held it for half a second before releasing it slowly. "He knows I lied to the cops about where I was the night Celeste was murdered."

I took in a sharp intake of air. I picked up my glass quickly and sipped my wine.

"He knew I'd lied because he saw me. Those damn binoculars." She laughed and gave me a sour look. "Tip asked me to say we were together that night. But Julian saw me, so he knew I lied."

"Why did he—"

"The cops were always picking on Tip. Every single time something bad happened, the smallest thing—a stolen bike, graffiti, *anything*, he was the first person they went to. He knew they would pound him about her murder. So he asked me to tell them we were together. I knew he hadn't killed her, so I did."

"You knew for sure?"

"Yes! He does stuff outside the rules, I know that, but not murder. He's not violent." She glared at me. "Don't even think something like that. Not in a million years. Not ever." She took a sip of wine. "But I do feel guilty. Maybe it somehow affected the investigation. I'm not sure how, I can't really see how it would, but if they didn't have all the facts about where everyone was, maybe it made a difference to their not being able to find Celeste's killer." She sighed and looked down at the table.

After a moment, she looked up again. "Anyway, it's too

late now. But Julian, he won't let me forget it. Every time I see him, he has to get me alone and remind me that I lied. And he says it like I'm going to get in trouble, that I might get arrested, might lose my business, that they might take Cole away from me, from us. I know it's all nothing, but he has a way of saying it that gets me so upset." She looked up at me again. Her eyes were brimming with tears. "It's all so crazy. I know it doesn't mean anything, but he makes me so upset. So yeah, that's why I look intense in that picture." She picked up her glass and took a long swallow, nearly emptying it.

She looked at me, holding my gaze for several long seconds, as if she were trying to measure my reaction, almost as if she wondered if this bit of information might change how I viewed my memories of that night.

I wondered if she was telling the truth. She downed the wine like she thought the police were surrounding the restaurant as she spoke. She said it was guilt, and I could see how what she'd done would make her feel guilty, but unless Tip had murdered Celeste, or knew who had, she was right. It didn't really matter. It didn't matter now, and it hadn't mattered then. Unless Tip had seen someone and wasn't saying ...

And, honestly, why did Julian's taunting upset her so badly after all this time?

I supposed guilt can behave strangely, making you feel things that aren't real. She'd done something wrong. At the time, she must have wondered if Tip knew something about it. She must have wondered if he'd seen something, or if he knew who did it. The police decided it was kids who were using, stealing Celeste's things to sell for cash. Maybe Karin wondered if Tip knew them.

I was confused and wasn't sure if I should ask her more,

but I also wasn't sure how to do that without sounding as if I were accusing Tip of murder or of protecting a killer. At the same time, maybe he was guilty. She was absolutely certain he wasn't. But every killer's lover is certain of their partner's innocence, aren't they?

As she took tiny sips to make what was left in her glass last a bit longer, I let her change the subject. At least now I could go back to Julian and ask him more questions. Now, if he said he couldn't remember, I had a few details to restore the things supposedly erased from his memory.

21

NOW: PARKER

The resentment in my heart was overwhelming, but I couldn't make it stop. Despite the feeling of shame that grew with every turn of my steering wheel, I'd followed Eden when she left our house, keeping two cars behind her all the way to the wine bar. I had to know what she was up to, and when I saw her with Karin, it gutted me. Apparently, it wasn't enough for that girl to lure Dylan away from me, or to keep showing Brianna how she was more amazing than me in every way. Now she was going after my friends.

I saw her and Karin sitting at a table for two at a bistro on the main street where all the restaurant patios opened onto the sidewalk, the tables covered by umbrellas during the day and warmed by gas heaters so they could be enjoyed almost year-round in our balmy California weather.

They were leaning over the table, laughing and talking like the best of friends.

I'd asked Karin to keep an eye on her, but it still hurt to see them like that. It was confusing. I guessed because they looked like they were having such a good time. I hadn't expected that. Karin was the one who'd made that crazy comment about the killer returning to the scene of the crime. I'd thought she was half-kidding, and I knew all her speculating was just gossip and the constant guessing games that people indulged in because no one had ever been arrested, but now they were laughing and talking like the thought had never crossed her mind. From where I stood, it looked like Eden was her best friend, like she might be sharing new speculations and guessing games with Eden, not me.

As I stood across the street, hidden by an SUV and a curbside tree, I saw the server approach their table. The server left, and before I knew it, she'd returned with two more glasses of wine. Well, weren't they having a great time. Eden was stealing my friend right out from under me. It looked like she didn't even have to try very hard.

Karin was my client as well as my friend.

Was Eden planning on going after my business next? She had that amazing, explosive Instagram account with ten times the followers I had. She'd waved it under my daughter's nose and pretended it was just a hobby, but maybe it wasn't. Maybe she wanted to steal my entire life.

I turned and walked away quickly before they saw me. It didn't look like they were planning to leave anytime soon, but I needed to get out of there.

I drove, hardly thinking about where I was going. I ended up at the mall, where I wandered around for almost an hour, stopping to buy a new pair of sandals and two tops. I wasn't really thinking about anything except how much I wanted Eden out of our house and out of my life, but by the time I was finished drifting in and out of stores, I knew I was going to stop by Karin's store. Just to see what she had to say. Hopefully, to see if she was still my friend at all.

The store was due to close in fifteen minutes, and there were only two customers. Karin was at the register, but she wasn't facing the door. She had her head bent over her tablet, working on something. I grabbed a pair of leggings and a headband so it wouldn't look to the other customers like I was wasting her time. Karin would notice that I was a true friend and cared about her business.

I went to the register and placed my purchases on the counter. "Karin, hi! Do you have a minute?" I asked.

"Absolutely. Are you getting these?"

"Yes."

She started ringing up my purchases. The other two customers left, so I guessed I'd bought some expensive yoga pants for nothing. But I would look at it as an investment in our friendship.

She put my purchases in a fabric bag with her logo stamped on it. "The bag's on me," she said.

"Thank you." Maybe that was a sign. She was still my friend after all. "I was right about Eden, you know."

"Oh?" She raised her eyebrows, and I carried on.

"She did come back home to get Dylan. I caught her kissing him."

"What?"

"Yeah." I found I couldn't stop talking, needing Karin to be on my side. "And she's doing morbid things with Brianna and Maverick, taking them to the murder site and—"

"Oh, wow."

"She's turning them against me, especially Brianna." My voice quivered as I said that, and I blinked back tears.

"I'm sorry," she said. "It sounds awful."

"It is." I looked at her, composing myself. "I wonder if you were right."

"About what?" She picked up her tablet and attached the power cord.

"You said that about the killer returning to the scene of the crime. About Eden ..."

"Oh. Right." She laughed softly. "I—"

"When Dylan and I were taking that little break right before Celeste died, Eden told me she was going to go after him."

"Really? You never—"

"She still loves him. It's obvious. And now that her marriage is over ... She was trying to seduce him after she thought I went to bed!" The words snagged at my throat. I felt like I was going to start sobbing.

"It does sound that way." Karin nodded. "It's weird that you dropped by today. I had wine with her just a little while ago. Too much wine." She laughed. "Keeping tabs, like you asked. But she kept talking, so I sort of got pulled into it. Anyway, she was very fixated on this picture of Julian from five years ago."

"What picture?"

"A picture from the memorial."

"Oh." I felt better and worse at the same time. I was happy that Karin obviously hadn't had a great time with Eden. She was still my friend after all. I shouldn't have assumed she was so easy to lure away. But now, it was a little clearer what Eden was up to. She *wanted* Julian to keep hinting that he knew something about Celeste's killer. She was running all over the place asking questions so that Dylan would start living in the past again. She knew I wouldn't like that. In fact, if she was looking at pictures from the fifteen-year memorial, she'd probably been looking at all kinds of things on social media, reading everything I'd posted over the years.

She knew when she came here that I'd been working hard at encouraging Dylan to move on. Now, she wanted to turn him back into an obsessed, grieving mess so she could pick up the pieces. She wanted my husband and my children. The question was—what was she planning to do about me?

I turned my attention back to Karin. "Why was she interested in it?"

Karin shrugged. "It was a photo of me and Julian, and she wanted to know if I remembered what we were talking about."

I laughed. "After five years?"

"I know. Right?" She bent over her tablet again and began tapping at it furiously.

"What did you tell her?"

Karin looked up at me. "Are you okay? You seem really upset."

"I just don't know what she's doing. She wants my family, and I ... this sounds a little ..." I leaned over the counter. It wasn't as if anyone could hear us, but I still felt compelled to whisper. "I don't know how far she'll go to get him."

"What are you ... never mind. I know what you're saying. It sounds crazy, but maybe not. People do crazy things when they've obsessed over someone their entire lives. Think about it. Twenty-five *years*." She was looking directly at me now, her tablet forgotten on the counter. "You need to get her out of your house, Parker."

"I know. I'm scared."

"Then listen to your gut."

"I'm trying. But the harder I try, the harder Dylan fights me."

She nodded, her eyes tired and a little sad, as if she knew exactly what it was like to fight a losing battle with the man you loved.

22

NOW: PARKER

Driving home, an idea came to me. The minute I was inside the house, I texted Karin, inviting her, Tip, and Cole for a BBQ on Saturday. It would be a break from the Eden-Dylan trip down memory lane that I had to endure every evening, and it would make clear to Eden that we were two couples, friends, that she was the outsider who didn't belong. It would show her that I had people who cared about me and would keep me safe.

I spent all afternoon boiling, chilling, and peeling potatoes for salad, cutting fruit, husking corn, and shaping hamburger patties.

Karin, Tip, and Cole arrived at five thirty. Maverick and Cole ran out to the backyard, and Brianna followed. Now that she was right at the doorway to her teens, it took her longer to get busy being a kid, but she still liked playing games in the backyard and goofing around with her brother. She would warm up, and by dinnertime, the three of them would be having such a good time, I would have to plead with them to come to the table.

I served wine to the adults, and we settled on the patio.

Karin talked about her studio, and she and Tip talked about their plans to go camping in Yosemite later that summer. The last time they'd been there, Cole had been only five, so they were looking forward to longer, more challenging hikes with more spectacular views.

Dylan barbecued the burgers while I got the rest of the food ready. We dragged the kids down from Maverick's bedroom, where they were playing Risk, and started eating just as the sky was turning inky blue.

The two glasses of wine I'd consumed, and the way Eden had faded to the background, were giving me a warm glow. I devoured my hamburger and took a second helping of potato salad. I sipped my third glass of wine more deliberately, vowing to enjoy my guests and not to get tipsy.

When there was a brief lull in the conversation, Eden scraped her chair away from the table. She turned so she was facing Tip, who was seated diagonally across from her. "Has Karin told you all the things Julian has been saying about Celeste's murder?"

I felt the wine turn sour in my veins. "It's a beautiful evening; let's not—"

Tip interrupted me without an apology. "What's he been saying?"

"He claims to have seen things that other people don't know about. He wonders if—"

"I don't want to start this all over again." My voice sounded sharp, but Eden was not going to do this.

She ignored me. So did Tip for that matter.

Eden took center stage, lapping up Tip's undivided attention. She began talking about Julian, how he felt about being wrongfully accused, about the unanswered questions that had haunted everyone for two decades now, about how the police were so confident they knew the type of person who had killed her but never identified that person in particular, and how frustrating that was and how it left Celeste without justice and her family without closure.

On and on she talked, as Tip nodded and *hmm*'d and *umm*'d in response.

I took a sip of wine and set my glass down hard. "Stop. Will you please stop? Julian just wants attention. Not having closure is hard, but talking about it constantly makes it worse because it doesn't change anything. Stop giving him airtime. Stop listening to him; stop encouraging him. Just stop." I stood, picked up the wine bottle, and topped off everyone's glass, finishing by asking Tip if he planned to do any fishing when they were in Yosemite.

Thankfully, Tip took the hint, and while he talked about fishing with Cole, Eden closed her eyes. A moment later, she opened them again, stood, and went into the house.

I smiled. It was just as I'd hoped at the start of the evening. She'd realized she wasn't wanted. Maybe she was upstairs packing right this minute. She'd felt the mood, she'd finally read the room as they say, and she knew that Dylan and I were so tightly knit there was no possible way she could ever divide us. He'd loved me from when we were children, and she wasn't going to be able to slither her way into his heart, even if she tried to do it by stealing my children out from under me or by trying to manipulate my friends.

Dylan and I had been through too much. A love that had survived the worst kind of grief and the greatest ecstasy, that had produced children that you both feel with every beat of your heart, a marriage where you've seen into the depths of each other's souls ... that can't be easily splintered. Dylan and I were everything to each other, and I never should have doubted that for even a moment.

I allowed the conversation to wash over me, moving on now from morbid topics, back to the casual chatter of long-time friends.

The sky was growing dark, and the stars looked soft and full of promises. I sensed that my vision was slightly fuzzy from a bit too much wine, but it was okay. We were safe in our home, and a little tipsiness wouldn't hurt anyone.

Karin had been going on about Cole's problems with a kid at school who was sort of bullying him. It wasn't serious yet, and she wanted him to handle it himself, but it was so hard, and she couldn't be sure when it would be the right time to talk to the teacher, and if she did and the other kid was punished, maybe that would make it worse. It was so hard to know what to do.

I glanced toward the end of the table and realized that, while I'd been gazing at the tree line at the back of our property, I hadn't noticed Dylan leave the table. How long had he been gone? Karin had been talking for an awfully long time. I was making sympathetic comments, but she didn't seem to want my input; she mostly wanted to describe her self-doubt in detail.

I put my wineglass on the table and pushed my chair back slightly. "Sorry to interrupt. I'll be right back." I went into the house. The great room was empty, most of the lights off, which I'd been aware of from my seat on the patio.

Following the voices of the kids coming from the second floor, I climbed the stairs.

I found them sitting on the floor in Maverick's room, continuing their game of Risk. Eden was cross-legged on my son's bed, hugging his pillow. Dylan was on the floor with his back propped against the bed.

The warm feelings that had washed over me only a few minutes earlier drained from my body so fast that I felt like I might faint, as if all the blood had run out of me. "Dylan."

He looked at me, smiling.

"What are you doing?"

"Watching Maverick take over the world."

"I can see that. We have guests."

He looked guilty, but he didn't make any move to get up.

"Let's go," I said.

A wave of irritation crossed his face. I knew I sounded like I was talking to one of our children. He hated it when I spoke to him in that tone. It wasn't deliberate. When you're responsible for shepherding children through their schedules, it's easy for that tone to slip into your speech in the business world and with your husband, too. It was unavoidable, as much as I tried. "Tip and Karin are sitting alone out there."

"Chill, Mom," Brianna said.

I tightened my jaw, forcing myself not to snap at her. I would not fight with her; I wouldn't lose control in front of Eden. Not again. I wouldn't spoil this evening and let her win, although it was obvious that she already had.

I glared at Dylan, willing him to return my gaze, but he stared at the board as if the fate of the world truly rested in Maverick's small hands and as if he, Dylan, might be called upon to give strategic guidance. I could demand he go with me, but he already knew that was what I wanted. If I said it again and he failed to come, Eden would have more to gloat over. And I would look like a bitch in front of my daughter, who was already teetering on the edge of viewing me that way. I didn't like the way she'd talked to me, and I didn't like that Dylan hadn't called her on it.

The only winning move was to keep my mouth shut.

I turned and walked out of the room. I went down the stairs slowly, listening to Brianna warning Maverick that she was coming for him. "Don't think you're going to intimidate me!" They all laughed as if this was the funniest thing they'd ever heard. Even Dylan and Eden were laughing.

I hurried down the rest of the stairs and out to the patio.

"Where are Dylan and Eden?" Karin gave me a knowing, concerned look.

For half a second, I wanted to smack her. What did she think? That my husband was inside making out with Eden? That I'd seen them and just left them to it, returning to my dinner guests like the perfect hostess that I am? I didn't like whatever she was implying. Now, I was tired and no longer pleasantly tipsy. I had a tiny headache coming on. I wanted them to leave. Obviously, Dylan wasn't coming back to the table.

"The kids are playing Risk, and Dylan and Eden seem to be very involved in watching." I laughed as if this was both understandable and ridiculous. My laugh sounded shrill and slightly frightened, even to myself. From the look on Karin's face, I imagined it sounded hysterical to her.

Maybe I was reaching the point of hysteria, but I didn't care. I had to find a way to get that woman out of our house.

23

NOW: EDEN

I was so eager to talk to Julian about what I'd learned from Karin that I could hardly pay attention to anything else. To change things up, to help ease Julian into a different frame of mind, I'd decided to invite him over for a drink. I knew he wouldn't step foot inside Parker's house, and I knew she would never allow that, but I thought he might agree to sit on her front porch. I just had to present it in the right way.

It was easy to initiate a casual encounter. He sat on his porch every evening, almost as if he was waiting for an invitation, just as he'd done his entire life. Now that I thought about it and looked at him through the eyes of an adult, I'd begun to see what a lonely kid he must have been. I'd begun to think about how he must have hurt, watching the three of us running off into the woods to play, while he sat alone, ignored, and often laughed at.

No wonder he hid behind those oversized binoculars and pretended they were so powerful they could see things no one else did. He almost acted as if they could see inside our very minds, even if they couldn't see inside our bedrooms.

After he'd been sitting on his porch for about fifteen or twenty minutes, I crossed the street and climbed his porch steps. "Hi, Julian."

He looked at me, but he was wearing large, very dark sunglasses, so I couldn't be sure if his expression was welcoming or irritated.

"You must be burning up. You get a lot of afternoon sun on your porch."

"Thanks for stating the obvious."

"I was going to make myself a gin and tonic. Do you want to join me across the street?"

He laughed.

"Is that a yes?" I smiled in the friendliest way I could manage.

He picked up his insulated cup and took a drink.

"Do you like gin? I could make vodka tonics if you prefer."

"She'll shoot me if she catches me on her porch."

I laughed even though it sounded so inappropriate. "It's fine. She's working. Besides, you're my guest."

"It's not your house, so how can I be your guest?"

"Do you like vodka?"

"As a matter of fact, I do."

"Come on. It's fine. We're all adults now."

"You wouldn't always know that."

"Well, it's time we acted like adults. We're neighbors."

"Are you moving in there?"

I laughed. "No. But I'm here for now. Come on." I took a few steps toward him and extended my hand as if he might need a lift out of the chair. "I know you want one." I could tell he wasn't as hostile as he'd been when I first spoke to him. Telling him that Marco's mom had Parkinson's had really helped. I could see that he had a different view of me now. We had a shared experience that many others couldn't understand, so I wasn't the enemy anymore.

"Why not. I'll take a free drink anytime."

I smiled even though I heaved a sigh inside. He'd turned it into something crude. Maybe he'd simply seen through me. It wasn't as if I were being genuine. I wanted information out of him, and I was luring him out of his comfort zone and oiling his tongue with alcohol in an attempt to get him talking.

He followed me across the street, both of us now aware that this was a transactional engagement. I wondered if he wanted something else from me aside from the free drink.

As he settled on Parker's wicker chair, he asked, "What kind of vodka?"

"Hangar 1. And Absolut."

"I'll take Hangar 1."

I went into the house and mixed the drinks as quickly as I could. I didn't have much time. Parker would be finishing work in the next half hour or so. Once she came out of her office, she wouldn't react well to this invasion of her territory by a man she'd hated all her life. And after the bitter end to her barbecue, I knew his presence might produce an even bigger reaction. I wasn't unaware that I was provoking her, but I didn't care.

I brought the drinks out on a tray and held it in front of Julian. He took a glass, and I settled beside him. I lifted my glass toward his. "Cheers."

"Same." He took a sip.

This wasn't going to go easily if he couldn't even give

enough to offer a pleasant, socially acceptable—false—wish of good cheer.

"So why so friendly? Years of treating me like dirt and now this?" He raised his glass.

"I don't think I treated you like—"

"Don't bullshit me."

"I was a kid, and kids do stupid, mean things."

"Got that right." He took a sip of his drink and stretched out his legs. He wiggled his toes so his flip-flops smacked the bottom of his feet.

"So did *you* lie to the police when you were questioned?"

He laughed.

It shouldn't have been a surprise. It was his go-to response to everything. Serious or not.

"What did you actually see when you were sitting around watching everyone? Or were you just pretending? Did you see something the night Celeste was killed?"

He laughed more softly and took another sip of his drink. He stirred it with his finger, nudging the lime wedge to the side of the glass. "I saw that you were in love with Dylan."

I felt my face get hot. Not the skin, not a blush I worried he would notice, although maybe he sensed it. But that warmth underneath that feels like something inside your body is mocking you, forcing you to recognize something you'd rather not.

"I saw that you were excluded from their little group once those two hooked up." He jerked his head toward the house behind us. "I saw how much that hurt. Maybe you knew how it felt to be me."

I said nothing. Maybe there was more of a connection than just a relative with a debilitating affliction.

"I was accused of killing Celeste for no other reason than because people didn't like me and thought I was a freak. Because I wasn't like everyone else. When I was cleared, do you know how many people apologized for thinking I was a murderer?"

"I don't—"

"Zero."

"Why did you keep going to her memorials if you're so angry and so ... why did you go?"

"Because maybe, at some point, someone needs to pay for thinking I was capable of killing a human being. A lot of them, most of them, thought I did it based on zero evidence. I've had to live with that for twenty years. Some of them still think that."

"I'm sorry."

"Are you?"

I put my glass on the table between us and took my phone out of my pocket. I brought up the picture of Julian and Karin. I held my phone out to him. "This is the picture I mentioned ... of you and Karin. It's from the fifteenth anniversary of her murder."

He glanced at it but didn't take the phone, even though I was holding it right in front of him, touching the edge of the case against his knuckle. He pulled his hand away. "Not that again."

"I think you do remember what you talked about. Karin remembers. She said—"

"I already told you. I'm not gonna remember a conversation from five years ago." He laughed. He shook his glass, rattling the ice, then slurped at the liquid

"Karin said—"

The front door slammed open, and Parker was beside

me, her hand on the back of my chair with such force I felt it move. "What's going on here?"

"We're having a drink."

She must have realized she was in danger of making a scene similar to the one at the barbecue, because she moved in front of me, a regretful smile spreading across her face. "We're going to have dinner soon, and this is really not a good time for company."

Julian put his glass, empty now, on the table. He scooted forward in his chair.

"I don't mean to be rude," Parker said, "but it's actually the worst time. Dylan and I, and our children, desperately need some family time. I'm sure you both understand. Or maybe you don't, but you can try." Her smile widened, exposing her gums.

Julian stood. "Yeah. I need to get going. Good vodka." He crossed the porch, and a moment later, he was already on the opposite side of the street.

Parker picked up both our glasses off the table, even though mine was still half full.

"Again, I don't mean to be rude, Eden, but we are very much in need of some family time. I'd hoped you would recognize that and offer to ... well, anyway. Please make some plans to be out of the house for the evening. We'd like to have a family dinner and spend some time alone with our children."

I looked up at her. "Of course. I didn't realize I was intruding. You should always feel free to speak your mind."

She smiled. "I do."

Her tone told me not to ask for a restaurant recommendation. I texted Karin for that.

An hour later, I was eating a leisurely dinner with a glass

of wine at an Italian place, enjoying the comfort of bread and pasta. After dinner, I went to one of those luxury theaters with lounge chairs that serve alcohol and appetizers. I was surprised our quiet town had one, but I suppose that was required now to lure people out of their homes to a theater.

I indulged in another glass of wine, not as good since it was the theater variety, and a tub of popcorn. It was an odd combination, but also strangely satisfying. When I arrived home, it was after midnight. The house was completely dark and silent. All the bedroom doors closed.

I went into the guest room and closed my door. I had the uneasy sensation that, despite the silence, others were awake and had watched me return. Finally, I got up and locked the bedroom door. Even then, it took a long time for me to fall asleep.

24

2019: EDEN

When I first left California, I'd put the past behind me. The brutal, shocking murder of my best friend's sister. A girl I'd played with at backyard barbecues and looked up to when she went away to college haunted my dreams. But during the daylight hours, I slowly, eventually forced myself to think about other things. After a while, my thoughts naturally turned toward my new life.

The thrill of studying clothing design at a well-respected school, the excitement of living in New York City and meeting so many new, like-minded people made it easier. When I met Marco, my childhood and high school years seemed to dissolve into a fine mist, almost as if they'd been dreams themselves. Images of Celeste's bloodied face still terrified me, appearing without warning in the middle of the most innocuous dreams—convoluted stories in which she was still alive, sometimes living in Italy, created themselves during my sleep on summer nights. But I had a new life.

As the years passed, I was still haunted by her murder, by

the ugly shock of death. Something that was supposed to happen decades in the future, at the end of a happy, productive life, not on a warm summer night in the days following high school graduation. Slowly, I began to feel as if her murder was something I recalled from a movie I'd seen, or an engrossing novel I'd read. The longer I stayed away, the less real it felt.

Moving to Italy magnified that sense of unreality. I was a different person with a different life. My parents and brother came to visit me there, and I never returned home. I learned to speak Italian and a smattering of other languages. After a while, I even found myself thinking in Italian. I was crazy in love with my husband. We had an exciting life with lots of friends and parties and careers we loved.

Then Marco pulled the rug out from under me.

Marco and I always knew we would have children, but we weren't in a hurry. When we casually started trying, neither of us were bothered that we didn't get pregnant right away. The months passed. Then a year. I went to the doctor. He went to the doctor. We did tests. And it turned out, I was the one to *blame*. And blame he did.

Slowly, ever so slowly, like water dripping on a stone, he began to remark more frequently and with increasing emotion about our friends' children. *What a delight they were. Such a blessing. The meaning of life, the joy of existence.*

In an effort to escape the sense of failure that burned in me under his constant disappointment, I began spending more time checking social media to see what my former friends and classmates were up to.

I retreated deeper into my online world, to the point that I wondered if I was becoming a virtual stalker. I wondered if I'd become like Julian, watching their lives from the shadows. I read every post and scrutinized the meaning of every emoji. I searched out friends of friends and scrolled through every photograph that was posted. I clicked to see the images in full size. Occasionally, I downloaded them and studied them further, trying to see in their faces and their gestures how they'd changed and how they'd remained the same. I read between the lines of their words, and I even noticed when they edited their comments and wondered at the moods and insecurities that had caused them to make the updates.

All of this started about six months before the fifteenth anniversary of Celeste's death.

So when the memorial event was held, I spent an entire weekend reading the tributes, of which there were hundreds, even after all that time. I enlarged every single photograph and studied the people I'd known, faint lines and shadows changing their faces from teenagers to settled adults.

I was especially attentive to photographs of Dylan and Parker. I marveled at how their children were near mirror images of Parker; I was stunned by how fast they were growing up.

I watched the videos that were posted.

There was one photograph that I kept returning to.

Karin Shapiro and Julian Taggart were sitting in the back row, facing a sea of empty white chairs. They leaned toward each other, their arms and shoulders tense, their mouths open, talking at the same time. It was clear they were having a very intense conversation and very likely arguing with each other.

I couldn't stop looking at it. Each time I went to the other photographs, each time I checked on Parker's latest updates, admittedly obsessing just a little bit about what she was saying, trying to figure out what her life was like now, I returned to that picture of Julian and Karin. I hadn't been able to stop looking at that photo of those two who had never been friends, who did not look at all like friends now, but who obviously had a lot to talk about.

It nagged at me.

And so, Celeste emerged from my dreams and began to haunt me in daily life. Not literally, obviously. I wasn't the type to believe in ghosts, and even when I thought I saw her in a crowd, I never once imagined it was actually her, but I felt disturbed. I felt like she'd so taken over my thoughts that I mistook every nineteen-year-old woman with dark, wavy hair and long legs to be Celeste—not really dead, her murder a nightmare that hadn't truly happened, or had happened to some other person who wasn't really me.

That photograph of Julian and Karin planted a seed that maybe it was time to return home, to find out if people were still wondering who had really murdered Celeste, to find out what they were saying. I started to wonder if people knew things they hadn't told the police. I wondered, if that was the case, maybe now, after all these years, might they be ready to tell the truth?

That was when I thought there might be a reason why Parker had replaced me with Karin Shapiro. She'd hardly given her the time of day in high school. Now, they were closer than sisters. I needed to know why. I needed to know a lot of things.

25

NOW: DYLAN

You can let go of something a thousand times, a hundred thousand times, but when that thing whispers there's a new secret that might be exposed, you dive back to the bottom of the murky lake, grabbing at every shrouded object, hoping this time you'll discover the answer. Finally, you'll know the truth.

As I stood in our bedroom, changing into a T-shirt from a button-down after work, I saw Eden and Julian crossing the street. They disappeared from view at the front of our house. I went out to the landing, still tugging the T-shirt over my head. I heard Eden come into the house, and I heard her filling glasses with ice. There were no voices, so I assumed Julian was on the front porch, and I assumed Parker was still in her office, unaware that the man she loathed was probably relaxing on our front porch.

When I heard the front door open and close, I crept down the stairs and went out the back. I walked around the side of the house and stood out of view, listening to Eden and Julian. Their conversation went in circles, which wasn't surprising, but it shook me when he suggested someone needed to pay for wrongfully accusing him. I hadn't realized he held such a grudge. I suppose I'd been so blinded by my own grief and frustration. I'd never once considered how he felt. We'd never been friends, and I'd assumed when he was questioned it was the same as when the cops had talked to me. Doing their supposed due diligence, not caring how it felt to be accused of murder. It had been far worse for me to be accused of my sister's murder. Any upset Julian might have experienced was so pale in comparison, it never registered with me.

I really needed to know what he was talking about. I needed to know if he'd actually seen something. Eden wasn't turning the screws tightly enough. It was time for me to confront Julian myself.

THE FOLLOWING DAY, I didn't even pull into our garage. I didn't want Parker to hear the door opening. Julian's car in the driveway assured me that he was home, so I stopped at the curb in front of his house and went to the door. I rang the bell and waited. I was a little surprised he wasn't sitting on the porch. Especially in the summer, he'd been a fixture there all his life. Maybe he'd arrived home only moments before I'd turned the corner.

Trying not to look like a creep, peeking through the front window, I glanced into the entryway but didn't notice any movement. I rang the bell again. After another half a minute, I knocked, then rang the bell, aware that I was becoming too aggressive. I stepped back, telling myself to relax. He wasn't going to come running if I made it sound like the police were at the door, banging and demanding immediate attention.

He had to be in there. His red Jeep Wrangler was sitting as if he'd pulled in moments earlier or was ready to go out, its oversized wheels suggesting he could easily escape into the wild, but as far as I knew, all he did was drive it the three-mile round trip to his veterinary clinic every day.

I rang the bell again, aware that he probably wasn't going to answer. Was he watching me through a security camera? I looked up, checking the eaves for a white plastic box with a dark eye, but there was nothing. Maybe he simply knew he wasn't interested because the only knocks on his door were for package deliveries, and he wasn't expecting any.

I walked down the steps, trying to decide what to do. Now I had it in my mind that I needed to speak to him, I couldn't bring myself to simply walk away. He was right there; why was he refusing to come to the door? It was possible he wasn't feeling well, possible he was in the shower or using the toilet or napping after taking emergency calls through the night and working all day.

Walking around the side of the house, I paused at the fence gate. It was crossing a line, literally, if I unlatched the gate and went into his yard. He wouldn't take it well, yet the longer I was here, the longer he failed to come to the door, the more desperate I was to talk to him. I was annoyed at myself for having waited so long. I should have gone over the moment Eden told me he was dropping hints that he knew things about my sister's death. What right did he have to keep secrets about a crime like that? He should have spoken to me or gone straight to the police. But he'd never been a person who did what he should have done. Not since he was a little kid, making everyone on the street uncomfortable with his binoculars.

Although that hadn't started until he was about twelve. What had he been like before that? Why hadn't any of us played with him? I honestly couldn't remember. Parker and Eden were my entire world back then. All the other kids in the neighborhood and at school were background shadows. I never thought about what they did or how they felt.

I unlatched the gate and stepped into the backyard.

I walked onto the patio, not trying to remain unseen, wanting to be aboveboard so that when he saw me, he wouldn't be enraged that I was trespassing. I was simply concerned. That was what I would tell him. And it was the truth, for the most part.

Crossing yet another line, I tried the back door. Locked. I peered through the glass. His cat stared back at me. It yowled, showing its long pink tongue and thin, sharp teeth. It continued crying, the sounds so loud and angry I could hear through the glass. I glanced toward the kitchen. The cat's food and water dish were near the bar that divided the kitchen and eating areas. Both bowls were empty.

Now, I was concerned. Maybe he hadn't gone to work at all. Maybe he was ill and needed help. Not feeding the cat suggested he hadn't come downstairs, that he couldn't eat or even get a clean glass of water.

Knowing I was creating future problems for myself, knowing there might be other explanations, but overcome by curiosity and my urgent need to talk to him immediately, my irrational conviction that he knew something important, and that every minute was a delay in finding out something that would finally, after all these years, help me identify my sister's killer, I hurried back to my car. I grabbed my jacket off the passenger seat and returned to Julian's backyard.

I pulled my phone out of my pocket and looked up the non-emergency number for the police. I called and asked for a welfare check for my neighbor. I explained his car was in the driveway, he lived alone, and his cat hadn't been fed. I was told they would send someone within half an hour.

But I couldn't wait. What if he needed help immediately and a half hour would be too late?

Wrapping the jacket around my fist and lower arm, I approached a narrow window on the side of the house. I punched my fist into the glass. It cracked slightly but didn't break. I should have known. I went to the backyard and unscrewed the spray nozzle from the hose. I took it back to the side of the house and used it to smash the window until enough glass broke that I could remove the rest, making an opening large enough to climb through.

Images of Julian's face and the rage he would spew on me over his broken window filled my head, but I pushed them aside. I was helping him. And maybe, if he was in a truly desperate situation, he would be so grateful he would stop his petty games and tell me straight up what he knew.

I entered the house. The cat's complaints grew fiercer as I checked the front room downstairs that he used as a home office, just as Parker did ours. Then I climbed the stairs.

"Julian?" A feeling of dread pressed against my chest from the inside. The certainty I'd felt when I smashed the window had faded.

"Julian? It's Dylan from across the street. You okay? I was worried. I know I'm out of line here, but I was worried. The cat was hungry, and ... Julian?"

About halfway up the stairs, I heard sounds of someone

moaning and then the slightly over-the-top cries of people enjoying sex coming through a speaker.

I was at the top of the stairs now. I paused. I didn't have a good feeling. There was an odor of ... I put my hand over my mouth and nose. I didn't think I was going to have to apologize, and I wasn't sure I was going to feel good about what I was about to discover. I should probably wait for the police, but something pushed me forward. Curiosity. Morbid curiosity. The need to know.

The door to the walk-in closet was open, and Julian was inside. His body was hanging from the top bar, the clothes shoved to the side. He was naked, with a belt around his neck, his tongue protruding through his partially opened lips. I gagged.

His skin was an awful color that I couldn't even find a word for. I gagged again. I slapped my hand over my mouth, starting to back out of the room, turning away from him. On a folding tray designed for eating meals in front of the TV was his laptop. An amateur porn webcam site was playing. I wanted to close the laptop, to make it stop, but decided the police might not like that.

I backed out of the room, still gagging, tasting vomit as I swallowed it. I wanted to use his toilet to be rid of it, but something made me stop, not wanting to leave any part of myself beyond what I'd already done—breaking the window, walking up the stairs, entering the closet ...

I stumbled down the stairs and out the front door, gagging and trying to gulp in fresh air at the same time. I went to my car and grabbed my water bottle out of the holder. I poured some into my mouth, then spit into the gutter. I swallowed more, spitting mouthfuls into the street.

It seemed like hours before the police arrived, but I think

it was a few minutes more than the promised thirty. Someone at my house must have looked out the window, because the next time I looked over, Parker, Eden, Brianna, and Maverick were all standing on the front porch.

They walked slowly down the steps, heading toward me in what seemed like slow motion, as if something about the way I stood, my posture, the expression on my face as they drew closer, told them what I'd found.

Things continued to unfold in slow motion. After a while, the officer instructed my family to return home, but kept me standing by the police car. A paramedic vehicle arrived, followed closely by a white van and another police car.

They asked me a few perfunctory questions, then sent me to join my family.

Parker took Brianna and Maverick inside before they removed the body.

Later that night, the growing chasm between my wife and I widened further when I told her that clearly Julian had known something, and that now the person who had murdered my sister had silenced him.

"Don't go there," Parker said. "He liked kinky sex, and he pushed it too far. That's all. Or else he had a guilty conscience and did it on purpose."

"You're wrong," I said. "Julian was a lot of things, but he wasn't careless enough to die in a situation like that."

26

NOW: PARKER

Dylan would not shut up about Julian being murdered. He felt compelled to repeatedly describe how he'd found the body and refused to even entertain the idea it was anything but murder.

He kept me up late after he found the body. He wanted to tell me every step of what he'd done, why he went over there, how he'd had a bad feeling when Julian didn't answer the door, about how pathetic the cat's cries were and how that should have told him ... "I should have known, I should have *known* it wasn't just a hungry cry."

I asked him to stop torturing himself with such gruesome memories, but he wouldn't stop. That had always been his weakness. He had to relive everything. He said that was how he processed things. He had to think through every little detail and tell the story over and over again until I wanted to scream.

He had to tell me about the smell and the sound of the porn as he was walking up the stairs. He even had to tell me about swallowing his own vomit. It was all so disgusting. I just wanted him to stop talking.

And Eden sat there eating up every word, encouraging him.

The next night, she brought it up at dinner. Right in front of our children.

I shot them both warning looks. I asked them to stop, but they ignored me.

"I know it was an elaborate scene," Dylan said. "But I think whoever it was wanted it to look like an accident. They want it to be over."

"What scene?" Brianna asked.

"We're not talking about this now," I said.

"Why not?" Brianna flicked her hair over her shoulder and picked up her fork.

"Because it's not appropriate."

"Why not? No one ever died on our street." She glanced at her father. "I mean ... sorry. I ..."

"It's okay," Dylan said.

"We're not talking about this. It's morbid and horrible, and it's not appropriate dinner table conversation."

"We talk about other bad things at dinner," Maverick said.

"No, we don't. We talk about—"

He interrupted me. "You talk about war, and you worry about nuclear stuff. That's a lot worse."

"That's different," I said.

"Yeah," Brianna said. "It's worse. I want to know what happened. I want to know if someone killed him. I want to know if there's an actual murderer running around here. I mean, should I be scared? Should I be carrying pepper spray or—"

"Stop," I said.

"They know what happened," Eden said. "It's natural they're going to have questions. You can't—"

"Stay out of this, Eden. It's none of your business," I said. Dylan talked over me, as if he didn't even hear me. "All I'm saying is that someone doesn't just suddenly die in a weird, unusual situation like that. Not when he's been telling anyone who will listen that he knows something about a murder. It's too much of a coincidence."

"I agree," said Eden.

"What is the weird situation?" Brianna asked. "I can't keep up with the story if you're hiding all the important details from us. I know what goes on in the world. Stop treating me like a little kid. Did he have someone in his bed or something? Were there two dead bodies? Three? Was he shooting up? What is it?"

"Nothing! We're not discussing this anymore," I said, raising my voice.

"You're making it worse," Eden said. "You're stirring up their curiosity. They have a right to know. He was your neighbor. They saw—"

I shoved my chair away from the table. "Brianna, Maverick, I want you to go outside and play." I began clearing the dishes even though there was still food on everyone's plates.

"Calm down, Parker. We're still eating." Dylan held onto his plate so I couldn't take it.

Brianna and Maverick pushed their chairs away from the table, although very reluctantly. They left the room slowly, turning to look back, clearly hoping to hear whatever conversation resumed once they were out of my line of sight. At least my children still listened to me some of the time.

I scraped food off my plate and stuck the plate in the

dishwasher. I picked up the next plate and began scraping food into the disposal.

"It's important to answer their questions," Dylan said.

"Will you please leave us alone, Eden."

She gave a tiny sigh, glanced at Dylan, then left the room.

"She's driving a wedge between us. Can't you see that?"

"What are you talking about? She didn't do anything."

"She's telling us how to raise our children!"

"She was right about that. They do have a right to know, and when you make a big deal of not telling them things, it makes them more curious."

"It's sick. And they don't need to know."

"They're going to hear about it from other kids. They're going to read about it online. You can't protect them from that. It's better if we explain it to them and give them context."

"Well, not in front of her. And I don't like her telling us how to parent."

"She was just—"

"I don't like it. And you shouldn't either. This is between us. She's driving us apart too."

"How is she doing that?"

"By feeding your unresolved feelings."

"She doesn't have to feed anything. Those feelings are there. You know that."

"I do. And you've worked hard to move past all of that."

"She's not the one who brought it all back to the surface. Julian did that."

"Because she got him going."

He stood and came over to the sink. "This is all very upsetting, but maybe it's a good thing. Maybe we'll finally get some answers. Maybe they'll reopen the investigation into Celeste's murder."

I turned to face him. "Come on, Dylan! They aren't going to reopen the investigation. They knew it was drugs. There was absolutely nothing to tell them it was anything else. Just because they never found the actual person doesn't make that not true. We've been over that a million times. I know it really hurts and you want an answer, but there isn't one. Julian had a horrible accident. That kind of thing happens all the time to people who play around with choking and sex. Look how you found him. It's so obvious."

"It's a coincidence that defies the odds. The police make mistakes. We hear about that all the time, and those are just the mistakes that get found out. There's a whole organization devoted to clearing people who are wrongfully imprisoned because of mistakes made during police investigations."

"No one was wrongfully imprisoned."

"That's beside the point. Mistakes are made. Every day. In *every* profession. You're always yelping about mistakes on social media."

"Oh my God! It's social media. Not a murder investigation."

"Human beings make mistakes. That's my point."

I took a deep breath. I grabbed a towel and dried my hands. "Okay. We're off track here. The point is, Eden is talking about things I don't want the kids to be focused on. And if they do have questions, you and I should be answering them, without her input."

"Why? I don't see the big deal."

"She's inserted herself into our family like a permanent

fixture. We have no idea when she's leaving. She acts like she's co-parenting our children. She—"

"Why all the hostility?"

"Because you can't see what's happening!"

"Nothing is happening. Our best friend, someone who was a central part of both our lives, who disappeared for two decades, is here, and we have a chance to make up for lost time."

"Making up for lost time is a myth. And why is she suddenly here?"

"She came to remember Celeste."

"But why is she still here? What does she want? Think about it."

He took a few steps away from me at the very moment I hoped he would put his arms around me and pull me close. I wanted him to tell me I was right, that she was in the way, that she'd long overstayed her welcome. Fish and house guests and all that.

"She wants to spend time with her closest childhood friends. Like I do. Like I would have thought you did."

"No. She's trying to take you away from me." I started crying. I hadn't meant to, but I was scared. I didn't understand why he couldn't see what was so blatantly obvious. Was he really completely unaware? Or was he pretending? I wondered what he would say if I told him what Karin had said about killers returning to the scene of the crime. He probably wouldn't be sympathetic toward Karin.

"She's not. I told you this kiss—"

"It's not just the kiss. She's trying to turn my children against me!"

"I can't believe how childish you're being!" His voice was louder than necessary. It made me grab my arms, wanting to give myself a hug. The more I tried to explain what was happening, the wider the space between us grew.

Seeing something from the corner of my eye, I glanced toward the doorway where I had a glimpse of the stairs, my vision blurred by tears. Maverick stood on the bottom step. When he saw me, he jumped off the step and raced through the room. "Stop fighting!" His voice sounded as teary as my own. He flung open the sliding door and ran across the patio and onto the lawn. A moment later, I lost sight of him.

"Now look," I said.

Dylan glared at me.

He strode across the room to the door that Maverick had left open and went out to the patio.

"Maverick!"

From where I stood, the backyard appeared deserted. I went out to the patio and stood beside my husband, leaving a space between us, feeling as if we were strangers, scanning the area for a child who appeared to have vanished into thin air.

There was a redwood fence for privacy that ran along both sides of our yard, but along the back where the yard met up with the wooded preserve, we had only a low chain-link fence meant to disappear into the scenery while keeping out some of the wild animals that came out of the woods looking for pet food and water during drought years. No fence kept the raccoons away.

The gate in the fence stood open.

"Do you think he went into the woods?" I asked, feeling stupid at the obvious nature of my question.

"Maverick!" Dylan shouted. "Where are you?"

I crossed the lawn to the tree at the back of our yard

where his tree house was located. I stood near the trunk and looked up to be sure he wasn't crouched on the platform with its simple walls and flat roof, the opening large enough to see all of the interior.

"He's not in there?" Dylan called.

I shook my head.

Dylan called his name several more times as he walked toward me. As anxiety crept up my spine, we both turned and walked toward the open gate. We went through and into the wooded area. It wasn't thick with trees. There were also plenty of clearings and groupings of rocks. We'd loved playing there as kids, inventing all kinds of games, wading in the creek, collecting stones and building forts out of fallen branches.

We alternated calling Maverick's name as we wandered aimlessly, not sure which direction he might have taken. We didn't allow either of our children to play in the woods unsupervised. I suspected Brianna had been in there with her friends, but I tried not to think about it.

The kids who occasionally hung out there smoking weed, and the few who smoked meth or did other more dangerous drugs when we were teenagers, no longer chose the tranquil setting for getting high. Still, because Celeste had died there, it gave both of us a bad feeling to allow our children to play there. At the same time, we didn't make it a hard rule because there's nothing like drawing a sharp line to entice your children to want to see how close they can get, to give them the desire to cross over.

After walking beside the creek for a while, my heartbeat feeling increasingly erratic, we turned and started along the path that led out and went between our house and the one next door, ending on the street so that everyone in the neighborhood had access.

My whole body was shaking now. Finally, Dylan put his arm around me, but it didn't feel as comforting as I'd hoped. I couldn't believe Maverick had gone far. At the same time, it was getting dark now.

"We need to call for help. Are we making a mistake by not continuing to look in the woods?"

"Let me text Eden." He pulled his phone out of his pocket. "And Brianna."

"I meant the police," I said.

"I think that's premature. It's only been fifteen minutes. He's just upset we were arguing. He's probably hiding."

"I'm scared." My voice trembled.

He squeezed my shoulders, then let go as he started texting.

"Maverick!" My voice was more of a shriek now, filled with panic.

Then I saw him. He was sitting between our trash and recycling bins, his back pressed against the side of the house, hugging his knees.

I ran along the last stretch of the path and into the partial enclosure where we kept the bins. I knelt in front of him and pulled him into my arms. I let my tears fall into his hair. "Why did you run away? You scared me."

"I don't like shouting."

"We weren't shouting."

"Yes, you were."

Dylan was standing behind me now.

I moved back, and Dylan held out his hand to help me to my feet. I pulled Maverick up, and we hugged him, hugging each other at the same time.

After a few minutes of reassurance, Dylan suggested ice cream.

Of course, Eden had to shove herself in our faces while the four of us ate ice cream, telling the kids they really needed to try gelato if they'd never had it.

Later, in bed, just as I was drifting to sleep, when I thought maybe Dylan had had a little wake-up call during our few minutes of panic, he turned away from me instead. "Maybe you should worry more about Celeste's killer hurting our children than whatever you're imagining about Eden."

After that, it took me over an hour to relax enough to fall asleep.

27

NOW: DYLAN

I didn't for a single minute believe Parker's accusation that Eden had come back and moved into our house to break apart our marriage or to steal her family away from her or whatever nonsense she was telling herself. I couldn't even figure out where she was getting those ideas. If it had only been the kiss, I would have blamed myself, but it was something else, something deeper. I didn't understand how she could imagine even for a moment that anyone could turn her children against her. Was she losing her grip on reality? Who thinks like that? It sounded like something out of a sappy melodrama.

Still, it worried me that no matter what her wild ideas were, if she believed them, then it probably would be best for Eden to leave our house. I didn't want to be unwelcoming, but an indefinite visit was clearly straining our marriage, at least from Parker's perspective. We'd had our ups and downs. All marriages do, but the added stress of what I'd gone through with my sister's murder, followed by losing both my parents in such a short time, and at a young age, had been rough. Parker had been a rock for me, and I didn't want to dismiss her concerns without any thought of how she might be feeling.

But I also didn't want to give up my belief that three people who'd had the kind of friendship we'd had couldn't find their way back to that. We'd been everything to each other. Parker and Eden were the landscape of my childhood. They formed some of my earliest memories, and they were part of the happiest years of my life before my heart was sliced open by my sister's death.

It wasn't as if I hadn't found happiness, but I remembered my childhood like it was my personal fairy tale. And I refused to believe we couldn't recapture at least some of that. Deep inside, at our core, we were the same people.

And, besides all of that, Eden was as certain as I was that Julian's death was not an accident. Her belief was gratifying. The coincidence was too unbelievable, but since Parker didn't see it that way, I liked having someone around who was as certain as I was.

The weird circumstances of Julian's death went too far beyond what we knew about him. Sure, of course he had secrets. Everyone does, and everyone knows that. His sex life was none of our business and might very well have involved the kind of game his death suggested. But I couldn't shake the feeling that even if that was his habit, then why now? If he'd done that sort of thing for years, why had he died now, just as he'd begun announcing to anyone who would listen that he knew things about my sister's murder? Things the police never discovered?

Parker refused to even discuss the possibility. She wanted it to be over once and for all. A small part of me understood that. I'd had therapy. We'd gone to couples counseling. We'd worked through the unfinished nature of my sister's murder. We'd worked through my grief, Parker's grief, all of it. I completely understood her desire for a *normal* life, as she called it. But the strange circumstances of Julian's death weren't something I'd gone looking for. This had blown up right in my face, and I couldn't ignore it.

Still, I had to be fair to Parker. I trusted her. Maybe her instincts weren't perfect, but there was a reason she thought Eden had some kind of ulterior motive in returning after all these years. It was only fair to dig into that a little more than I had, rather than taking everything our old friend said at face value.

I found Eden in Celeste's bedroom, sitting on the bed, reading her tablet. A mug of tea was on the nightstand. The door to the room was partially opened, which was why I'd thought to look in there. Normally, Parker liked that door closed, the room off-limits to Brianna and Maverick. Because the door to Celeste's room was beside the stairs, out of the way after we'd done our remodel when I inherited the house from my parents, it was easy to forget it was there. I'd wanted it kept as my sister had left it. Parker did not, but she gave in to me, as long as the door remained closed and it wasn't treated like some kind of holy shrine, as she put it.

I knocked on the doorframe. "Can we talk for a minute?"

"Sure." She closed the cover on her tablet.

I shut the door behind me and pulled out the ladderback chair from Celeste's desk and straddled it. I leaned on the back, resting my chin on my forearms, possibly to make myself appear more casual than I felt. It seemed as if I was about to attack her, accusing her of something absurd—the imaginings of a slightly paranoid woman that I was forced to pretend were my own. "We haven't really talked about what made you decide to come to the memorial after all these years."

She raised her eyebrows. "Several things came together at once, I suppose."

"Oh?"

"My divorce. Obviously. I felt a little lost. I still do."

"You haven't said much about it."

"I thought I'd made a life for myself in Milan, but it turned out I'd only been adopting Marco's life." She shrugged, and I saw the sadness cloud her expression. "Most of our friends stopped inviting me out when we separated. They didn't turn on me or anything ugly like that, but they just, you know, drifted away. Faded out of my life."

"That must have been tough."

"It was."

Her eyes looked watery. She picked up her mug and took a sip of tea, obviously trying to soothe herself.

"I realized I'd left my whole life behind when I went away to school. It felt ... I don't know, unfinished. Celeste was murdered, and that whole summer was so awful, and then I left. And it felt like I'd moved into an entirely different universe."

"I can see how it would feel that way."

"All new people, all new scenery, learning so many new things, thinking about my future. Loving my classes. Then meeting Marco."

I nodded.

"Anyway, when things got difficult with us, I started thinking about the past. After he left, I was almost obsessed. I realized I wanted to say a final goodbye to her. I said goodbye at her funeral, but I never ... when I saw it was the last memorial, that was part of it. And selfishly, maybe I thought coming back to the past would help me figure out my future. It sounds like a fantasy, but I'm still hoping." She smiled.

"So, no brilliant revelations?"

She laughed. "Not yet. But as I said, still hoping."

"I feel a little awkward saying this, so I'll just put it out there. Parker thinks you're trying to break us up." I laughed, and I sounded as awkward and nervous as I felt. "That you came back to break up our family."

She stared at me for several seconds. Then she started laughing. "Why would I do that? Seriously? Why would I want to break up your family?"

"I'm not sure." I laughed with her, still sounding awkward. I felt like my wife's marionette. At the same time, I was glad to be supporting her. I wasn't blowing off her concerns. This was what our marriage needed. Mutual understanding of the other's point of view. That's what we'd been told by our counselor. And it was the truth. "Maybe because of whatever happened between you two after Celeste was killed."

"I don't even know what happened."

"What? Over the wedding?"

She shrugged, then shook her head slightly.

I sat up and curled my hands around the top edge of the chair. This was a waste of time. I'd given Parker's crazy ideas enough airtime. She needed to stop looking at life through such a negative, suspicious lens.

I stood. "I hope you're getting lots of time to think. To figure things out. It's good to reconnect, and I'm sure Parker will come around."

She smiled at me, and I knew that she knew Parker had put me up to this.

"I'll let you get back to your tea and your reading," I said, and then I went into our bedroom and changed into running clothes. I needed some fresh air and sweat.

I was not giving up. The three of us had been too close, too connected, formed too many memories and lifetime bonds over all those years together. I refused to stop believing we couldn't rebuild that. I absolutely believed what I'd said to Eden—Parker would come around.

The truth was, Parker was acting out some teenaged spat. And she didn't like it that Eden agreed with me about Julian's death. She didn't like it that there were unanswered questions about my sister's murder that might still be answered, even now.

28

NOW: PARKER

Because Dylan had been the one to make the gruesome discovery of Julian's corpse, Detective Harrow made a courtesy call to tell us the death had been ruled an accident. He didn't use the word *gruesome*, of course. But it was. Dylan felt ill every time he thought about the scene he'd come upon in Julian's bedroom. I felt sick thinking about what he'd had to go through and how those vivid images were making him more upset.

Now, more than ever, he could not stop talking about Julian and his supposed secrets. He almost moaned as he spoke, chastising himself for not speaking to Julian sooner, not going over there a day earlier, hours earlier. I don't know what he thought he could have done.

After the detective left, Dylan went into the kitchen and opened a beer. He didn't offer me one, so I grabbed one for myself.

He took his beer out to the front porch. Instead of sitting down to drink it in comfort, or even leaning on the railing, he stood in the center of the porch, staring at Julian's house. He drank his beer and said nothing.

"Let's go out back and relax," I said.

He ignored me and took another long swallow from the bottle.

"It's morbid to stand there and stare at his house."

"It wasn't an accident. How can they not see that?"

"They said it was."

"They're lazy," he said.

"They're not."

"Julian was strange, but there's no way he was into that kind of thing. He had medical training. He wouldn't do something so risky."

"Medical training for animals and people is not the same thing," I said. "Besides, sometimes people who are experts are the worst."

"Someone killed him and made it look like an accident."

I heard the front door open. I turned, already knowing who I would see. Eden was standing there, holding a beer. That woman had radar or something. We couldn't be alone for three minutes without her appearing as if she could hear us from anywhere in the house, even when we whispered or closed the door. The only place she hadn't appeared was in our bedroom. Yet.

"What did the detective say?" Eden asked.

"Accident." Dylan swigged his beer. "I told him it wasn't, and he went on about lack of evidence suggesting anything else. Just like with my sister."

"That's not at all like your sister," I said.

Eden took three steps toward my husband and touched his arm. She rubbed it gently. She turned and looked at me, then yanked her hand away as if she'd scorched it.

I stared at her, not smiling. She took a few steps away from Dylan. I went to the double swing and sat down, expecting Dylan to join me, but he remained where he was, like a pillar of salt in the middle of the porch, staring at the now-empty house across the street. A chill ran through me as I had the horrifying thought that Eden might decide to buy it.

I got up and went into the house. I needed some moral support here. Karin had been shocked by Julian's death, overcome by guilt she couldn't really explain. I sent her a text and asked her to bring us a plate of her amazing chocolate chip cookies for dessert. She often did this, but hadn't been by since Eden planted herself in our house. She replied with an emoji that was a shower of cookies. I added a message telling her about the accidental death ruling, but she didn't respond.

Returning to the front porch, I found Dylan and Eden on the swing. Eden looked up at me but didn't make a move to get up. I leaned on the railing with my back to Julian's house, sipped my beer, and willed Karin to drive faster.

A few minutes later, I heard her pull up in front of our house. I turned and watched as she got out of her small SUV, walked around to the passenger side, and removed a cookie tin from the front seat. She approached the porch, greeting everyone in a somber tone. "Parker told me the cops decided it was an accident."

"It wasn't," Dylan said.

Karin handed the cookie tin to me. "Your favorites."

"Thanks." I gave her a light hug. "Do you want a beer?"

She shook her head.

She hopped onto the railing, letting her feet dangle, crossing her ankles. I stared at her toe rings, wondering why I'd wanted her there. It was an impulsive decision because I'd felt ganged up on by Dylan and Eden and their murder obsession. Now, I saw that having Karin there would make it impossible to change the subject, impossible to move Dylan on to some other, productive activity. Now, I was trapped with a semi-social gathering. Often strangely curious about adult conversations, Brianna and Maverick might wander out to the porch to hear what we were talking about.

I was glad Karin had declined the beer, but not happy she was sitting on the railing and not happy I'd asked for the cookies because I felt rude not offering one to Dylan and Eden. I placed the tin beside me, hoping no one would ask.

"I can't believe he's gone," Karin said. "And it's so ... I feel so guilty. Don't you?" She looked at each of us in turn, letting her gaze linger too long, making sure we made eye contact with her.

"Why would I feel guilty?" Dylan asked.

"We were so awful to him."

"He was a creep," I said. "I know, I know. We shouldn't speak ill of the dead, but he was. I don't feel guilty for anything. He never tried to be friendly. He tried to scare us and make us uncomfortable. All I did was protect myself. You're not required to make friends with someone who makes you feel threatened."

No one said anything. Their silence made me feel as if they were all judging me, as if they thought I had absolutely spoken ill of the dead. All I'd done was tell the truth.

Dylan tipped his beer back and swallowed the rest. He stood and went into the house.

"I don't think we should feel guilty." I said this in a softer voice. "It was an accident, so there's nothing to feel guilty about. Things happen. It's not like he killed himself because he felt shunned or something like that."

"What if it wasn't an accident," Karin said. "What if Dylan's right?"

I looked at Eden, expecting her to jump on, but maybe she only did that for Dylan's benefit. Now that he was gone, she couldn't be bothered.

Karin looked at the porch floor. Her hair covered the sides of her face, and her voice was so low, I had to lean forward to hear. "I feel guilty because Julian wanted me to tell the police I lied for Tip the night Celeste died."

I glanced at Eden. She looked unsurprised by this information. I was confused. Why was Karin telling us this? Did she still think Eden had killed Celeste? Was she going to accuse her of that to her face?

"I've always wondered if that caused them to miss something. And I'm thinking ..." She looked directly at Eden, giving her a hard stare. It looked threatening, even if I wasn't reading into it. I didn't think I was.

"I have to convince Tip to talk to the detective. It's a different guy now. And there's the way Julian tried to pressure me all these years to tell them I lied, and now he's dead ... I think we need to tell them. I don't know if Tip will agree, but it really is the right thing to do. It's the only way I'll stop feeling this guilt, I think."

Eden still hadn't said a word. Her expression hadn't changed at all.

Karin's eyes were cold and hard, staring at Eden, as if she was daring her to convince her not to go to the cops, daring her to forget everything and move on.

I desperately wished I could know what both of them were thinking. Karin sounded like she was threatening Eden.

One thing was certain, and it was something that made me feel hopeful. Maybe Karin and Tip going to the police would get them focusing on Eden, get them asking her all kinds of uncomfortable questions. Maybe ... if I was lucky, it would get Eden out of my house. Maybe they would even charge her with killing Celeste. And Julian. Was that possible?

I reached down and picked up the tin of cookies. I removed the lid. I stood and walked to the swing. "Do you want a cookie, Eden?"

She shook her head. I smiled and offered one to Karin, who also declined. I returned to my spot by the railing and ate one myself.

29

NOW: EDEN

For some reason, the conversation on Parker's front porch felt staged. I couldn't say why I felt this way. I wasn't sure if it was Karin's sudden arrival with a tin of cookies, as if we were a family grieving Julian's death, or if it was Parker's speech about how none of us were guilty for shunning Julian all our lives. Maybe it was Karin's sudden desire to go to the police to tell them she'd lied.

After twenty years, why was she going now?

I got it that she felt guilty, and maybe she realized she'd made a mistake. Maybe the shock of Julian's death had pushed her toward that decision. But it still felt off. The way she'd looked at me when she said she would convince Tip to go with her, it felt like she wanted me to react. But what was she expecting? I didn't get it, but there was something threatening in her tone. Did she think *I* was the one who had killed Julian? And Celeste? The thought shouldn't have surprised me, and once it appeared in my mind, the look on her face clicked into focus.

Except for the barbecue, I hadn't spoken to Tip in

twenty years. I'd hardly spoken to him in high school. I had no idea how easy or difficult it would be to convince him to talk to a detective and admit he'd lied in a murder investigation. It seemed like a long shot. Especially with a new suspicious death hanging over the community. At least it looked suspicious to me. To Dylan, too. And to Karin.

It was understandable that the police had decided it was an accident. They'd said there was no physical evidence anyone else had been in the bedroom the night Julian died. He was alone in his closet, without a condom, the laptop facing him. There were no beer bottles or other clothing. They hadn't found hairs or any fingerprints that didn't belong to either Julian or Dylan. There was no evidence of anyone else in the house, aside from the window Dylan had broken.

But Julian could have invited a guest over, and maybe they just didn't leave any loose hairs behind. Was that possible? I had no idea how often hairs drop off our bodies or how likely it is that a guest will touch a door handle and leave a fingerprint rather than the host opening all the doors.

I really didn't even know how much they'd looked, how much they'd tried to collect. Did they comb the entire house with evidence bags, or only his bedroom? I knew nothing about how the police functioned.

What I did know was that his death was just too strange and too unexpected and too coincidental. It was possible I was experiencing one of those instances in which the brain wants to make a connection due to the shock of the situation, but making connections seemed to be all I could do. And I couldn't stop thinking about the hints Julian had dropped, as if they were loose hairs, which he was begging for someone to collect and analyze.

I sat in the armchair in the guest room and tapped a list of the things he'd said to me into my phone, the things Karin had told me he'd said to her over the years. I noted the hate mail he'd mentioned receiving every time a memorial on the anniversary of Celeste's death was held. They'd spoken to Dylan because he was the one to find Julian's body, but not to the rest of us. I doubted they knew about the hate mail—unless Julian had saved it and they'd found it. I noted that he believed others hadn't told the police everything, even though he'd never named anyone aside from Karin.

When the list was complete, I went looking for Dylan. He was in the backyard, digging dandelions out of the lawn with a weeding tool.

I stood beside him, letting my shadow fall over him.

"I'm going to the police station," I said.

"Why?"

"I think it might help if I talk to the detective and tell him the things Julian was saying."

I hadn't told him about Karin and Tip's lies the night Celeste was killed. He had a right to know, but it was so upsetting. I wanted to tell him. I'd wanted to tell him when she first mentioned it to me, but each time I opened my mouth, I couldn't manage to get the words out. In this one thing, Parker and I were in agreement. I was certain she hadn't told him either. In fact, I'd had the impression she'd known nothing about it until Karin blurted it out on her front porch just a few hours earlier.

"Do you really think it will make a difference?"

I shrugged. "It can't hurt. I just wonder if they were so focused on his body and the way he died and the whole"—I waved my hand around—"the whole scenario, if that made them only think along the lines of what he appeared to be doing when he died. They didn't really think about all this other stuff. They looked at evidence to see if anyone was there involved in the suffocation game with him, but they weren't thinking about Celeste's murder or the other things going on in his life at all. They didn't talk to people because it looked like his death was about sex."

Dylan sat down on the lawn, still looking up at me. He adjusted his ball cap, pushing it off his forehead slightly, rubbing his finger across his left eyebrow. "That's a really good point." He sat up straighter, then got to his feet. "I should go with you."

"No. I think I should go alone. If you're there, it will seem like …" I wasn't sure how to say it gently. Maybe there was no way to make it sound kind. "They might get the impression you're trying too hard to make it about your sister. If it's just me, it won't seem as emotional."

His lips tightened; then he nodded slowly. "Yeah. I guess you're right."

"I know I am." I wanted to pat his arm, but I also wanted to look toward the house to check whether Parker was watching us. I should assume she was watching. I took a step away from him. "Hopefully, Detective Harrow will listen. Hopefully, if he's there and I can get him to meet with me. I don't want to call and ask, because he might say no, the case is closed."

Dylan laughed. "Of course he'll say that."

"I'm leaving now. I'll see you in a while."

"Thanks, Eden. I'm glad I'm not the only one who thinks this way. It seems obvious to me that there's something weird about it, or at least weird that it happened right now, right after her memorial."

"They can't make the same mistake twice. Even though it's a different detective, even though it's been twenty years, it feels the same. There's nothing obvious to indicate it's not the picture they painted, so they just run with that."

"I know."

"Bye." I lifted my hand in a little wave, turned, and walked away.

I hoped the detective would see me. I wasn't confident he would, but I could be pushy when I made an effort.

30

NOW: PARKER

Once again, Eden and my husband were having a private conversation. I wanted to cry. I also wanted to slam open the guest room door, throw her clothes into her suitcase, drag it down the stairs, and put it on the curb. I'd call her an Uber and tell her to develop some self-awareness about when she had overstayed her welcome.

Why didn't Dylan get it? Couldn't he see that her constant presence was eating away at our marriage? Our family? These subtle little things were so destructive. Whispers and secrets and private smiles between the two of them that they thought I didn't see. Or maybe they didn't care whether I saw. Maybe he wasn't even thinking about me.

What were they talking about in the backyard? He looked so upset, and then suddenly he was all smiles. What had she told him? What was she doing out there? If she had something important to say, she should be talking to both of us.

I went into her room and flipped open her laptop. It was

password protected, of course. I stepped into the bathroom and opened the cabinet over the sink. There was nothing interesting, nothing that told me anything about her life. I wanted to dig through the pockets of her suitcase, but if she caught me, Dylan would take her side.

I looked out the window again. Dylan had returned to his weeding. Eden was nowhere in sight.

I hurried downstairs and out to the backyard.

"Thanks for digging those out." I pointed to the bucket of weeds. "They were getting out of control."

"Yup."

I sat on the grass beside him. "Give me the weeder. I'll help."

"It's fine." He stabbed the metal rod into the ground and wiggled it around the roots of a dandelion.

"Where did Eden go?"

"She's going to talk to Detective Harrow."

"Really? About what?"

"About the things Julian was saying."

"That's strange."

"Why? It's really obvious there's something not right about him dying like that. They should have talked to people instead of just looking for physical evidence, finding nothing and then calling it a day."

I took a deep breath. I didn't think he was going to like what I was going to say, but knowing she'd gone to the police, knowing they were going to keep stirring the pot, that Dylan was not going to let go of this, I had to speak up. I was also absolutely certain Eden was not going to leave our house as long as both of them believed there was some secret they needed to uncover. Karin's theory was as good as any, and maybe Eden had stupidly set herself up.

"Karin had something weird to say. It's kind of out there, a little disturbing, very disturbing, I guess, but it also—"

"What are you talking about?"

"She was talking about how the killer always returns to the scene of the crime."

"What?"

"That's what they say."

"I know." He glared at me. "But what is she—"

"That maybe Eden ..."

He dropped the weeding tool and gave me the ugliest look I'd ever seen cross his face. For a moment, it looked as if he hated me. For a moment, I felt his hatred wash over me. Pure loathing, as if he couldn't bear to share the same world with me.

"You're out of your mind. Karin thinks Eden murdered my sister? And now Julian? That's disgusting. How can you even say that? How could you even listen to that?"

"I know, but ... Eden wasn't here the night Julian died."

"I can't believe you're saying this. Besides, I thought you were absolutely sure it was an accident."

"You seem so sure it wasn't. And I'm just saying, she's the only person who no one knows where she was."

"I'm not going to listen to this. Why is Karin saying something so awful?" He grabbed the weeding tool, stood, and dropped it into the bucket full of dandelions.

"Julian didn't start talking about all these things he supposedly saw, or whatever he was going on and on about, until Eden showed up."

"You don't know that. We never talked to him. Eden was the only person who bothered to give him the time of day."

I'd known he wouldn't like it, but once I started, I felt like I had to keep going. The story Karin had imagined unspooled inside my mind, and my tongue kept going even though my brain was shouting at it to stop, even though Dylan's eyes were telling me that I might be destroying our relationship with every word I spoke. As if each word were a sharp blade, slashing at the cords binding us together, leaving a bloody mess that could never be mended.

"Why do you hate her so much?" His voice was thick with emotion. "She was our closest friend. The three of us were everything to each other, and now you act like you wish she'd never come back. It feels like you don't want her in our house. She can't have children; did you know that? And you don't even have the kindness to allow her to have a connection to our kids. What happened to all those conversations we had when we were little about growing up and watching our own kids become lifelong friends like we were? What happened to all the things we said and all the hours and hours and *years* we spent telling each other everything and having the best times of our lives?"

"Better than our marriage? Than the times with our family? Is that what you think? Do you wish we were still children and that you'd never married me? That we never grew up, like you're some kind of Peter Pan wannabe?"

He threw the bucket on the ground. The weeding tool clattered against the sides, then fell out as the weeds spilled around it. "Why are you so petty? That's not what I'm saying." He bent and set the bucket upright. He gathered the weeds and stuffed them back inside.

"I'm sorry. I'm not saying any of this right. I—"

"Just shut up." He grabbed the bucket and walked toward the back of the garage. A moment later, he'd disappeared through the rear entrance.

I sat there, the sun beating on my head, making my scalp

burn. I felt as if I'd destroyed parts of us that Eden hadn't begun to touch. But it was still her fault. None of this would have happened if she hadn't moved herself into my house and kissed my husband and fed him all her questions about his sister's murder. She'd swept in like some Italian princess and made herself sparkle in my daughter's eyes, making me look provincial and dull. She was in the process of driving my husband mad with his desire to know something that couldn't be known.

I closed my eyes and tried to take a deep breath. I had no idea how I was going to fix things with Dylan. I had no idea how I was going to work my way back from the things I'd said, because now he didn't want to listen to me.

One thing at a time. I had to focus. The most important thing, still, was to get Eden out of my house. She was tearing us apart. It would be impossible to heal as long as she kept creeping around, listening to every conversation, undermining everything I said.

I didn't care how ridiculous Karin's suggestion was. If she believed it, and more importantly, if Detective Harrow considered it even a remote possibility, it had the potential to get Eden out of our house.

Dylan had left the detective's card on his nightstand.

I went upstairs, took a photo of the card, and went into my office. I closed the door and called Detective Harrow's direct line.

31

NOW: EDEN

Not only did Detective Harrow make time for me, he seemed far more interested in my list than I'd expected. I'd thought I would have to sell him on the idea. He led me past a tiny office, gesturing toward the door farther down the short hallway. "It's a little cramped in my office. I'll take you into the witness room, if you don't mind."

"That's fine."

He was tall, with straight blond hair that brushed the back of his collar. I felt a bit like a child following him down the narrow hallway. He opened the door to a room that was about the same size as his cramped office, so I didn't see what the difference was, but I said nothing.

There was a table and four chairs. Mounted in one corner was a camera.

"I'll record our conversation, if you don't mind," he said.

"Is that important?"

"That way I don't have to take notes."

It made sense. I hoped I wasn't being naïve. He was a

detective, even if our town was small and the police force was generally friendly and focused more on community engagement than on making a show of force. Although that was rarely necessary because the crime rate was low—petty theft, vandalism, occasional bar fights, and drugs. Celeste's murder, and now Julian's death, had been sensational partially because nothing like that ever happened. Not ever.

He pulled out a chair for me.

"Do you want coffee? Water?"

"No, thanks." I pointed to the water bottle sticking out of my purse.

He seated himself across from me.

"So, Nancy Drew, what do you have to show me?"

Now, I wasn't so sure he was as friendly and interested as I'd first thought. "This isn't a joke," I said.

"I'm not laughing."

I decided to let it go. I tapped my phone to bring up my list. I explained about being away for twenty years. He asked me several questions about where I'd been, why I hadn't returned home until now, and what had made me come back for the memorial. I simplified my answers, figuring most of it was none of his business and the rest of it wasn't relevant to why I was there.

After I went over all the comments Julian had made, I took a deep breath. I'd decided to break Karin's confidence. She seemed bent on doing that eventually anyway, and I'd decided they'd had twenty years to do the right thing. The odds that Tip was going to step up now were slim, so I wasn't going to protect him. He meant nothing to me, and really, neither did Karin. She was Parker's friend. She shouldn't have lied, and once she saw they weren't finding any suspects, she should have returned and admitted she'd lied.

"Why are you here and not Tip?" Detective Harrow asked.

"He's had twenty years," I said.

"Fair enough."

"I don't know if it even means anything. Maybe he only asked Karin to lie because he didn't want to be bothered, because he was afraid of being picked up on a drug charge. Maybe he didn't see anything. In fact, he probably didn't; I don't think he would have kept that to himself. But my point is, Julian seemed pretty sure that there might be several people who did the same thing. And a lot of people leaving out a lot of small details could leave a very large hole in the picture your predecessor ended up with."

He nodded. "Or not."

"What do you mean?"

"What else do you have?"

"I think the timing of Julian's death is really strange. Since he started talking about all these things just now. After twenty years."

He smirked. "The human brain is designed to make patterns. We want to find meaning where none exists. The timing of his death in relationship to most likely baseless accusations is meaningless. Those are unrelated events."

"But you didn't question anyone."

"He was very obviously by himself when he died, Ms. Leone."

"But—"

"What's your interest in Mr. Taggart?"

"He did a lot of hinting around that he knew something."

"Hinting around is not a set of facts we can investigate. You must realize that."

I nodded. At first, I'd felt he was truly interested; now I felt he was close to mocking me.

He patted his pocket and pulled out his phone. He pushed his chair away from the table. "Excuse me for a minute."

He left the room without saying more.

I sat there, unsure where to look or what to do with my hands. I felt conscious of the camera still recording me. Suddenly, I wondered if I looked relaxed. It was an unset-tling thought. I didn't need to look relaxed. I wasn't a suspect. What was going on here? I picked up my phone and tried to calm myself by scrolling through social media, forcing myself not to make eye contact with the camera staring at me from the corner of the ceiling.

A moment later, Detective Harrow returned. He took his seat, and without saying anything about why he'd left, he asked me, "Where were you the night Mr. Taggart died, just out of curiosity?"

"Are you serious?"

"I am. Where were you?"

"I went to dinner. And a movie."

"With whom?"

"By myself."

He looked at me, as if he wanted me to squirm.

"I have a receipt for my ticket. And the server at the restaurant probably remembers me."

"What time did you arrive back at the Campbell home?"

"I can't believe you're—"

"What time?"

"Around eleven thirty. Maybe eleven fifteen. I don't remember exactly."

"But you didn't see anyone?"

"No. I ... this is ridiculous."

"You're the one who suggested Mr. Taggart's death might not be accidental, and that people should be questioned. I'm starting with you."

"Does that mean you'll be questioning others?"

"That has nothing to do with you."

"I came in here to tell you that Julian seemed to think Celeste Campbell's killer might still be around. He implied that person wasn't an anonymous drug user who stole her watch and her other things as a source of easy cash."

"I understand that."

"So why are you acting as if I might be the one who killed him? That means you think I killed her? I would never ... I'm not a killer."

"I'm trying to understand why you're so eager to turn an obviously tragic accident into a murder."

"If I'd killed him, why would I come to you and try to change your mind? That makes no sense."

"People who commit murder don't always make logical choices. They aren't like the rest of us."

I tried not to let out a loud sigh. He'd seemed sympathetic and professional at first, but it had ended quickly with that Nancy Drew comment. I didn't understand why he was even talking to me. He obviously thought I was crazy. I couldn't believe he actually thought I was a killer. He was just trying to upset me, trying to make me go away so he didn't have to do anything else.

He raised his voice slightly. "Interview with Eden Leone terminated." He gave the date and time. He stood and went to the control panel on the wall to shut off the camera.

He turned to face me. "Email me the list of things that are troubling you. I'll give it some thought. But in case I decide there's anything that merits further investigation, I advise you to check to see if anyone can verify the time you returned home the night Mr. Taggart died. Thank you for coming in. I think you can find your way out." He left the room, letting the door fall closed.

I sat there for a moment, trying to figure out how things had gone sideways.

Back at the house, Dylan was waiting eagerly to hear what I had to say. The moment she heard my voice, Parker appeared in the great room. She leaned against the bar, fiddling with a toy truck Maverick had left there.

I was nearing the end of the story, telling them what the detective had said, trying my best to leave out the demeaning comments. "I can't believe they're asking me for an alibi."

"Did he say that?" Dylan asked.

"He didn't use that word, but he was pretty clear there's no proof I came home when I said I did—and he'd like me to provide some."

"We were asleep," Parker said. "So we can't help."

"I didn't feel well that night." Dylan's words were hesitant. "We'd been playing a game, but we didn't finish because I felt like crap."

"Not supposed to say that, Dad."

All of us turned to see Brianna standing in the entryway. She moved into the room, sliding behind her mom, heading toward the fridge.

"So we all have alibis," Parker said.

"Is being asleep an alibi?" Dylan asked. "Just rhetorical, not that we need one."

"Who needs alibis? For what?" Brianna opened the fridge. She pulled an apple out of the bowl and took a bite.

"Eden."

"Why?"

"All of us, maybe," I said. "If they decide to investigate Julian's death as a murder."

"Wow. Well, I saw you come home the night he was killed. If that counts," Brianna said.

"You were asleep," Parker said.

"But I wasn't."

"You were supposed to be. I don't want you involved in this mess," Parker said.

"But if they don't believe Eden, I—"

"I don't want you talking to the police."

"I saw her come home. It was eleven forty," Brianna said.

"How can you remember the exact time?" Parker asked. "You just happened to wake up right at that time and look at the clock? I don't want you lying to the police to protect Eden."

"I'm not lying! I was waiting for my nails to dry, and I—"

"Why were you painting your nails at that time of night? Never mind. The point is, I don't want you involved with the police. Eden will have to figure out something else."

"Well, if she can't, I'm not going to let them arrest her or something." Brianna took another bite of her apple and walked out of the room. We heard her thumping up the stairs.

No one said anything more.

Parker turned away from me, but not before I saw a look of anger grip the edges of her mouth.

32

2022: EDEN

The online announcement that the twentieth anniversary of Celeste's murder would be the final memorial event shocked me. I couldn't stop reading the words Dylan had posted on his page, written below a photograph of Celeste when she was sixteen. Her head was thrown back. She was laughing. Rays of sunlight were laced through her hair so that it glowed as if she were already in another realm.

He'd written a long, emotional post about how the memorials every five years had been touchstones for him, helping him to know that Celeste wasn't forgotten, helping him to know that others shared his loss, even after so much time. Those events, even though he couldn't explain how, made him feel as if her life continued to have meaning, maybe simply because they brought the community together with a shared memory and shared feelings of shock and loss that had become a permanent part of all of them.

Reading those words, I knew I had to go.

Maybe it was only because they came at a time in my life

when I'd been avoiding making a decision. Maybe because it seemed like the only decision I was capable of making.

Marco and I had finalized our divorce only seven months earlier. During the course of our separation and divorce, I'd begun to feel like the outsider. I didn't speak Italian with quite the fluency and nuance that my friends did. I didn't share the cultural roots. At my core, I was American. I wasn't one of them. They didn't shun me, and they didn't even turn their backs on me. It was more subtle than that. Less enthusiasm. Not as many parties. Growing evidence that, when there were parties, they invited Marco more often than they invited me. It was only going to get worse.

I'd found myself spending hours doing nothing but brooding. Sitting with a cup of tea and looking at old photographs. Sitting in the garden, my gaze collapsing into an unseeing stare, then my eyes drifting closed as my thoughts turned to vivid memories.

One of the sharpest memories was the clean, final split between Parker and me.

When I'd left for college, we stayed in touch. Although our phone calls became less and less frequent, there was no deep animosity or sense that our friendship was over. Just a gradual shift in our lives that was causing the space between us to grow deeper and wider. The betrayals rose to the surface and became more prominent.

Then Dylan had assumed I would be in their wedding party.

What he didn't know was that Parker told me not to come. Yes, at first, she'd thrown up excuses about the cost of international flights and the lack of space in their house, which meant even more expenses for a hotel room for a lengthy stay. If I was going to be a proper bridesmaid, I really should be there for the shower, the bachelorette party, and that wasn't possible. She supposed she couldn't expect that of me, but it didn't seem fair. Surely, I could see that.

All of this happened in text messages and email.

Then she called me to tell me the truth. Her truth.

First of all, I was an embarrassment. How clueless was I? How could I even consider being in their wedding. Yes, Dylan was assuming it, and he'd been copied on some of those emails because that's who we'd always been—a hive mind, discussing everything among the three of us. But where was my shame?

Maybe Dylan didn't see it, but my crush on him was so obvious it was painful.

I told her that was ancient history.

She laughed. "You forget, I know you better than anyone. I know you better than you know yourself."

"That's a brainless truism people love to toss around, but it's not true."

"You're blind to how you come across, Eden. I can't have you at our wedding, hanging on Dylan, looking at him with those lovesick eyes. It's embarrassing."

"I don't do that," I said, my voice hoarse and pained as I tried to fight through the thick coating of lies she was telling herself.

"You can't see it. But everyone else does. And I won't have you ruining my wedding, standing beside me looking like you want to kill me so you can rip my dress off and pull it over your own head."

I couldn't figure out what was wrong with her, or maybe I could, but I was done defending myself. My crush on Dylan had dissolved a long time ago.

"Dylan just lost his mom and dad," Parker continued.

"Sadly, he still hasn't gotten over Celeste's murder. He doesn't need your drama. It's better if you tell him you're not coming. That it won't work out."

I wanted to argue with her, I wanted to talk to Dylan myself, but I was suddenly too tired. It was clear she felt threatened by me, although I didn't fully understand why. Maybe she knew I saw through her the way she wanted to pretend she saw through me.

Didn't she realize I was in love with Marco? And I was. At that time, when I was twenty-two years old, just out of college, living in Italy, I felt like my life was a dream come true. Dylan Campbell was a tiny speck on the horizon of my memory. I couldn't even recall what it had felt like, fantasizing about him on hot summer afternoons and long into the night when I should have been asleep.

Now, Marco consumed me. Our life was exciting and fun. Our sex life was beyond what I'd ever imagined as a teenager. We'd just bought a home and were decorating it carefully and deliberately.

So we didn't go to the wedding. I didn't know what she told Dylan, and by the time they got married, I didn't really care. I wondered if I would ever see them again, and it didn't seem all that tragic if I never did. Maybe I would never set foot on the North American continent again. Maybe my parents and brother would always visit me in Europe. Maybe, as they grew older, I would move my parents there to be with me.

But those were all maybes for another time, existing in a far-distant future. I was in my early twenties, living in a beautiful city and madly in love with my man, my career, and my life. I didn't want to think about a teenage crush and gaslighting comments and broken childhood promises and chilling looks and a murdered girl.

A decade and a half later, I was a different person. I had a sharper eye and a more nuanced conscience.

It was time to lay a lot of things to rest, not just the memory of Celeste's brutal murder. That nagging photo. The shards of my broken relationship with Parker, the way she'd cut me out of her life, first slowly, then swiftly, like the clean slice of a razor.

33

NOW: DYLAN

It didn't seem possible the detective was seriously considering Eden as a suspect in Julian's death. Was he trying to make her uncomfortable because he thought she was wasting his time? Did he think her concerns about Julian's cryptic comments were just gossip, searching desperately, as I had done, for an answer to an unanswerable question? Was this an instance of resenting an *outsider* interfering where she wasn't wanted?

For the most part, he'd tried to intimidate her, but hadn't charged her with murder. He hadn't even told her they would investigate the death as a murder based on what she'd said. But why had he acted as if she needed to provide the details for where she'd been that evening? Why had he gone so far as to say she needed a witness before he would believe that she'd come directly back to our house and remained there all night?

What was even more troubling was that Parker didn't believe our daughter. Apparently, her animosity toward Eden ran so deep, she wanted to twist our daughter's words, coming close to accusing her of lying before she would help Eden in a difficult situation with the police. It sickened me.

To escape, I took Maverick to the library. After we came home with a cloth bag full of books, I went for a run. I needed to talk to Parker, but a part of me didn't want to see her at all for the rest of the day. I wasn't sure I wanted to sleep beside her in the same bed. I wanted her to explain herself, but she didn't seem to be able to do that in a way that didn't turn my stomach or make her sound wildly irrational. I kept asking the same questions and getting the same, unsettling answers.

When I stepped out of the bathroom after showering off the sweat from my run, Parker was waiting for me. She was sitting on the side of our bed, both feet on the floor, her hands folded and resting on her thighs. She looked as if she was waiting to hear what I had to say, as if I owed her something. But I didn't. She was the one who needed to start talking.

"Why are you avoiding me?" she asked.

"I'm not."

"We need to talk."

"Then talk."

"Don't you have anything to say?"

"No. And I don't want to play guessing games. What's on your mind?"

She heaved a sigh. "Sit down."

I shoved my hands into my pockets and leaned against my dresser. "I'll stand, thanks."

"I don't want Brianna involved in anything with the police. Besides, I know she's lying."

"You have a really low opinion of our daughter."

"I don't. It's the opposite. She's a kind person. Eden has

wowed her. Brianna thinks she's our friend. She wants to help. She's trying to do what she thinks will make you happy."

"That's a twisted low opinion of her."

"It's not. She's a child."

"Almost a teenager. And she's not a liar. Not under any circumstances. Not even to make us happy."

"We have *no* idea where Eden was the night Julian died. If he was murdered, it looks a little strange. She hasn't left this house for more than an hour since she moved in here, and suddenly she disappears for an entire evening. She comes home when everyone is sound asleep. You don't think that's a little ... suspect?"

"You think our best friend murdered Julian?"

"I don't know what she did or didn't do. I'm saying I understand why it looks suspicious to the police."

"I thought you were absolutely certain it was an accident?"

"I don't know what to think. But I know Brianna wasn't painting her nails in the middle of the night. And I know she didn't see her come home. And I think it's really strange that the moment Eden returned, Julian started obsessing over supposed information that only he knew about Celeste's murder. When he turns up dead and you keep insisting it was murder, the only person who can't say where she was that night is Eden."

"I'm not going to listen to this."

It was obvious that if I wanted to keep my marriage on anything resembling solid ground, I should tell Eden to leave. It was obvious that Parker was going to keep upping the ante in her battle against our friend. I wasn't ever going to understand the complexities of their relationship. But I still could not seem to let go of wanting to get back what we'd had when we were kids. And I couldn't understand why Parker didn't want that too.

Parker and Eden had been like sisters. Neither of them had a sister, and Celeste used to comment to me that the two of them had each other's backs and teased and fought and made up, treating each other as if they had stepped into that role for each other. I think, in some ways, Celeste was jealous of them. She said having a brother was cool—she wouldn't trade me for the moon or all the planets and stars, but she always wondered what it would be like to have a sister. She never went so far as to say she wished she had one, implying she wanted to replace me. But a sister would have been nice.

I started toward the door.

Parker flew off the bed, grabbing my arm. "Wait. I don't want things to be ... I feel like we're drifting away from each other. I don't like what she's doing to us."

"How many times do I have to tell you? She's not doing anything."

"How can you say that after that kiss? You don't see what's happening." Her voice turned to a whisper, and her lips quivered in that way they did when she was going to cry, which wasn't often.

I moved back toward her and put my arms around her, pulling her close. "She's not doing anything to us. I told you that kiss ... we drank too much. I was ... I'm so sorry. Is that why you hate her so much?"

"She shouldn't be here."

"I promise it won't happen again. I've forgotten all about it. I don't feel anything for her beyond friendship. That's it. I love you. Only you. It's always been you. I just want the three of us to be friends like we were. I don't understand what happened."

"She tried to take you away from me! That's what happened. And now she's trying to do it again. And you've always been blind to that."

"What?" I pulled away from her, still holding her shoulders, looking into her eyes. I could see the fear, like a trapped animal. Why was she so afraid of losing me? I didn't understand. I so regretted the kiss, and I knew I should ask Eden to leave, but still, something inside me whispered that Parker needed to grow up. She needed to look at this rationally and stop discounting an entire lifetime together and all that we'd done to build a strong relationship.

"When we broke up for a few days, right before ... before Celeste died."

"She didn't try to take me away. What are you talking about?"

"Eden told me she was in love with you. And she didn't care how I felt or anything." She whimpered, then gasped for more air. "She was going to tell you, and she was so sure that since you and I were broken up, she could have you for herself."

"Okay. I didn't know that. She never said anything. But we were *teenagers*. Everything was overdramatized. I'm sure she's forgotten all about it. She loved Marco. She was happy with him."

"Was she? How do you know that?"

I didn't. She was right.

"It would really make me happy if you would ask her to move out of our house. It doesn't mean we can't see her, I just don't want her living here."

It sounded so childish, so ... She sounded bitter and

unwilling to do the very thing she'd nagged me about for years—to let go of the past. I didn't think she would like it if I pointed that out. "What would make me happy is if you would accept there are unanswered questions about my sister's murder that still trouble me. If you would trust that I love you and I'm not interested in Eden. She's my friend. And she used to be yours." I brushed my lips across hers, let go of her shoulders, and left the room.

LATER, when I found Eden sitting alone on the back patio, I closed the glass door so we wouldn't be overheard, and sat on the lounge chair facing her.

"Do you think Harrow is seriously going to question people about where they were the night Julian died?" I asked.

"I'm not sure. It felt a little like he was just asking those questions to make me go away. But it's hard to know. He recorded our conversation."

"That sounds serious."

She shrugged. "Maybe it's required."

"Could be. If he does ask everyone to provide proof of where they were, it's good Brianna saw you. I hope you think it's worth it now that he's started with you."

"I do. He needs to look at it more closely. It's just too coincidental. But maybe that's not how the police look at things."

"I would have expected to hear from him by now, though."

She nodded.

"I guess Parker's made it more than obvious she doesn't want you staying here anymore," I said.

She laughed. "Very clear."

"But you're not going to take her *hint*?"

"I keep hoping she'll ... I don't know. I'm not sure why, but I do. Maybe losing my marriage and most of my friends in Italy has made me overly sentimental. Maybe I'm clinging to something that died a long time ago."

"I should probably tell you it's time for you to leave, but I have to admit, I like having you here. It's helpful having someone else on the same page. That you're as convinced as I am someone killed Julian because of what he was saying about Celeste's murder."

She nodded.

"So thanks for that. And thanks for putting up with Parker's hostility."

She didn't say anything more, and I wondered if she really believed Parker was going to come around.

34

NOW: PARKER

Clearly my husband was not going to do the right thing for our marriage and for our family. His childhood sentimentality was overriding his responsibility to our children and even his love for me. Love that he claimed was lifelong and unwavering, despite standing at the foot of our stairs with his tongue down another woman's throat and his arms wrapped around her delicate body.

I was going to have to do it myself. Telling her to leave wasn't an option, because he would immediately undermine me, as would my daughter. Not that my preteen daughter made the decisions for our family, but with her and Dylan sharing their wide-eyed admiration of Eden, and Maverick seeming to be of the same opinion, I had no one on my side.

Forcing her out was the only way. Setting up a situation in which Dylan had no choice but to recognize the danger she posed was the only path left for me.

Thanks to my close friendship with Karin, thanks to Tip's illegal side business, I had easy access to something that would help me make Eden look very bad. Of course, she already should have looked bad for what she'd done—trying to seduce my husband—but for some reason, he saw that as a tiny little slip-up that meant nothing.

I told Karin I wanted a small amount of Liquid X. Just for Dylan and me to have a fun, romantic night. Despite her healthy lifestyle, Karin admitted they'd used it a few times. Just for fun. Even though Tip sold all kinds of substances, one rule he'd always followed was never to use his own products.

I quit work early, went upstairs, and knocked on the guest room door, resenting for the hundredth time that I was knocking on a door in my own home.

"Come in." Eden's voice was a cheerful singsong. She wasn't expecting me; I'd been avoiding her as much as I possibly could. She probably thought I was Brianna, wanting to share more secrets in French. Or maybe even Dylan, wanting to sit on her bed for more whispered conversations with the door closed. Every time I turned around, they were talking beyond my earshot—in the middle of the backyard, on the patio with the doors closed even though it was a warm summer afternoon, in Celeste's room where he knew I never went ... it was relentless.

I opened the door but didn't go into the room.

"Hey." She gave me a cool smile.

"I guess things between you and me have become a little tense." I tried to give her a regretful smile. "I'm in the mood for a margarita. We could have chips and salsa and sit on the patio and talk."

She stared at me. I was sure she was waiting for me to acknowledge what an understatement that was, but I thought I'd said enough. I wasn't going to gush out a bunch of nonsense. I wanted her sitting on the patio drinking. That was it.

She continued holding my gaze. She wasn't going to fall for this as easily as I'd expected. Maybe she was as done with me as I was with her. I laughed. It sounded nervous and slightly off-key. "For old times' sake? It can't hurt. A fun drink, like civilized adults?"

"Sure. Can I help get anything—"

"I'll take care of it. Go sit down and enjoy the afternoon sun."

She closed her laptop, still looking at me as if she didn't trust me. She shouldn't. But she also shouldn't be so suspicious. She was staying in my house, eating my food, taking over my family, shoving me to the side. The least she could do was pretend she would enjoy having a drink with me.

When she was seated in one of the patio chairs, all of which I'd arranged so the backs were to the windows, I put tortilla chips in one bowl and salsa in another. I filled the blender with ice and the margarita mix and tequila. Just in case she decided to pop back inside, or turn to check on where I was, I had the glasses on the counter near the stove, an area that wasn't visible from the patio. I dropped the Liquid X into her glass.

I took a sip from the other glass, making sure my dark lip gloss left a smear on the salted rim.

I carried the tray outside and placed it on the table.

I laughed as I picked up my glass. "Sorry, I jumped the gun on our toast. I needed to taste it to be sure it was good."

She picked up her drink.

I raised my glass. "To old friends."

She smiled but didn't echo my words. She took a sip and put her glass on the table. I had to give her credit for being true to herself. She wasn't going to pretend anything. I'd made my feelings obvious, and she wasn't going to jump all over me and lick my hand like an eager puppy just because I'd thrown her a scrap from the table after shoving her out of the way for weeks.

"What did you want to talk about?" She took a chip and ate it without dipping it in the salsa.

I took a healthy swallow of my drink, hoping she would mimic me. I didn't want this torment to go on longer than necessary. I needed her to drink that margarita, fast. I was confident the salt and the tequila would overpower the slight soapy taste the drug sometimes had, but it would be a little while before it took effect. I had some time to play with, but not a lot.

Fortunately, I had a plan for this part as well. I didn't want to talk about anything with her. I absolutely did not want to talk about my husband and how she was trying to seduce him right out from under me. I didn't want to talk about how she was trying to charm my daughter and undermine my authority and make herself look like she was a whole lot more fun and interesting and savvy than me.

I planned to bore her to tears. And I hoped that would make the drug work faster, too. I took another long swallow of my drink. "I love margaritas. Karin got me into drinking them. I'm sure in Italy everyone drinks exotic wine, not plain old margaritas, but they're so refreshing. Don't you think?"

She took a sip. "It's very good." She took another sip.

"I didn't mean that to sound derogatory toward Italy. I'm sure it's beautiful and quaint."

"It is. But it's not perfect. No place is."

I was shocked she admitted to imperfection. It would be nice if she would share that news with my daughter, who was probably ready to move to any city in Europe with her if she asked. I then launched into a monologue about my work frustrations and how challenging it was to get some of my clients to understand what I was trying to do for them with their social media accounts. As I talked, I furiously sipped my drink.

I didn't want to hear about Italy, and I didn't want to talk about Julian and whether or not he'd been murdered, and I definitely didn't want to talk about the past. We'd had enough of that. I wanted to talk until she drank out of sheer boredom.

As I talked, I could see she was finding my monologue tiresome.

I put down my glass. "Oh, no."

"What?" Eden took a sip of her drink. Her glass was about two-thirds empty.

"I just remembered, I'm making a salmon dish for dinner, and I forgot a few things. I wanted it to be really nice. Salmon is Brianna's favorite."

"That's a mature taste for her."

"Isn't it? Do you mind keeping an eye on Maverick while I run to the store? Brianna's at Rachel's."

"Sure. No problem."

"Just a second."

I went into the house. I grabbed a notepad and pen from the kitchen drawer and plastic wrap from another drawer. I returned to the patio and handed the pad and pen to Eden. "Will you jot down my list for me while I put the salsa in the fridge?"

"Okay."

I rattled off a list of five items, tearing off plastic, and covering the dish, sealing the plastic around the sides.

"Thanks so much. Can you put this away? And finish your drink. There's a little more in the blender in the fridge, if you want."

She nodded.

"I shouldn't be too long."

She followed me into the house.

Now, I had to hope for the best. Relying on hope wasn't the ideal way to carry out a plan, but this was calculated hope, so I was fairly confident. Once the Liquid X took effect, she would be tired. She would sit on our comfy couch, and then she would tuck a throw pillow under her head, and soon, she would be passed out so that even Maverick running down the stairs wouldn't wake her.

When she did wake, she would be facing my wrath for leaving my son unattended. Hopefully, that would be a wake-up call for my faithless husband.

35

NOW: EDEN

There were a lot of voices. Loud voices. My head felt heavy and my brain thick and soggy, as if someone had poured mud into my nostrils. I tried to sit up, but I could hardly lift my head. When I opened my eyes, the room spun around me, so I closed them quickly.

Parker's voice was the loudest. "Anything could have happened! What if he'd fallen out of his treehouse?"

"He's nine years old, not three. He's not going to fall out of the treehouse."

"I asked her to watch him, and look at her. She's still not awake."

The shouting was making my head pound. I tried again to sit up, cupping my hands over my ears to dull the shrill screech of Parker's voice.

"Nice of you to wake up."

The sunlight was gone from the room. I didn't recall lying down, but ... or maybe I did. I'd asked Maverick to stay in the great room, where I could keep an eye on him. But it had been late afternoon. Now, the patio was covered by shadows. "What time is it?"

"Six forty-five!"

"Stop shouting," Dylan said. "Where were you?"

"I told her I had to run to the grocery store, and she said she would watch Maverick! Instead, she took a nap. Anything could have—"

"You already said that."

I sat up slowly, feeling the room swim around me. I grabbed a throw pillow and wrapped my arms around it to stabilize myself.

"He's been on his own for over two hours!"

I couldn't be sure if Parker's voice was incredibly screechy or the thick, cloudy feeling in my head was making it sound that way, as if all my own thoughts had sunk so deep into that pit of mud, her voice was the only thing left.

"It took you two hours to go to the grocery store?" Dylan asked.

"Rachel's mom texted and asked if I could pick Brianna up instead of her being dropped off, but that's irrelevant. The point is, Eden fell asleep. And looking at her, it's more like she passed out. Are you drunk?"

Her face was suddenly so close I could smell a whisper of alcohol on her breath, her eyes boring into mine as if they wanted to drill right through my skull.

We'd had the margaritas ... and ... "We both had a drink, didn't we? But I hardly—"

"How much did you have after I left?" She rolled her eyes. "It doesn't matter. I can't trust you around my children. I knew I couldn't. My gut was telling me that all along. You have no experience with children, and you have no clue how vigilant you have to be. I'm terrified just thinking of all the things that could have happened."

"Parker, he's *nine*. It's unlikely—"

"I asked her to watch him, and she chose to get so drunk she passed out!"

I squeezed the pillow more tightly. I wanted to stand but wasn't sure I could. My legs felt weak. Everything was so heavy. "I'm really sorry. I don't know why I fell asleep. I didn't have any more to drink after you left. It's really strange. I was sitting here, and I just—"

Parker held up her hand. "Stop. I don't want to hear any excuses or apologies. It doesn't matter. Responsibility for a child is the most important thing in the world. I want you to leave. By tomorrow."

"Slow down," Dylan said. "You're overreacting."

"I'm not." She began crying softly. "I trusted her. I trusted her with one thing. My kid." She pressed her fist against her chest, her eyes welling up with tears again. "All you two can talk about is the killer—the killer is still around, the killer is still around. And now, she passes out when she's supposed to be watching my little boy, and I'm supposed to smile and say it's okay. Everything worked out in the end?"

"There's not a maniac prowling the neighborhood," Dylan said.

"That's exactly what you've made it sound like," Parker said.

"We're getting off track here. I get it that it was upsetting to find her passed out ..." He looked at me, his head tipped to one side as if hoping I'd jump in with an explanation, but I had none.

"I've lost all trust. What if she leaves the door unlocked

and someone comes in while we're sleeping? What if she leaves a candle burning in her room and passes out again; what if—"

"I didn't pass out." My voice trembled as I tried to form the words.

"You absolutely did. I had to shake you before you knew I was even here."

I clenched the pillow, feeling irrationally angry. I couldn't argue that I'd been in a very deep sleep, and I couldn't blame someone else, but it somehow didn't feel like my fault. I'd never passed out like that. And I hadn't even finished my margarita. Something wasn't right.

"I've never fallen asleep like that. Something happened." I sat forward on the couch. The room swam again. I hugged the pillow tighter and forced my eyes to focus on Parker's face. The constantly swaying objects around me were proof that my sleep hadn't been brought on by overtiredness or a little alcohol.

Dylan folded his arms across his chest. He turned toward Parker, moving slightly so she was forced to look at him. "You're making this into more than it is. You both had a drink. You have some responsibility for serving them and then disappearing for two hours."

"I didn't *disappear*." Parker turned and walked out of the room.

"As soon as I've recovered from what's going on in my body," I said, "I'll start packing."

"Not necessary," Dylan said. "She's overreacting. She'll calm down."

"I don't think so."

"She will. I'm tired of this."

When he turned away, following Parker up the stairs, I lay back down on the couch and closed my eyes. As soon as I had a chance, I would have a look through Parker's medicine cabinet. Despite the thickness and my inability to recall what had happened, I had one clear thought—I'd been drugged. Parker was upping her game in trying to get me out of her life. She wanted the past dead and buried. She hadn't wanted Julian speculating. She didn't want Dylan looking for answers. And she didn't want me stirring up memories.

That evening, the atmosphere at dinner was icy. I was surprised I'd been allowed to eat with them. Parker went out of her way to avoid speaking to me or looking at me. Dylan suggested we play a board game with the kids. I couldn't imagine why he thought that would make things any better. Any normal person would have moved out of that house long before this, but something held me there. A childhood bond that I'd thought was broken was turning out to be stronger than almost anything else in my life.

And something else ...

The chill melted slightly during the game as our focus shifted to rules and competition, but it was still tense, and soon, the tension became exhausting. When Brianna won, I excused myself with a headache. A truthful complaint after waking up half drugged a few hours earlier.

I went upstairs, waited at the top until I heard the level of chatter increase with the start of a new game, and then I slipped around the corner into Parker and Dylan's bedroom.

Before heading into the bathroom, I checked her nightstand drawers and slid my hands between the layers of clothes in her dresser drawers. I found nothing that suggested it might be holding sleeping pills or some other drug she was hiding from Dylan.

In the bathroom, I glanced over the prescriptions in the medicine cabinet. There weren't many, and nothing that claimed to cause even mild drowsiness or warned that the user needed to avoid alcohol. I closed the cabinet and began opening drawers.

None of the drawers yielded anything. I stood in the center of the room, my heart racing. The longer I was in their luxurious master bathroom with its jacuzzi tub and shower with two heads, facing the counter with his and hers sinks and mirrors, my head truthfully pounding, the more certain I was that there had been something in that cocktail that put me into the deepest sleep I'd ever experienced. I hardly even remembered drinking the margarita. I couldn't remember what Parker and I had talked about as we sat on the patio, and I didn't recall her leaving for the store. I had a vague impression of Maverick in the great room with me, and then ... nothing.

I stepped into the walk-in closet. On the floor was a large case with wheels designed to hold cosmetics. I undid one of the clasps and pulled open the largest drawer at the bottom. Inside was a purple plastic box. I popped it open and found a narrow glass bottle with a black screw cap. Printed on the glass with permanent marker were the words—LIQ X. A small plastic bag with a zipper seal held ten or twelve tiny clear capsules with less than an eighth, maybe a sixteenth of a teaspoon of white powder inside. The bag was labeled ACID in black marker. There were also two eyedroppers.

I took the bottle and the plastic bag, closed the box, and put it back in the makeup case.

After another glance around the magnificent bathroom with its potted plants and decorative candles, I turned off the lights and walked out through their bedroom to the landing.

I sat on the top step and listened to Parker, Dylan, and their children playing their game. When the winner was declared, I would seal my place in their house for a while longer.

36

NOW: PARKER

The kids went up to bed before Dylan and me, which was our usual routine, even when they stayed up playing games or watching a movie. Dylan usually got the coffee set up, so it was ready to brew at the flick of a switch the following morning, and I rinsed whatever glasses and snack bowls we'd used and put them in the dishwasher. Together we moved almost like ghosts, because we didn't need to speak, through the ground floor, checking locks and ensuring the windows were closed and secured.

I heard the kids' voices at the top of the stairs, and when I finally went up myself, I realized I'd heard them talking because Eden hadn't gone to bed with a headache as she'd claimed. She was sitting on the top step, her bare toes curled around the edge of the next step down, her arms resting on her knees.

"Are you okay?" Dylan asked.

"Yes. I wanted to talk to Parker for a few minutes."

"I'm exhausted," I said.

Dylan stepped around her and waited.

Eden stood and grabbed the railing. "Just Parker." She started moving down the stairs toward where I stood, halfway up, anger surging through me again, just when I'd thought it had settled for the night.

Dylan went into the bedroom, abandoning me. I did not want to talk to her. I had nothing to say to her. I couldn't understand why she was still living in my house when I thought I'd made it clear she was a menace to our family. Maybe I'd been too passive-aggressive. Maybe my trick with the drinks had confused her. It was possible she'd believed me when I said I wanted to talk and relieve the tension between us. It was hard to know with her.

I started up the stairs.

"Let's go downstairs." Eden began descending, moving past me, brushing her arm against mine.

"I said I'm tired."

"This will only take a few minutes, and it needs to be done now."

"You aren't going to tell me what to do in my—"

"Now." She'd reached the ground floor. Instead of going into the great room, she walked along the short hallway toward my office. I heard her open the door as if it belonged to her.

Gritting my teeth, I followed.

She closed the office door and held out her hand.

Resting on her palm was my bottle of Liquid X and my micro-dosing capsules. I grabbed at them, but she closed her fingers and yanked her hand away so fast, I wondered if she'd practiced. "Clearly I didn't pass out from sipping half a margarita."

I didn't say anything. I would let her run through her

angry complaint, get my stuff back, then go to bed. I was truly exhausted. And it was her fault. Having any guest in your home is tiring. You can never truly relax and unwind, but Eden had added twenty more layers to that normal sense of needing to always look nice and be ready to carry on a pleasant conversation and be concerned about another person's comfort and well-being. Your *guest.*

"You drugged me."

"Can I have my stuff, please?"

"I want you to say it."

"Think whatever you want. You can't prove anything."

"Why are you being like this? I'm not stupid."

"I know."

"Then why can't you say it?"

"I just want you to give me my stuff so I can go to bed."

"And the pills? You take acid? Don't you know how dangerous that is?"

"It's called micro dosing. Don't be so naïve. All the Silicon Valley hot shots do it."

"All of them? You know them personally?"

"It's very common. And it's not dangerous. It makes me more creative. It helps me focus. It's very challenging looking after two active children and being a businesswoman. You have no clue how hard I work and what's required of me. I need to compartmentalize and focus. Micro dosing makes me a star at that. It gives me an edge in a very competitive field. Not that I'm required to explain my life to you."

"It sounds more like a justification. For using illegal drugs."

"Like I said, it's more common than you realize, so you should probably do some research before you shoot off your mouth. It was made illegal because of a bunch of political nonsense. There are a lot of experiments showing that mushrooms can help people with depression and other mental illnesses. You should probably look into that."

"This isn't mushrooms."

"Acid, too. Small quantities. Now give me my stuff. I'm going to bed."

"First, let's be clear—I'm not going anywhere. If you try again to make me leave, I'll take your little stash to the police."

I glared at her. I wasn't sure how she would prove it was mine, but I knew she would tell Dylan. For now, it looked like she had won. Again. "Why are you even here? Can't you see when you're not wanted? I guess you were always a little obtuse." I laughed.

"Am I? Not wanted?"

I felt myself gasp, but kept my lips tightly closed, hoping she didn't hear it. I held out my hand. "I'll take that."

"So it's our secret?" she asked.

"You got your way."

She handed the drugs to me.

"It's nice to know I'm not moving out tomorrow. In fact, I think I'll go relax right now with a nice hot bath. I was admiring your beautiful tub. Too bad I can't use that tub. A jacuzzi ... nice." She smiled.

I shoved the drugs into my pocket and pushed her shoulder, nudging her toward my office door.

She went willingly. I wished I could get her out of my house that easily.

37

2003: DYLAN

It was weird having my sister home from college. Celeste had always seemed like she was almost the same age as me, even though she'd tried to act as if she were five years older, telling me what to do, pretending she knew so many things about the world that I didn't. She said it was because she read a lot of books, that she wasn't trying to pretend she was older or smarter, just sharing information she'd gleaned. She liked that word—gleaned.

When my sister came home after her first year in college, she really did seem older.

Maybe it was the expensive watch my parents gave her for high school graduation that made her look more like an adult. Or maybe it was that she crossed her legs in exactly the same way as my mom when she sat in the armchair, or that she offered to help my mom with dinner. It was definitely weird.

But in other ways, she was the same

She still liked fishing, and she didn't mind getting worm slime and fish guts in her fingernails.

We were sitting on two rocks beside the creek, much farther into the woods where the water was deeper, almost four feet. There were a decent number of trout there, and usually we caught three or four every summer, just enough to make us optimistic about going out there once or twice a month to mostly talk, but also to drop our fishing lines into the water.

"I have a much different perspective on things after being away," Celeste said.

"Why?"

"Because my horizons have broadened. From my classes, because I've met people from, literally, all over the world."

"Good for you. I'm sure you've gleaned a lot of new insights."

"Actually, I have. But I also see people here differently. With better clarity."

"Oh yeah?"

"I've realized Parker has a real mean streak."

"That's not new. You never liked her."

"I like her."

"Don't bullshit me. You've always put her down. It's very subtle, so you think I won't notice."

"I don't think I have."

I looked at her. I lowered my sunglasses on my nose and peered over the top edge. We always did that to each other, mimicking our father, who did that when he thought we weren't being strictly honest.

Celeste laughed. "Okay. But it's clearer now."

"She's not mean. She's strong. She says what she thinks and doesn't try to be nice just because she's worried about other people's feelings."

"Sometimes you should worry about other people's feelings."

I shrugged. I reeled my line in slightly, watching the bait move through the clear water.

"They both have too much influence over you," she said.

"Did you come out here to fish or to talk shit about my friends?" I asked.

"No. But it's always bothered me that Parker and Eden were pretty much your only friends."

"So you've mentioned."

"I just ... going to college is mind-blowing. There are so many interesting, different people out there in the world. You have no idea. You think our high school has a lot of kids and our town is a decent size, but this is really a whole new experience."

"And I'll find out for myself in three months."

"Exactly!" She shouted as if she'd scored a point.

"You're going to scare the fish."

As if to argue with me even on that, there was a sharp tug on her line. She stood and turned her reel a few times. She pulled her pole back slightly, then let the line out before turning it multiple times, drawing the fish toward her. After a few more turns of the reel, the trout broke the surface of the water, thrashing to break free, driving the hook deeper through the side of its mouth.

When she'd pulled it out of the water, it flopped angrily on the rock, then gave up its life. I never liked that part. I loved eating trout when my mother cooked it, but I could never cook it myself. My entire family laughed at me, telling me I couldn't be a fisherman if I didn't learn to fry my own catch. But I couldn't do it. I couldn't cut off the head, couldn't clean it.

I didn't mind the fishing, but I hated watching the death throes, and I hated the cleaning and cooking. It made me wonder why I did it. I could just as easily hang out by the creek and toss stones into the water, perfecting my skill at skipping the flat ones across its surface.

Staring at the fish, its mouth open, the eyes vacant, I felt incredibly sad and slightly afraid for some reason. I'd never experienced that before. I gripped my rod tighter as Celeste put more bait on her hook.

"You'll see when you get there," she said. "I mean, you did see when you toured the campuses, but when you actually start living there, it's a whole new world. It's incredible. It will feel like you were living in a cave."

"Good to know."

"Don't sulk."

"I'm not."

"Maybe when you start school, it will be a good time to take a break."

"From what?" I knew exactly what she wanted me to take a break from, but I was getting more and more irritated. I'd actually had thoughts of cooling things between me and Parker. It would be hard with me two hundred miles away at school and Parker staying at home with her parents, studying at a two-year college while she worked part time and saved money for university.

Parker hated that I was leaving. She never complained that I got significant tuition breaks because I was going to the school where my parents were both alumni, allowing my family to afford what hers could not, especially with four kids. But she resented that I was leaving. She whimpered sometimes that she was being left behind. I hated it when she did that. I wasn't going to give up my chance for a great education.

As if she'd read my mind, as if she knew all my thoughts, which was the reason we were so close, even though we argued and sometimes put each other down, Celeste said, "If it's real, your relationship will survive hitting the pause button for a few years."

"Four years is a long time." I had to argue with her. She'd echoed the thought I'd had almost every day for the past three months, but I had to argue.

"She's going to be jealous and assume you're seeing other girls anyway. That will cause fights, if you think about it. This way, it would be out in the open."

"Maybe. She's not really jealous."

"Yes, she is."

I didn't argue with that.

"You've never even looked at another girl, as far as I know. You can't be sure unless you have other people to compare with. I know you're in love. And I won't condescend to say you just *think* you're in love, but you need to experience other people. You don't want to wake up when you're forty and realize you never kissed another woman and you never found out what it was like to spend time with someone different."

"Being forty is not top of mind."

She laughed. "I know. But it happens."

"That's what the evidence suggests," I said.

She laughed harder. "When I look at the pictures of Mom and Dad, I can't even ..."

"Yeah."

"You can't get locked in before you meet other people. And you don't want to miss the whole college experience because your head and your heart, and really your entire life, is still back here. You might as well not even go."

She stopped talking. That was another thing I loved about my sister. Even though she was always telling me what to do, she didn't go on and on about it. She said what she was thinking, and then she shut up. It was peaceful. It was what tipped the scales for fishing from the parts I didn't like to the parts I did.

Then she did something that she hardly ever did. "I'm not trying to tell you what to do because I think Parker has a mean streak. I just want you to be sure. I want you to be happy."

So I decided to let her score a point. "I was thinking I would break up with her. Now. And tell her then we'll know for sure. Even though four years is a long time."

"It feels like forever," she said. "But not really."

38

2003: PARKER

That bitch.

This was not the thought I should have had when my boyfriend, the boy I'd loved since I was thirteen, the boy whom I'd *wanted* to love since I was ten years old, the boy who had lived next door to me and held my hand when I was scared and kissed my lips for the first time and made love to me and told me I was beautiful and listened to me and looked into my eyes like he wanted to drown there, said he wanted to break up. I should have cried. I should have felt my heart break into a hundred, thousand, million pieces.

But all I thought was—this isn't him. I could see it in his eyes. They weren't really looking into mine.

I wasn't going to cry, and I wasn't going to throw a fit. I definitely wasn't going to beg as so many sad, sad girls did when their boyfriends dumped them. Because Dylan wasn't dumping me. He was doing what his sister told him to do. That girl thought she knew everything. She spent her whole life telling him what to do. When she went away to college, I thought she would stop, but of course she came home for the summer and picked up right where she left off.

I gave him a sad smile. "We're going to change a lot in four years. We'll be in our twenties. Completely different people."

"It's not like we'll never talk to each other," he said.

"No, but we won't see each other much. We'll change."

"We won't change who we really are. We haven't changed since we were kids. Not really. And then we'll know for sure if we're meant to be together. Because we'll have more experience."

That might as well have been her voice coming out of his mouth. I could hear her talking. I could even see her face in his. "I already know for sure."

"I mean—"

"You don't have to explain. I get it. The college experience."

"Yeah."

He wanted to be with other girls. He didn't want to be tied down. Maybe those words made sense in his head, maybe not. But it was all her idea. He didn't really *feel* that way. He was in love with me. I could almost taste it. I could hear the sound of his heart. I could almost read his mind. I honestly believed that sometimes. I wasn't scared that he didn't love me anymore. I knew he did.

When he left my house, I stayed in my bedroom, where we'd been talking. I turned up my stereo. I fell onto my bed and stared at the ceiling. I watched a spider walking across and wondered if it had any idea where it was going, or if it was just wandering around, hoping for the best.

I was not going to sit around hoping for the best. Celeste Campbell was not going to poison Dylan anymore. She'd been doing that her whole life. She'd never liked me. She never did anything obvious so that other people knew she didn't like me, but she made it very clear to me. She interrupted me. She changed the subject when I was trying to tell an interesting story. She took pictures of me that made me look bad. She was always catching me with my mouth open or chewing food or my eyes closed with some weird expression on my face that made me look slightly brainless.

She'd told Dylan to break up with me. There was no doubt in my mind. I was sad that she had so much power over him.

I waited a few days. I needed time to get my courage up.

On Tuesday, June 17, the weather turned unbearably hot. It was the kind of weather that made Celeste leave her house to sit by the creek to read her big, brainy books.

I was ready.

During dinner, I poked at my food, moving it around my plate with my fork, staring at my green beans as if they were maggots.

Finally, my mother glanced my way. "Are you alright, Parker?"

I shook my head. I laid my fork down as if it were so heavy, I didn't think I could manage to lift it to my mouth. "I'm going to bed."

My mother got up and came around to my chair. She put the back of her hand on my forehead. "You feel warm."

I nodded.

"I'll bring you some—"

"I just want to sleep. 'K?"

"Okay, sweetie. I'll check on you before I go to bed."

Once I was in my bedroom, I put on socks and tennies. I pushed the window up as far as it would go. I lifted the screen out of the frame and dropped it to the ground, where it landed softly on some plants. I climbed out and ran across our backyard, then climbed over the low fence, and I went into the woods where no one could see me from the house.

I found the path and walked along it to the huge flat rock by the large curve in the creek where Celeste sat. Sure enough, she was there. She was leaning against a boulder. Beside her was her backpack, the zipper undone with the cord to her Walkman trailing out of it up to her headphones. She had a book open on her lap and was eating Starburst candies.

I watched her reading. She never stopped. She didn't even look up to notice it was getting darker. I wasn't sure how she could see the words anymore. Her head moved slightly to whatever music she was listening to.

How had she gotten such a hold on Dylan? I didn't have that kind of hold on my brothers. They didn't care at all what I said. If I told them what to do, they would laugh in my face or completely ignore me. She had so much power over Dylan, she made him break up with me—the person he said he loved more than anyone in the whole world. He said he loved me so much, it hurt. But now, he'd suddenly decided we needed to be *sure*. Those two things didn't make sense. They couldn't exist as the same opinions inside the same person. One of them wasn't the truth.

We were going to get married after college. Celeste would always be there, trying to poison our love for the rest of our lives. If she didn't completely obliterate it first, before we even had a chance. She might convince him not to get married. She might convince him now that he'd broken up with me, why bother? There were plenty of fish in the sea. I could hear her saying it. I could hear her voice inside my head, screaming—*You can do better, Dylan. There are plenty of fish in the sea. Wait till you meet all those smart, hot college girls. You'll see.*

It proved her arrogance that she felt safe sitting beside a stream she couldn't hear, reading a novel. The Walkman pumped music inside her skull while the words in her book filled the rest of her brain with an imagined world so that it might have been only her body sitting there alone, with all her instincts for self-protection silenced.

I watched for quite a long time, although maybe it only felt like a long time. Unlike her, I was hyperalert to every sound in the woods surrounding us. The trickle of water over rocks, the occasional rustle of undergrowth and dead leaves as squirrels raced for their last bit of food in the semi-darkness that was spreading fast.

Her head was bent forward. She hardly moved except her fingers flipping the pages. She was always reading thick books, maybe to prove to the rest of us how smart she was. Maybe only because we bored her, and she wanted to live in whatever world she found inside enormous novels.

As I moved toward her, I felt all the things I should have felt when Dylan told me he wanted to experiment with other girls. I felt my heart break in two, then into four pieces, then eight, then a million. I felt as if blood were filling my eyes so I could hardly see. She had no right to tell him anything, no right to destroy my life. I loved him, and she was ripping him away from me. He loved me, and she was trying to poison that love. What kind of evil person tries to destroy another person's love?

Pure evil.

I moved even closer. I stood beside a pine tree now, the top impossible to see unless I tipped my head all the way back. At its base was a rock the size of a woman's shoe. I picked it up and held it in my hand. The weight of it pulled at my shoulder. I wondered if it was too large. I let my arm go slightly limp, raising it up and down to see if I had the strength to control it.

Confident that I did, I moved closer. I watched where I placed my feet, even though I knew she couldn't hear me. I wondered if a sixth sense would tell her she wasn't alone, but I hadn't seen her look up for the entire time I'd been watching. Did that mean she might look up soon? Was the idea that someone could sense another's presence real, or just something we believed after the fact?

I knew he was there all along? I felt her watching me?

We believe a lot of things after the fact.

I moved more quickly now, not wanting to risk that she might sense my presence.

A moment later, I was right behind her, and still her fingers touched the corner of the page, ready to turn to the next. I raised my arm. Without pausing to think or to plan how this might play out, I brought the rock down on the back of her head with every ounce of strength I possessed.

She didn't scream, as I'd thought she might. She grunted. Her upper body fell forward.

Without thinking, without hesitating, I raised my arm again and brought the rock down as hard as I could. This time, I heard a crack. Or maybe I imagined it.

Then it felt as if I drifted out of my own body. I brought the rock down again and again until she was lying on her side. The huge, flat rock where she was sitting was covered with a thick pool of blood. Her headphones were dislodged from her head, but she still heard nothing. Her eyes stared blankly at the trees surrounding us.

When I looked down at her, when I saw how much blood was spreading across the rock, my heart started pounding so hard I couldn't breathe. The woods were quiet. The birds had stopped chattering. I wasn't sure if that was because it was almost dark or if it was because of me.

Still holding the stone in one hand, I pulled a plastic bag out of my pocket. I held my breath and unclasped her watch. I dropped it and the Walkman inside. I ran across the large flat rock and down to the side of the creek. I ran until I reached the spot where the water got deeper. I threw the blood-covered stone into the water. I ripped off my clothes and got into the freezing water. It felt good to have everything in my body freeze up, it helped my thoughts freeze too, so I didn't think about her ... lying back there ...

I washed all the blood off my face and hair and hands.

I put my clothes back on and turned on my pocket flashlight. I went farther into the woods and found one of the hollowed-out tree trunks. I dropped the bag with the watch and Walkman inside. I would figure out later how to get them out, how to be rid of them.

When I got home, I collapsed onto my bed. I pressed my face into my pillow and cried. My mind spun around and around like I was drunk, wondering if I was evil. I didn't think I was. Celeste was evil. Anyone who tries to destroy love is evil. It's the definition of evil. I was sure of it.

Finally, I stopped crying and sat up. I looked at my shorts and saw there was still blood on my clothes. I didn't think there was. I didn't know why. Maybe I wasn't really thinking at all. I felt it on my face ... I shivered, remembering that wet, awful feeling. My eyes filled up with tears again. I couldn't help myself. I loved him too much, and she took him away. She had no right.

I wiped my eyes and tried to think.

Before sunrise, I would put my clothes in a black trash bag. I could take them to the dumpsters behind the shopping center. There were so many of them, and all those huge stores had their backs to them. People never went out there.

I didn't like the feeling in my stomach, planning what I would do with my clothes, when I thought about her things left in the tree that I hoped would stay hidden. It seemed stupid now. Thinking I could make it look like she was robbed.

The sick feeling got stronger as I started to see what an awful, horrible, unforgivable thing I'd done. It was the opposite feeling of waking up from a nightmare, when you're so happy it wasn't real, and the more the seconds tick past, the cleaner and freer and happier you feel. This was not like that. It was real, and it would never go away.

39

NOW: EDEN

From the moment I'd pulled those drugs out of Parker's makeup bag, I had no intention of keeping her secret. I wanted to scare her a little, to make sure I got a good night's sleep without any more discussion of my leaving in the morning. But once she'd had a good night's sleep, she would realize she could easily hide the drugs somewhere else. Or get rid of them. Stop her micro dosing for a while. Besides, the police couldn't just come in and search based on my word.

The moment I had a chance to talk to Dylan out of range of Parker's sharp ears, I did.

Parker had taken Maverick to a birthday party, and she had an appointment with a client after that. I was surprised she'd allowed Dylan to stay alone in the house with me, but maybe she'd given him strict orders to never be in the same room. It certainly seemed that way because when I walked into the great room for a glass of water, he nodded at me, then went out to the patio. He'd already made a similar escape when I'd encountered him on the landing just as Parker and Maverick were leaving.

I took my water out to the patio and sat down. "There's something you need to know."

"Yeah?" He was looking at his phone, scrolling through messages, and he didn't stop.

"I felt like I was drugged yesterday. I've never passed out like that."

"You don't need to keep apologizing. Everything's fine."

"I'm not apologizing."

He kept scrolling, still not making eye contact.

"Parker put something in my drink."

"Why would she do that?"

"So she could accuse me of negligence."

He looked at me. "She's not going to endanger our son to make you look bad. Things have really deteriorated between you two. I'm really sorry to see this happening. I wish I—"

"I passed out. Even now, I can barely remember having margaritas with her. I don't remember anything we talked about, and I didn't feel well all evening. Something wasn't right. So I looked through her things, including her makeup bag."

"That was—"

"Let me finish. I found Liquid X. Do you know what that is? A date-rape drug. I also found acid."

He laughed.

"Why is that funny?"

"Parker doesn't take drugs."

"She drugged me. There's no doubt in my mind. And when I asked her about it, she admitted to taking the acid. It's called micro dosing. She's almost proud of it. She compared herself to high-tech superstars, who I guess take it to get a creative edge."

He stared at me.

"I'm not making it up. I can't make it up. You can go look right now. Maybe she's moved it, but it's somewhere in the house."

"Why are you telling me this?"

"I wanted you to know that your wife drugged me."

"Okay. I ... she's obviously far more upset than I realized. I misread how badly she wants you to leave. I—"

"And I think it shows that you don't know her."

"I'm ... I didn't know. I can't ... I need to talk to her."

"What else is she hiding?"

"She has one secret. A rather minor one, in the scheme of things. I don't think that means she has a closet full of them."

"If she's been hiding something so huge—the fact that she needs illegal drugs just to raise her children and function in her job—"

"Is that what she said?"

"Yes. She's taking a serious drug just to function ... and you had no clue? To me, that says you don't know her at all."

He sat forward on the chair and shoved his phone into his pocket. "I don't think it means I don't know her at all. It's one secret."

"I just think—"

"Okay. I said I should talk to her." He stood.

"What she did to me is very upsetting. And she's respon-sible for your children while she's taking a drug like that. Doesn't that—"

"I *said* she and I need to talk."

He went into the house. I suppose I'd also misread

things. He and I might be close, we might have connected on a deep level and be in the process of rebuilding our friendship, but the connections and secrets of a marriage run deep. There was no way I could understand that or hope to figure out what was going on between the two of them or how he might interpret this.

Although it was possible that he was upstairs that very minute, looking through her makeup bag to verify what I'd said, preparing himself for a confrontation.

Parker had willingly told me all about her micro dosing because she didn't want me asking about the Liquid X. But as I thought about how powerful the substance could be, my thoughts wandered to Julian. The police hadn't said anything about whether he'd been drunk or had smoked weed or taken something else to get high before he ended up hanging from that door. A drug like Liquid X would give someone like Parker the upper hand over a man like Julian.

Parker hadn't wanted him stirring up questions about Celeste's murder. She was losing her mind over the fact that he wouldn't stop talking about it. And then he was dead.

Parker had been trying to keep Celeste buried for twenty years. She'd dragged Dylan to therapy, trying to make him forget. She wouldn't take her children to the place where Celeste died or hang photographs that did her memory justice. She seethed at the memorials every five years, finally convincing him it was time to end them. It definitely was, but maybe if she hadn't fought his grief, he would have kept Celeste's memory alive in other, quieter ways.

Parker had believed Dylan was still in love with her, even when he'd broken up with her. Four days later, Celeste was dead, and they were back together. Had some twisted teenage notion of tragic love made her believe that Dylan would fall into her arms in his grief? Hadn't he done exactly that?

I felt ill. But I had for some time now, every time the thought presented itself, each time with more clarity and greater certainty.

40

NOW: DYLAN

I didn't have to look in Parker's makeup container to know Eden was telling the truth. But I did. And as I stared at the evidence on the palm of my hand, I felt like I was watching a scene from a movie. My immediate instinct was to flush it all down the toilet, but instead I closed the plastic box and put it back where I'd found it. This required a conversation at the right time, when the kids were in bed, when we could talk without getting pulled away by work or some other distraction.

That evening, I heard Parker in the kitchen, making dinner. I went into the great room, standing in the doorway, looking past the dining table, over the bar, as she stood with the chef's knife in her hand, slicing the ends off green beans. It was a large knife for that job.

She moved quickly. Usually, I enjoyed watching her prepare dinner, but now I felt l was watching a cartoon figure. Was she moving at a more rapid pace than a normal person, whacking through the tiny ends of the green beans with more force than necessary? Was there something frenzied about her movements? What was she seeing as she chopped? What was she thinking?

I'd read about micro dosing. It wasn't new to me when Eden mentioned the term. I'd heard the claims it didn't alter your perceptions whatsoever. It simply enhanced your focus or whatever bullshit they liked to tell themselves as they rewired their brain chemistry.

How did they know they weren't hallucinating?

Every aspect of life is altered by perception. If you're changing how your brain interprets and processes the world, at what point do you cross the line into hallucination? It was insanity. I couldn't believe she was doing this. And for how long? Months? Years? When she was pregnant with our children?

I wanted to rush into the kitchen, grab the knife out of her hand, and shake her until she told me what was going on underneath all that wavy blonde hair, behind those beautifully darkened, mysterious eyes.

Eden was right. I didn't know her at all.

I walked slowly toward the counter.

"Hi, hon."

I didn't answer. I stood at the end of the bar, watching that knife.

"Are you okay? You look like you're in a bad mood." She pulled four green beans from the pile, lined them up, and chopped off the ends. "Ow! Oh!" She rested the hand holding the knife on the counter and put her index finger that had been holding the beans into her mouth, sucking on the edge.

"Why are you having so much trouble with that knife?"

She took her finger out of her mouth. She grabbed a

scrap of paper towel and wrapped it around her finger. "I'm not having trouble. The knife slipped."

"How much have you had to drink?" I looked at her wineglass. "Hardly anything. Did you take something else?"

She laughed. "What are you talking about?"

"Did you take something that's making you clumsy with the knife?"

She glared at me.

As if she'd heard us, Eden walked into the room and came up to the counter. She leaned against it, staring at the droplets of blood on the cutting board. "Can I help with anything?"

"I don't need any help," Parker said.

I left the room and ran up the stairs. As I skipped steps in my rush to our bedroom, I thought of my determination to have a quiet, lengthy conversation with Parker. A conversation that didn't go anywhere near our children's radar. But I'd underestimated how angry I was. I needed to hear what she had to say right now. Even though it was probably nothing, watching that knife slide through her finger had been chilling. It felt like she had no control over it. She seemed to be lacking awareness of what she was doing, and it terrified me to think of her driving Brianna and Maverick around in that state.

I returned with the plastic box. I placed it in the center of the cutting board, right on top of the blood. I didn't care if it was making a mess of the board and our dinner. I needed to hear how she would explain jeopardizing our kids, not to mention the stability of our entire lives, by using drugs that could get her arrested if she were caught with them. She could destroy everything.

Parker put her hands on her hips, the paper towel coming partially unwound. "You told him? You said—"

"Why have you been lying to me?" I asked, my voice too loud.

"I haven't lied to you."

"Not telling me something critically important that affects me and my life and our kids' lives is lying."

"I didn't lie."

"Why are you doing this? And you get behind the wheel of the car with our kids in the back seat?"

"It's not like that. I'm not getting high."

"Don't give me that micro-dose bullshit."

"It's not bullshit. It's totally safe. A lot of high tech—"

"I don't want to hear that. Some of those people have zero morals, so I don't think they're a great recommendation for a lifestyle to mimic."

"It gives me an edge. It makes me creative. And it doesn't make me high or make me hallucinate. It's not like that at all. I can show you a lot of research."

"You should have told me. You shouldn't be *doing* it!"

"I don't have to discuss every choice that has to do with my own body and my own life with you."

"This affects all of us."

"It doesn't. You need to understand how it works. And stop being so provincial."

"I'm not provincial. And why on earth would you have a club drug in there too? Does that give you an *edge* with our guests?" I let out a bitter, angry laugh as I thought of how I'd argued with Eden, insisting that one secret didn't mean my wife was a stranger to me. I was wrong.

"It's not mine. She put it in there to make me—"

I laughed. "Leave Eden out of this."

"I can't. She planted it to make you think—"

"That's not true," Eden said.

I turned so that my back was to Eden. "This has nothing to do with Eden. You're the one who has been taking acid behind my back. For how long? Never mind. Doesn't matter right now. What else have you not told me? What else don't I know about you?"

"Nothing!" Parker screamed. "One little thing. One thing to help me be the wife and mother of the decade! Raising outstanding children, running an incredibly successful business that has thousands of outstanding testimonials, cooking fabulous meals, and being a loving, caring, devoted wife, who has helped you cope with terrible tragedy. That's why I need a little extra dose of focus and creativity. I need an edge!"

I stared at her. I couldn't believe she actually thought this was true. "I'm going for a run."

"But dinner is—"

"I'm going for a run."

As if I were already starting my run, almost as if I were being chased, I jogged out of the room and back up the stairs two at a time to change my clothes.

41

NOW: PARKER

My mind was flooded with memories. The past twenty years had all come rushing into my head, and it was hard to sort out what had happened only a few days or hours earlier and what had taken place two decades ago.

The day I went to Julian's house to find out why he was suddenly hinting around to Eden that he supposedly had some inside information about Celeste's killer had been one of the most upsetting days of my life. It had taken all my strength, and all the clarity of focus I had developed over the years, to maintain my equilibrium. And yes, the focus and sharpness that was assisted by micro doses of acid. It truly sharpened my mind. It filtered out distracting thoughts and helped me keep my mind on a single track.

Every mother, every mother who balances a challenging career with motherhood knows—the most difficult part is the nonstop flood of things to do, running on a loop through your mind, distracting you at every turn. When you're cooking dinner, you're thinking about medical appointments that need to be scheduled. When you're meeting with a client, you're thinking about what you need to pick up at the grocery store. When you're working on an important project that requires absolute focus, you're thinking about your son's last math test, and when you're making love to your husband, I'm ashamed to say, you're sometimes thinking about the client you forgot to respond to. At least I was. Maybe other women didn't. But for me, it was constant.

Micro dosing stopped most of that. It helped me focus. And focus brings peace of mind. Focus helps you accomplish what you need to and want to. It helped me enjoy my family more. When I was with my children or alone with my husband, I was truly present. And I resented that Dylan didn't understand that. I resented that he and Eden turned it into something sordid through their ignorance.

That day at Julian's, I'd managed to keep a pleasant, neighborly smile on my face as he babbled on with nonsense about things he saw and things he knew. All statements without any details. While I sat there, trying to figure out if it was just talk or if he actually knew something, my gaze wandered around the room.

And then I saw it.

Sitting on a shelf between the kitchen and dining area was a Walkman.

It was hers. I knew it the moment I saw it. That distinctive orange foam of the old-fashioned earphones. Of course, lots of Walkmans had that. Maybe Julian had even had his own Walkman at one time. But I knew that wasn't the case. Instinct is accurate, and I knew it was hers. I also knew he'd put it there because he suspected it was me.

He wouldn't have left it out for just anyone. He wouldn't

have left it out, fearing someone might think he was the one who had murdered Celeste.

Besides, Eden hadn't mentioned seeing it. And she surely would have. I knew her. She absolutely would have said something about it if she'd seen it.

He kept talking, saying things that meant nothing, saying things to make me worry that he'd seen me that night, and now I knew that he didn't really know, but he thought he did. And he also thought that if he kept on talking, I would suddenly blurt out the truth. I would give myself away. So, on and on he talked while I fell into memories of that day.

The day I'd gone back to the hollowed-out tree.

I'd been so sure it was safe. The tree was over five feet tall. I couldn't quite see to the bottom of the inside. I'd had to drag another log over there. When I'd gone back to get her things after they closed the case, I'd brought one of the pincher tools that people use to pick up trash. Even with that, I wasn't sure I was going to be able to get the Walkman and watch out of there, but I couldn't leave them sitting there forever. It just felt like a piece of me and what I'd done hanging out there. It felt like something that could get me in trouble. Someday. I wasn't sure how; I just didn't like it sitting there.

Especially because they'd decided that Celeste had been killed by a kid or kids wanting her expensive watch to get cash for drugs. If the watch was still out there, then that meant she wasn't killed for drug money. So I had to get her things and be rid of them.

Every night I'd lain in my bed and regretted leaving them. I'd been in a panic and hadn't wanted them with me. But I should have taken them.

Looking into that rotted tree, into the dark depth of it, at first I thought I couldn't see because of the dark and the debris that had fallen inside during those months. But as I scraped round with the pincher tool, I realized they were gone!

My heart started beating so fast I thought I might have a heart attack. I was too young. Teenagers didn't have heart attacks, but I honestly thought my heart was going so fast it was going to run out of energy and stop right then. Someone had found her things. That meant someone had seen me kill her. It couldn't mean anything else. The chances of someone finding things inside that tree were impossible.

I sat down beside the tree and started to cry. Then I panicked even more. What if no one had seen me? But what if that person took the things and spent every day watching the tree, waiting to see who came back?

I stood and ran as fast and far as I could away from there.

Then I spent twenty years feeling scared. Not terrified. Not every minute of my life. After a while, it faded. First a little, then a lot. The micro dosing helped me focus on other things. Finally, I mostly forgot about it except when I had bad dreams.

I never understood how someone found her things. I never understood why they didn't watch the tree, waiting. Maybe they weren't patient enough. All I knew was that I didn't feel safe.

But now I knew. Julian had found them. Maybe he didn't know it was me. Maybe he was lucky. Maybe when he wasn't sitting on his porch watching all of us, he'd spent as much time exploring those woods as we had. Maybe he also knew every hollowed-out tree, every rock that was smooth and level for sitting by the creek, every spot that was good for wading or skipping stones.

It no longer mattered. When I saw that Walkman, I knew I couldn't have him talking to anyone anymore. I couldn't have him speculating and playing his silly games. And most of all, I couldn't have him dropping hints to Eden, who couldn't wait to be rid of me so she could fall into my husband's arms.

While I sat in his great room, I began making my plan.

When I demanded that Eden make herself scarce that night so we could have family time, I'd lain awake until she came home. After she'd settled in bed, I went out. I went into his house with a pint of whiskey laced with Liquid X. I knew he'd still be up. He wasn't the only one who kept an eye on the neighborhood. I'd seen his lights on late at night every night of the week. I knew he often had evening appointments at his veterinary practice, and I knew he was often awake until well past midnight.

The only part I wasn't sure about was whether he would let me inside. But when I told him I needed to talk about Celeste's murder, that my husband was losing his mind, he swung the door wide, always eager to gossip. He probably thought he would trap me into a confession once and for all.

We shared the whiskey, but I only pretended to take swigs, and he didn't really notice. He was too excited to have someone in his house, talking to him, paying attention to him.

I didn't know what he thought when I suggested we go upstairs. With the whiskey and the Liquid X starting to kick in, he probably didn't think anything at all. The rest was the most physically, mentally, and emotionally exhausting thing I'd ever done, but there was no choice. And I was confident that, in the end, it meant I could finally move on. We could finally move on. Dylan and I, with our precious children beside us, could live the life we'd dreamed of when we were young, before everything went wrong.

But it wasn't over. Eden wasn't going away, and she wasn't going to stop wanting my husband. I was pretty sure she believed I was the one who had murdered Celeste.

Luckily for me, she'd kind of set herself up.

Karin knew and Dylan knew that she was in love with him. She'd loved him for over twenty years, but she couldn't have him. She'd tried to forget him in Italy, and it hadn't worked.

A woman who has lost her marriage and all her friends and has finally realized she has nowhere to go would easily sink into a deeply depressed state. A hopeless state.

Fortunately, she'd willingly given me a sample of her handwriting when I'd asked her to jot down a shopping list for me. I wrote a short note, copying the distinctive parts of her writing.

I thought killing Celeste would bring Dylan into my arms. I came back for him, but he won't ever love me.

I put the note in my nightstand. Leaving the drawer open, I went into the bathroom and opened the bottom cabinet on Dylan's side of the counter. In the back was a soft leather case his father had given him for his eighteenth birthday. A frivolous, old-fashioned gift he'd never used but couldn't part with because it came from his dad—a brand-new, never-used straight razor. I placed the razor in my nightstand on top of the note.

42

NOW: EDEN

Parker had obviously woken up with a plan, and it scared me. It started with a knock on the guest room door. She stood outside, all sugary sweetness, a lopsided smile so phony she looked almost psychotic. She held a small tray with a mug of coffee and a croissant on a white plate.

"I brought you a little something to go with your coffee. Wait until you taste it. This bakery creates pure magic with their chocolate croissants."

"Thanks."

"Can I come in? You can snuggle back in bed for a while and relax."

I took a step away from the door. "I'm up now, so—"

"Come on. Back to bed. You deserve some pampering." Her smile grew more manic. "Have a relaxing morning. We have big plans this afternoon. A family hike! You're invited, of course."

"Oh. Okay." I felt slightly dizzy. An image flooded my

mind—Dylan and the kids pulling ahead of us, disappearing around a curve in the trail, Parker urging me toward the edge of a cliff to point out a marvelous view, then shoving me to my death.

"Don't look so suspicious. I know things have been tense." She laughed. "I've made some mistakes, but so have you. Let's vow to start over."

"You said that before."

"For real this time." She put the tray on the nightstand and swept out of the room.

I didn't feel like getting back into bed when I was already up. I threw on my robe and moved the tray to the table beside the armchair. I sat down and picked up the croissant. I was almost afraid to drink the coffee, but I assured myself she wouldn't poison me. She couldn't. How would she explain that to her family?

UNDER OTHER CIRCUMSTANCES, the hike would have been a fabulous experience. But my anxiety grew with every step. The higher we climbed into the foothills, the more Dylan and Brianna and Maverick pulled ahead, the more real my imagined premonition became and the faster my heart beat. It wasn't caused solely by the steep incline and the sun beating down on my back. There was sweat on the sides of my face and across my scalp, tracing the ridges of my spine. There was sweat everywhere, and it attracted the fine dust that drifted up from our footsteps.

Parker worked hard to prevent me from keeping pace with the others. Every few steps, she grabbed my wrist, pointing to a delicate wildflower or a gnarled tree she thought I would find interesting. Every clearing among the trees beside us was a reminder of our childhood, eliciting a memory.

After a while, I couldn't even see Dylan and the kids.

"We need to catch up to them," I said.

"It's fine. We've hiked this trail so many times, I know it like the back of my hand."

"I thought you wanted family time."

"I do, but I also wanted to talk to you."

I lengthened my stride.

She grabbed my wrist again. "Don't be in such a hurry. You'll tire yourself out. And it's hot. You're all sweaty. You need to pace yourself."

I lifted my ball cap and wiped my forehead, then wiped my palm on my shorts.

"I owe you a huge apology for the way I've treated you," Parker said.

I laughed, but it sounded more like a snort.

"I deserve that, I know. I could never tell Dylan about the micro dosing. I knew he wouldn't understand. No matter how things change, most of the responsibility for raising children still falls on the mom. And trying to be successful in a competitive field like social media influencing and management is hard. You have to be *on* all the time."

"Dylan seems very involved with Brianna and Maverick."

"He is. I'm not complaining. Anyway, now that it's out in the open, everything is good with the two of us. It really is a blessing that you told him. So I want to thank you for that."

She grabbed my hand, squeezed it, then let go. Was she expecting me to tell her she was welcome, that I was happy to have saved her marriage? What did she want? I didn't believe a word coming out of her mouth. Why was she telling me all this? Why bother if she planned to push me over the side of a cliff, down a sheer drop of hundreds of feet?

My heart was pounding, and I could feel myself almost gasping for breath.

"Do you need to rest?" Parker asked.

"I'm fine. I just think we should catch up to them."

She laughed. "We will. Just a few more minutes. 'K? Don't be in such a hurry. It's not good to push yourself so hard. Especially in this heat."

I continued pushing. She grabbed my wrist again, gripping it so tightly this time, I feared this was it. She was going to drag me off the path, through the scrub, over the rocky surface to the edge.

"I want you to know, and this is so hard for me to say, but I'm trying to be open here ... I was feeling insecure. So alienated from Dylan and, honestly, I guess a little worried about our marriage. I directed all that at you. But now that he understands how it is for me, now that he's more educated about micro dosing and how it makes your brain so much more alive and creative, he gets it. He understands that it doesn't make you incapacitated or change your personality or any of those things he worried about. Everything is good with us. Better than it's ever been. I can thank you for that! I could just hug you right now. But you're awfully sweaty." She laughed again, the edge of mania becoming even sharper. "So thank you, Eden. My childhood friend. My lifelong friend. The one who knows me better than anyone. You know everything about me, right?"

I was afraid to answer. I was afraid of saying the wrong thing, afraid of making a wrong move.

Finally, she seemed to have said all she wanted, and we

gradually caught up with the others. By the time we returned to the parking lot, I was exhausted by my constant imaginings of myself fighting my way back from the edge of the cliff.

At home, Parker continued to orchestrate our activities as if she were the director of a Broadway production. She ordered Dylan and the kids to take quick showers. She told him he should take Brianna and Maverick bowling and out for pizza.

"Eden and I are in desperate need of some girl time, right, Eden?"

I tried to smile. I had no idea what my face looked like, but she smiled back at me as if I'd given the impression I was thrilled and touched by the thought of spending an evening alone with her. Mostly, I was so relieved that I hadn't been shoved to a terrifying death, I felt on the verge of tears every time I took a breath.

She hustled them out of the house so fast, I wondered why Dylan didn't question her manic planning. I supposed he was still so stuck with his own fantasy of recapturing our lost friendship, and relieved at whatever had been worked out between them regarding her secretive drug use, he was living in a slightly altered reality.

When they were gone, she sat me down, still sweaty and grimy from our hike, on the great room couch. She placed a large white box with a wide pink satin ribbon around it on the coffee table. "Open it." She giggled like a child.

I touched the ribbon. I was feeling so unstable, I half expected that when I lifted the lid of the thick cardboard box, it might explode. If not that, a venomous snake might dart out and bite me. Parker would leave me writhing in pain, letting me succumb to the poison while she sat sipping a glass of wine as I died before her eyes.

"Why are you waiting, silly?"

I pulled the ribbon. I lifted the lid off the box. Inside was a jar of bath salts and a bottle of bubble bath.

"You were obviously jealous of our jacuzzi tub. I have it all set up for you." She clapped her hands. "You can have a luxurious soak to get rid of all that sweat." She wrinkled her nose. "I'll make us some pasta and open a nice bottle of Chardonnay. We can have a good heart-to-heart talk. How does that sound?"

It sounded awful.

It hadn't been the cliffside fall to my death. This was it. She was either going to drown me in the tub or poison me with dinner. I wasn't sure how she would make either of those look like an accident for Dylan's sake. Or for the police, for that matter, but I had no doubt she had some sort of plan. She'd had plenty of time to work out the details. I was absolutely certain she had not forgiven me. She had not decided we would be friends again.

She'd murdered Julian. She'd murdered Celeste and lived without guilt, looking Dylan in the eye every day of his life for the past twenty years. And she was almost certain that I knew.

I smiled and walked slowly up the stairs, with Parker following closely behind.

She'd filled the bathroom with candles. It looked almost magical as they flickered in the fading afternoon light. I told her it was spectacular. I listened to her instructions for working the jets on the tub, and then she left, assuring me that I would have absolute privacy once I'd locked the door behind her.

I filled the tub with water and bath salts and bubbles. I washed my face. I locked the door.

Then I took my phone out of my pocket and opened the recording app. I turned it on and placed my phone under a folded towel on the shelf. I stepped behind the frosted glass panel of the shower and waited for Parker to return.

43

NOW: PARKER

Liquid X and acid weren't the only drugs I had access to. With Karin and Tip as our best friends, I had a candy store of goodies to choose from. In order to ease my former best friend's path to her death, I had a small bottle of amyl nitrite. It would relax her and put her in a slight state of bliss. But the effects wouldn't last long, so I had to move quickly.

I'd soaked a washcloth with it and added some lavender. The lavender's pleasing scent would allow me to get close to her, although she would probably already have her guard up once I picked the lock and walked into the bathroom uninvited. Still, I thought she would be startled enough at my bold entrance that I could take the two long strides required to reach the side of the tub and have the cloth to her face, promising the soothing aroma of lavender, before she had a chance to realize something was terribly wrong. I'd practiced it multiple times and knew my movements would be sure.

The half-empty bottle of amyl nitrite would be left on

the floor, leading Dylan and the police to believe she'd used it to relax and numb herself—before slashing her wrists.

I stood in the bedroom and took a few calming breaths. The sound of the jacuzzi jets could be heard through the bathroom door. I closed my eyes and pictured her lying there, already partially disabled by the soothing effects of hot water. Naked and wet, she would feel vulnerable and unsure. At what point would she know something was wrong?

I took another breath. It was time to stop thinking and trust my instinct. Overthinking never helped.

The tiny screwdriver slid into the lock, and with a quick twist and the tiniest click that I didn't think could be heard above the noise of the jets, the door was unlocked. I pressed down gently on the handle and opened the door. Steam filled the bathroom. Candles flickered, and the scent of gardenia assaulted me. I tightened my grip on the razor, spread open my fingers holding the washcloth, and stepped inside.

The tub was empty.

I froze. Had she slipped under the water to wash her hair?

I moved closer, trying to see through the layer of bubbles covering the surface. There was no sign of her, but the bubbles were thick. Still, shouldn't I be able to see the shape of her body, some movement in the water?

Suddenly, I felt a punch to the center of my upper back. It knocked the air out of me, and I stumbled forward. I turned, waving both arms, still expecting to see a naked, slippery Eden. Instead, she stood there fully clothed. Unable to let go of the steps I'd planned so many times in my mind, I shoved the amyl-nitrite-soaked washcloth toward her face, but she easily blocked me with her forearm.

"You're supposed to be taking a bath!" My words sounded stupid even as I said them, my shouts echoing off the tiles. "How did you ...?" I slashed the razor across her upper arm, but it only caught the fabric of her T-shirt, tearing the sleeve, nicking her arm only slightly. Tiny drops of blood bubbled out, but she didn't seem to notice.

She tried to grab my wrist, but I yanked my arm away from her. She grabbed my other arm and twisted it. I dropped the washcloth as I tried to break free of her grip and keep the razor out of her reach.

"You killed her!" The edge in her voice was cold and hard, her voice lower than normal and deadly quiet. Tears bubbled out of her eyes with the same slow pulse as the blood seeping from the wound on her upper arm. "I don't even know who you are! How could you do that to her? To him?"

I needed her to shut up. I needed her to stop. I slashed the razor at her again; this time it caught the back of her hand. She screamed and released her grip on my arm, but then she grabbed at my hair, pulling me toward her so hard my eyes flooded with tears. The pain was unbearable, and I thought she was pulling it out of my head as I heard a tearing sound. I screamed. The entire room was filled with the sounds of both our screams.

She grabbed my wrist and twisted so hard I heard a crack. I cried out again, and the razor fell out of my hand. She crashed to her knees and grabbed it by the handle, throwing it toward the tub. It splashed into the water.

"You smashed her head in and acted like nothing happened, like you felt nothing!"

"She tried to take him away from me! She was evil. She tried to destroy his love for me."

"You're insane. You're actually insane."

I fell onto my knees and turned the knob to unplug the drain, sweeping my hands across the surface to move the bubbles out of the way until I saw the silver curve of the razor's handle. I pulled it out and stood.

She lunged for the doorway, but I grabbed the back of her shirt, pulling her down. She fell. Her shoulder hit the side of the door, and it swung closed. She grabbed for it, clawing her way closer. The razor was slippery with bubbles. I wanted to wipe it dry, but I couldn't let her get it away from me.

She kicked at me, hitting my jaw. I screamed again. My whole body screamed with pain, but I couldn't let her go. I had to get rid of her. I couldn't let her talk to Dylan. I couldn't let her out of the bathroom, out of my house.

But she shoved the bathroom door open and threw herself out into our bedroom. I got to my feet and ran after her. She was already out of our bedroom, headed toward the stairs. I lunged at her again, tackling her and pushing her to the ground. She grabbed both my wrists and rolled me over, so she was almost on top of me. We struggled, rolling closer to the top of the stairs.

Both of us were crying, screaming with pain and rage.

Then she was trying to pry my fingers off the handle of the razor. She shoved her knee into my stomach. I groaned and gasped for air, trying to slash the razor across her stomach, but I was too low, and all it did was slice at her denim shorts and belt.

A moment later, still not able to catch my breath, Eden had a tight grip on my forearm, forcing my hand back toward my own body. As I tried to pull my arm free, she kept pushing it away, closer to me. And then she relaxed slightly, and my hand moved back. I felt the razor slide down my inner arm, deep into my flesh with a pain so intense I couldn't breathe.

The weight of her was off me, and I felt myself falling. It wasn't the crashing, thudding feeling I would have expected, but a floating feeling, as if I were flying down the stairs, but at the same time, flying up, flying to meet Dylan, flying into his arms.

44

NOW: DYLAN

Eden had called me to tell me what had happened, but it wasn't enough to stop the tsunami of grief and shock I felt when I turned onto our street with our children.

Paramedics, an enormous firetruck, and two police cars were parked haphazardly in front of our home.

It wasn't enough to stop me from feeling as if I were being punched in the gut over and over, as if some great hand was squeezing my heart, forcing the blood out, tearing at my throat until it felt so raw that I thought I'd swallowed the straight razor Eden had described to me.

I didn't know what I would say to my children after this, for the rest of their lives. How would I ever find words to comfort them? To explain? To make any sense of anything? Seeing their faces and hearing the sounds coming out of them was too much.

I tried to hold onto both of them, but they didn't want it. At first, they did. They clung to me like infants; then they wrenched away, running to see their mother, which they were prevented from doing. I wasn't sure if that was the right thing or not. I wasn't sure of anything. I was furious the officials wouldn't let them see her. I was relieved they wouldn't let them see her. I wanted to take them away, but I couldn't.

Eden tried to hold onto them while Detective Harrow led me to the front porch, but they didn't want her either. Then they did. She took them inside the house, but I could still hear them crying. Sometimes they grew silent, and then there would be a scream of pain so gut-wrenching I felt I was being split in two.

The detective told me what Eden had said, and that too made me so furious I wanted to punch his concerned face. I wanted to hear the details from Eden, not him. At the same time, I didn't know if I could look at Eden.

It was all just too much.

Celeste. Parker. Eden. Celeste.

Their names spun in my head.

Parker. My wife was a murderer. A stranger. A monster.

My entire life spun inside my head; unanswered questions that had tormented me now had answers, but I hated those answers with every cell of my body. I wanted to go back to my agonized ignorance. I wanted my wife back. I wanted my childhood back. I wanted my sister back. I wanted my innocence back.

Maybe there's no such thing.

The detective asked me a thousand inane questions, and he seemed dissatisfied with so many answers, so he kept pushing, as if he had to know the stupidest most unimportant details about where I'd been that evening and what Parker's plans for the evening had been and what kind of relationship she had with Eden. God. What was wrong with this man? Wasn't it obvious that none of that mattered? Why the hell did he think he needed answers to those questions? Ever? But especially now?

Right now, as the female paramedic gently and firmly closed the back doors of the truck. As both paramedics climbed into the front of the truck and drove away. There was no siren. The lights that were flashing when I arrived home had been turned off. The body of my wife was inside. The woman I'd loved since I was a teenager, the only woman I'd ever loved, was gone. I hardly knew how I would go on without her. Inside that truck was the body of my sister's murderer, and I wanted to fling open those doors, shake her, and scream into her vacant face, demanding to know why. I wanted to kill her myself.

How had she looked at me a million, ten million times, knowing what she'd done? How had she cooked meals for our family and laughed with me and comforted me? How had she made love to me and held me and brushed her lips across mine? How had she given birth to our children and held them and kissed their precious faces?

What kind of monster lived inside her?

Did the woman I'd spent my life with even exist? Was she an actor playing a role the entire time? Was anything real? Hairline cracks were racing and spreading, shuddering like an earthquake through every moment of my entire existence. Soon, everything I'd known would shatter and break apart; there would be nothing left but dust.

And our children. How could I ever explain this to them when I couldn't explain it to myself?

Their questions would be legion.

I felt like sobbing, but the pressure of that tidal wave of emotion was so great, my body didn't have the strength to allow it to move from inside me out into the world.

As the detective droned on and I said things that might not have even been true because I could hardly make sense of his questions, I was overcome by a strange calm. Nothing was real. This couldn't be real, so maybe none of it mattered. Even my feelings. As I sat there in a near-trance, he gave up, telling me he would talk to me again when I was feeling better.

I laughed, wondering how my psyche had the capacity for laughter. Maybe it was an instinct, like sneezing.

He walked into the street to talk to the other police officers. The fire truck was gone.

Eden came out onto the porch. She stood a few feet from me, looking toward the cluster of law enforcement officers. She spoke in a low voice. "I told them what happened, but I haven't said everything yet."

"I can't ..."

"I have to give them something, but I wanted to ask you first."

The scene in front of me turned blurry. I blinked, unsure what was wrong with my eyes. Maybe because it was dark and all the lights were distorting my vision. I rubbed my eyes. My fingers came away wet.

"I recorded the ... I recorded ... I wanted to record what she said in case ... You can listen to it before I give it to the detective if you want. But it's not just her admitting what she did ... you'll hear ... everything."

I thought about what I'd already heard. A straight razor. When Eden first mentioned that, I'd tried to think why the hell she had a straight razor. Then I'd remembered the gift from my father on my eighteenth birthday. I'd forced myself not to picture Parker and Eden fighting in our bathroom, the cuts and the blood.

Glancing at Eden's hand now, I saw the thick bandage where she'd been cut. There was another on her arm, covered by the sleeve of the hoodie she'd thrown on now that it was past midnight and getting cold.

"Brianna and Maverick. Where are they?"

"Watching TV."

"Are they ...?"

"They're numb. For now. I made them hot chocolate."

"Thanks."

Two patrol officers got into their car and started the engine. They backed out at an angle and drove slowly down the street. The neighbors that I'd only been slightly aware of, as if they were there with the police, assigned to stand watch and drink in the details of our tragedy, were drifting back to their homes. There wasn't anything much left to see. Now they would sit up for another hour, have a drink or a mug of tea and talk about the shock of it all, speculate on the pieces they'd overheard, trying to figure out the rest, texting each other to compare notes.

"I think I need to tell the detective now," Eden said. "Before he leaves."

"I don't know."

"Never mind. I'm not thinking straight," she said. "I'll just send a copy to my email. You can decide later."

I nodded.

She tapped her phone, then stood watching the screen while the file loaded. A few minutes later, she walked slowly down the steps toward Detective Harrow.

I closed my eyes.

I needed to talk to our children. My children. They were my children now. My sole responsibility for the rest of my life. I hoped I would be enough for them.

45

2003: EDEN

I was sitting at my desk, trying to fill out the form that would match me with a dorm roommate. Mostly, I was staring out the window, feeling stupid that I hadn't told Dylan how I felt. I'd talked about every unimportant thing I could think of until he was staring at me like I was brain-dead. Then his mom told him to go find Celeste, and I lost my chance. I would go over there tomorrow, but it would be harder. I'd feel even more self-conscious, and he would look at me again like he couldn't figure out what I was doing there. Maybe it was too late. But thinking that made me want to cry. It wasn't too late. I was not going to think that.

Staring out the window, I saw Julian sitting on his front porch, the light shining on his head. Like always, he was holding his binoculars to his eyes.

His mom and the woman who lived next door to him were standing in front of his house, talking. Their voices sounded screechy, and they looked upset.

Then I realized Julian was aiming the binoculars at his mom and the other woman.

A police car drove down the street and stopped in front of Dylan's house. What was going on? I put down my pen and leaned closer to the window, trying to see Dylan's front porch on the other side of Parker's house.

A man from three doors down ran out into the street, stopped to talked to Julian's mom and the other woman, then walked across the street really fast toward Dylan's. I couldn't see him after that without taking off my screen and leaning out the window.

It didn't seem good that a police car was parked in front of Dylan's house. Did that mean he couldn't find Celeste? It must. Why else would they call the police? If she was hurt, they would have called the paramedics. I went downstairs and out onto the front porch. I could hear voices from the police car radio, but I couldn't understand what they were saying.

I walked across our lawn, then Parker's, and into Dylan's yard. No one was on the porch, but the front door was open, and I could see two cops standing in the doorway. While I watched, they moved into the house, but the door stayed open.

Slowly, I moved closer, trying to see in the living room window. The man who had been hurrying across the street was in there. I could hear someone crying really loudly, almost screaming or wailing like a little kid, but worse. Taking a deep breath, I went up the front steps and into the house. I hoped they didn't tell me to go away, but I had to know if she was missing. Had she been kidnapped? No one I knew had ever been kidnapped, but it happened. Or was she just missing?

In the hallway, the crying was louder. Dylan's mom. She was crying and screaming. "My baby. My sweet baby. My little girl."

Mr. Campbell looked awful. Like someone had punched him in the face. He was talking but not really looking at anyone. "God dammit. God dammit. God dammit. I'll kill him. I'll kill him. God dammit."

One of the cops was a woman. She took Mrs. Campbell's arm and Mr. Campbell's arm and walked them out of the room and across the hallway, right past me, to the family room.

I went into the living room.

Parker and Dylan were on the couch. She was snuggled up to him with both her arms around him.

The other man and the other cop left. I heard them talking in the hallway. "If you could ask your wife to come over, that would help. But we need to talk to her."

"Sure. Sure," the man said.

"What happened?" I asked even though I had a pretty good idea what they were going to tell me.

"She's dead!" Dylan cried. "Someone killed Celeste. Her head was all smashed in." He started sobbing. "She was ... all this blood! She's dead!" He sobbed harder. "Why would they do that? I don't ... how could this happen? Her head." He pressed his hands against his face.

Parker squeezed him tighter. "Cry, baby. It's okay to cry. I got you." She leaned her head against his chest, curling her body around his like a snake.

Dylan wiped his hands down his face. He stiffened and sat up straighter. He peeled himself away from Parker and stood. "I need a beer." He walked out of the room so fast I thought he might trip and fall because he was leaning forward at a funny angle. Maybe he was going to be sick.

I looked at Parker.

"What are you staring at?" she asked.

"I ..."

"Stop staring at me. This is so, so awful, and you're acting weird."

"I'm just ... I thought you broke up."

She jerked forward on the couch. "That's what you're thinking about? His sister is *dead*, and you're thinking about breaking up? What's *wrong* with you? That's disgusting. So disgusting. I can't believe you said that. I know you must be in shock, but oh my God."

"I just ... it's a shock."

"Dylan finding his sister dead is a *shock*."

"I know. I can't ... it's too awful. I can't even believe it."

She settled back on the couch. "Focus on what matters, okay? Besides, I told you, Dylan loves me. Nothing, and no one, can ever break us up. You need to know that. 'K, Eden?" She looked at me, her eyes stabbing into mine like knives.

A chill so cold ran down my spine I thought I might pass out. I'd never felt so cold in all my life. She wanted me to think she meant me. I could never break them up. But I didn't break them up. I never tried to break them up. What she really meant was Celeste couldn't break them up. Parker always thought Celeste wanted to be rid of her.

She complained to me about Celeste all the time. Celeste didn't like her. Celeste was always telling Dylan what to do. Celeste, Celeste, Celeste. And now she was dead. I couldn't believe she was dead. I'd never known anyone who died except my grandfather. And he was old. He was sick for a long time. We knew he was going to die. It wasn't right for someone our age to die.

There were always stories about teenagers dying. Murder. Car accidents. Drowning. But it never happened to anyone we knew. It never seemed ... real. This didn't seem real.

Dylan came back, gulping his beer. He flopped onto the couch and slammed his beer on the end table. "It sucks so bad. How can this happen?!" He punched the arm of the couch. He grabbed his beer and chugged some more.

I sat cross-legged on the floor and leaned my elbows into my knees and rested my face in my hands. Tears ran out of my eyes, covering my fingers. It felt so awful I wasn't even sure what I was feeling. I wanted to hug Dylan, I wanted to tell him how sorry I was, but all the words that came into my head seemed like they weren't good enough.

All three of us were quiet for a long time. The only sound was the thud of Dylan's beer bottle each time he put it on the table. And then that stopped too. After a while, we could hear the cops talking, his mom crying, his dad cursing. People were coming in the front door. The phone was ringing.

I heard his dad again. "I'll kill that son of a bitch. I'll rip his head off. I'll—" The police officer interrupted him, telling him to let them handle things.

Even though I was still resting my face in my hands, all I could see inside my head was Parker's face and that icy stare in her eyes. I looked up. "Do you think it was someone we know?" I whispered.

Dylan, who was mostly mumbling things I couldn't hear, stared at me with his mouth open. He snapped it closed, then said, "If it was, then someone we know is a fucking monster."

It was after midnight when I went home. Parker was still there. The police were gone, and one of Mrs. Campbell's friends had brought over a few of her sleeping pills.

The detective had talked to Dylan, which made him so angry he refused to look at anyone after that. They talked to all the neighbors. They wanted to know if anyone had seen anything. They wanted to know if Celeste had any enemies. What teenagers have enemies? It sounded like something from a cartel or the mafia.

I wondered if I should tell the police that Parker thought Celeste didn't like her. It sounded so petty. Every single kid at our school thought someone or the other didn't like them. Every single one of us. That's how it is for teenagers. That didn't mean they committed *murder*. What proof did I have? Should I tell them? Would they think I was trying to create drama? Would everyone think I was trying to make Parker look like a horrible person so I could have Dylan? Parker would think that for sure. Would Dylan think that?

And what if she didn't?

I didn't know.

I did know. That look in her eyes. It was the look of a monster. It sounded silly to think there's such a thing, but in my heart, I knew. There was no proof, but I knew.

When the detective asked me if Celeste had any enemies, I said, "Not that I know of."

46

ONE YEAR AFTER PARKER'S DEATH: EDEN

For obvious reasons, the one-year memorial for Parker was not as well attended as the memorials for Celeste had been. Those who did attend knew why Dylan wanted to bring neighbors and friends together to remember Parker. Even though most saw only the monster in her, for Brianna and Maverick, it was complicated. Beyond complicated.

She adored them, as Dylan—and I, from time to time— assured them repeatedly. They loved her. The only person they'd known was the woman Parker had presented to them. That woman was a kind, fierce, gentle, supportive mother. To them, the woman who murdered two people and tried to take the life of a third was a separate entity, which lurked somewhere so far below the surface, they hadn't known she existed.

Dylan didn't want to turn their experience of Parker into a lie. And a lot of people understood that, without him having to spell it out. They felt it in his understated tone asking them to—*Help Mav and Bri remember the mom they loved.*

We gathered in the clearing in the woods where Dylan, Parker, and I had played as children, where we'd shared our secrets, and, it turned out, our lies, as teenagers. A friend of Dylan's played the guitar. The lyrics to his song were about summer; they were comforting and hopeful and didn't bring any heavy baggage with them. Dylan read a poem that Parker loved about motherhood, we had a few moments of silence, and that was it.

There was a table with cookies and punch, nothing like the lavish buffet lunches that had marked the years after Celeste died.

While Brianna and Maverick sat in the shade, talking to their friends, Dylan and I wandered over to the creek. Without either of us suggesting it, we took off our shoes and waded into the cold water. After the initial shock, it felt refreshing on my hot skin, the pebbles giving the bottoms of my feet a gentle massage. I closed my eyes and felt as if I were fifteen.

"Thank you for hanging around," Dylan said.

I opened my eyes. "Why wouldn't I?"

"I mean this past year. I don't know what I would have done without you. What the kids would have done."

"I'm glad I could be here."

"Are you planning to stay?"

"I don't know yet. I always thought I hated being in a small town. I loved being in New York for school. Milan was thrilling. But I don't know ... my old home is growing on me."

He was silent for several minutes. Then he said, "Tell me why you *really* came back."

I took a deep breath. "The night Celeste was killed ... Parker gave me this look ... and, somehow, I felt like I knew. I didn't, but I did, if that makes sense. She blamed Celeste for your breakup. I think she worried Celeste would convince you to never come back here after college. That she would lose you forever."

"You knew?"

"I didn't ... it was a feeling. And a look in her eyes. So cold I could hardly breathe. But how do you tell that to the police? There was no proof. When I saw that picture of Julian and Karin, I wondered about it. I started wondering if other people didn't tell the police everything."

"Why didn't you say anything?" His voice had a hard, sharp edge.

"It was a feeling. I was a kid. They wouldn't have paid any attention. You know that. You *know* that."

He kicked at the water, sending droplets flying across the surface. He let out a deep sigh.

"I started to think that the only way was to make Parker so uncomfortable, she would slip and say something. I thought if she was afraid I was trying to take you away, she would get so upset she might somehow give herself away. Not a very great plan, but I just thought ... I never imagined ..." I choked slightly. "I didn't think she would *kill* Julian."

He didn't say anything.

I took a few tentative steps toward him.

He was staring down into the water. Finally, he spoke. "That's difficult to hear, but thanks. You've always been a stand-up friend." He looked toward the clearing.

I followed his gaze.

Brianna and Maverick were walking toward us. It made me gasp sometimes when I caught sight of them and noticed how much they resembled Parker. Especially Brianna. It was unsettling. But they were nothing like her at their cores. They were grounded. They were loved, and they knew how to love other people. They would be okay.

"I wonder if they feel her presence when they're here. If they think about when we were out here a year ago scattering her ashes," Dylan said.

"I imagine they do."

"Do you? Feel her presence?"

"Maybe. A little."

"I guess this was the only way the three of us were all going to be connected again." He took a step toward me, and we stood there, letting the water flow around our ankles, pulling us toward a fresh start.

A NOTE FROM THE AUTHOR

Thank you so much for choosing to read *Don't Trust Her*. There are so many books to choose from, and I'm thrilled that you chose to spend time with my story. I hope you enjoyed reading the book as much as I loved writing it.

I'm eternally interested in the childhood and teenage experiences that shape us and often haunt us throughout our lives. It was a fascinating journey to explore Eden's escape from an oppressive childhood friend and her almost-too-late determination to find a way to do the right thing.

My acknowledgments are brief because sometimes I just can't find the words to express my thoughts.

I'm so appreciative of the entire team at Inkubator Books. Their investment in story development and marketing, as well as their talent and style in all the facets of publishing has introduced so many readers, including you, to my books. I'm forever grateful.

Most of all, thank you to Don Grant, my first reader, my sounding board, my sanity. "You were my voice when I couldn't speak."

Reviews are so important to other readers. If you could spend a moment to write an honest review on Amazon, no matter how short, I would be extremely grateful. They really do help get the word out.

Best wishes,

Cathryn

www.cathryngrant.com

ABOUT THE AUTHOR

Cathryn Grant writes psychological thrillers, psychological suspense, and ghost stories. She's the author of over thirty novels. She's loved crime fiction all her life and is endlessly fascinated by the twists and turns, and the dark corners of the human mind.

When she's not writing, Cathryn reads fiction, eavesdrops, and tries to play golf without hitting her ball into the sand or the water. She lives on the Central California coast with her husband and two cats.

ALSO BY CATHRYN GRANT

INKUBATOR BOOKS

PSYCHOLOGICAL THRILLER TITLES

THE GUEST

THE GOOD NEIGHBOR

THE GOOD MOTHER

ONLY YOU

THE ASSISTANT

THE OTHER COUPLE

ALWAYS REMEMBER

BEST FRIENDS FOREVER

THE FAVORITE CHILD

THE SECRET SHE KEPT

DON'T TRUST HER

CATHRYN'S OTHER TITLES

She's Listening

(A Psychological Thriller)

THE ALEXANDRA MALLORY PSYCHOLOGICAL SUSPENSE
SERIES

The Woman In the Mirror ◆ *The Woman In the Water*

The Woman In the Painting ◆ *The Woman In the Window*

The Woman In the Bar ◆ *The Woman In the Bedroom*

The Woman In the Dark ◆ *The Woman In the Cellar*

The Woman In the Photograph ◆ *The Woman In the Storm*

The Woman In the Taxi ◆ *The Woman In the Church*

The Woman In the Shadows ◆ *The Woman In the Hotel*

SUBURBAN NOIR NOVELS

Buried by Debt

The Suburban Abyss ◆ *The Hallelujah Horror Show*

Faceless ◆ *An Affair With God*

THE HAUNTED SHIP TRILOGY

Alone On the Beach ◆ *Slipping Away From the Beach*

Haunting the Beach

NOVELLAS

Madison Keith Ghost Story Series ◆ *Chances Are*

Jealousy Junction

SHORT FICTION

Reduction in Force ◆ *Maternal Instinct*

Flash Fiction For the Cocktail Hour

The 12 Days of Xmas

NONFICTION

Writing is Murder: Motive, Means, and Opportunity

Printed in Great Britain
by Amazon

29133926R00169